A CHARM AGAINST DROWNING

by the same author

BROND
JILL RIPS

FREDERIC LINDSAY

A CHARM AGAINST DROWNING

ANDRE DEUTSCH

First published 1988 by
André Deutsch Limited
105–106 Great Russell Street London WC1B 3LJ

British Library Cataloguing in Publication Data

Lindsay, Frederic
   A charm against drowning.
   I. Title
823′.914 [F]   PR6062.1484

ISBN 0 233 98254 X

Printed in Great Britain by
Ebenezer Baylis & Son Limited, Worcester

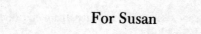

For Susan

. . . Have not all races their first unity from a polytheism that marries them to rock and hill?

W. B. Yeats, *Autobiographies*

CONTENTS

PROLOGUE

'They're England's glory,' old Turner said with a dry stress that suggested the opposite. 'See those?' Black scuff marks at head height on the staffroom wall seemed the only likely target of his waggling thumb. 'Chap who's been ill. Wears sandshoes. Sand-shoes!' Turner, an ex-headmaster come out of retirement to labour in that ungracious place, wore boots that laced up high on his bony ankles.

'What does he do?' I asked, not caring but respectful of my elders.

'Tries to see how far he can run up the wall. Does it at the intervals. Instead of having a cup of tea. Makes a hell of a crash every time he lands. Can't say I'm sorry he's off at present.'

'Broken leg?' I asked, hanging my coat on the peg farthest from the door. As a temporary intruder, I'd chosen it as the least convenient to which no one seemed to have laid a claim.

'Flu,' Turner said balefully.

My nose twitched to the same smell I'd been catching since my arrival a week earlier. It leached out of the drab green walls: poverty laced with disinfectant. Here in the staffroom it was the sour undermix to lingering scents of tobacco and cheese snacks toasted on an ageing hot-plate of dubious legality.

'God wants you,' the old man said suddenly.

A frightening thought. 'What?'

'Our leader.'

'Mr Walsh wants to see me?'

'He expressed that preference. As soon as you came in, he said.'

'God!' I looked at the clock.

'You, to see you, you to see wanteth he.' His face imploded in creases. After a moment I realised he was laughing at his own wit.

'Came in here looking for you ten minutes ago. Only you weren't here, being late as it happened.'

1

'Mrs Calder said she didn't want me in first thing . . . Not to worry, eh?'

'Why should you worry?' Turner made a face as if some sour left-over from breakfast had lodged itself under his dental plate. 'You'd be a fool to worry about anything that happened here.'

I had only been in Walsh's room once before, a week earlier on my first day at the school. That time, too, he had called 'Enter!' and I had hesitated a moment staring at the word 'Headmaster' in ornate script worked into the frosted glass of the door. Why couldn't he say 'Come in' like anyone else; or write 'hand in on time' instead of 'hand in timeously' on the little memos he circulated? He should have been funny. He *was* funny. It was just that I was no good with authority figures.

'Enter.'

He was up out of his chair, smiling, a square man with a bald head bobbing like an egg in a pan of hot water.

'Campbell! Come in, come in. Come in, my dear boy!'

I didn't like it. So much welcoming unnerved me.

'Take a pew. You sly dog! Eh? Eh?'

It was the wrong moment to remember Turner telling me that Walsh had vanished during the previous session with a nervous breakdown; and not for the first time apparently. He came to school by bicycle and today, I noticed, he had forgotten to remove the clips from his ankles. I wondered if that was one of the early signs.

'Eh?' He subsided, salting his twinkling with reproach. 'A sly dog. Keeping your light under a bushel. I don't look for that sort of thing from the people here. It never occurred to me you might.' Might what? 'But you have!'

And he was up on his feet again, the egg bobbing round the desk at a disconcerting rate, sinking towards me as I blundered to my feet. Ducking and coming up under his outstretched hand, only the narrowest and most merciful of margins prevented me from butting him full on the shell.

'Good man!'

He whirled back a step and settled quivering with good humour. 'Why?'

'Why!' For a fraction of an instant the smile congealed and drooped until a threshing of flesh beat it up from chin to chin and,

2

buttery, to his lips again at last. 'I like that. What I call a sense of humour. Take a First for granted, eh?'

A First? Joy; superstitiously choked down for fear of a mistake.

Walsh cocked his head to one side and made a judgement.

'You didn't know? Then I'm the first. Or rather you are.' And he grinned enormously like an appetite and held out the morning paper folded at the place.

University College, London. English literature and Language. With Honours of the First Class. George Campbell. I had done it.

'But the results weren't supposed to be out yet.'

'Here they are!'

'And I've—'

'You've done it!'

And the ends of my fingers were caught between two moist plump palms and squeezed and tugged up and down. What a nice man! A joy that was like pain swelled in my chest and I felt my lips stretch, matching his as if in a mirror until I thought my cheeks would crack. I wanted to laugh, but he might have misunderstood. I wanted to take him by the ears, like Moe in the Three Stooges, and plant a squashy wet kiss on the wrinkled sag of his forehead. I wanted to brace my feet against the earth and lift him straight-armed above my head – George Campbell, weight-lifting champion of the world in the Academic Olympics! And still undefeated – the Champ-een! I wanted to do something for the old man. It was a moment when I wanted everyone to be happy.

'I should be with Mrs Calder,' I said solemnly. 'I'm supposed to be giving her a hand with the younger ones today.'

'She wouldn't mind,' Walsh said. 'Not for one day, not if I tell her why. You could go home. Find someone to share the good news.'

'My mother.'

'There you are!'

I thought about it, then said like a fool, 'That's very good of you, but—'

But I'd go to Mrs Calder's. Which I did. Because I was a good boy. Walsh, of course, didn't put it quite like that. It's a long time ago now; some things blur. I think he may have said something like, 'Two qualities of a good teacher, being timeous and being conscientious.'

Timeous. The White Rabbit hurrying past, mustn't be late,

3

unforgivable to be late, a bundle of report forms tucked under his arm. And Alice tumbling down the rabbit hole, turning in the air, falling so slowly, her skirt drifting down to uncover the long white child's length of her legs. I wasn't going to be a teacher.

'I know,' Walsh said, 'you're only with us for another few weeks. What made you choose us?'

'I needed a job after the Finals –. until the summer. I'm saving for a holiday.' By the look on his face I could see that wasn't what he wanted. I tried again. 'But, of course, the chance to work with handicapped children . . . I did want to do that. I felt that was very worthwhile.'

Back in those days, you see, there was a shortage of teachers. Someone to fill in was always welcome.

When I came out of his office, the corridor was empty. I swung my arms and punched the air in triumph with my fists. Then, at once, looked about in case I had been seen. The corridor was still empty. Sunlight came from the playground side, painting the opposite wall in stripes of brightness. It was a beautiful day.

Mrs Calder's room, though, was on the dark side of the building, so that it seemed as I came in to be stacked with shadows and the air of it touched coldly on my cheek.

Laura pulled at my hand. Of the six children in Mrs Calder's group, she wasn't my favourite. Since what happened the day before, that had been Timmy.

'Being a good girl?' She looked up at me, not understanding, and I tapped my own ear and indicated her hearing aid where it dangled unheeded. She put it back in and then, beautifully, unexpectedly, gave me a smile as if we had just shared a joke together. 'Having fun?' I asked her out of the bounty of my exuberance.

'Laura!' Mrs Calder called. 'Laura!' her voice thinning irritably.

I took the child by the shoulders, brief bones that seemed ready to break in my hands, and turned her gently until she saw the teacher.

'Laura!'

All of the children were profoundly deaf; but, as if that weren't enough, each of them had something else wrong as well. With Laura, it meant the urine bag tied to her leg and the tube that ran from it to the hole in her stomach. For Timmy, my current favourite, it went back to the pram and the one violent shake too

4

many that had left his brains partially scrambled. A loner, he was sitting over by the far wall kneading a grey hunk of plasticine into an unappetising sausage. My small victory with him had been won on the previous day when he made the sound he had been taught for 'man' and turning I found Walsh had slipped into the room and was standing behind us. 'Oh, yes,' Mrs Calder had said, 'we can manage that. But no one outside would understand a word he was saying. I shouldn't forget that if I were you, not unless you want needless disappointment. It's not as though you were going to be with us for long.'

Timmy's aid, too, had come adrift. As I tried to ease it back in, the child shook his head fretfully. 'Must – wear,' I mouthed. 'Be – a – good boy.' I had been well told how important the hearing aid was for the profoundly deaf, moulded to fit exactly into the child's ear, the adjustment very necessary and precise. As I finished, something made me turn round, I have no idea what, that was a silent classroom; perhaps some alteration in the air itself.

Laura must have displeased Mrs Calder. Must have, since I witnessed a sweeping full arm blow with the open hand on the side of the head. Blood ran in a bright thread from the child's ear.

'Look at what you've done!'

She looked at me without expression. At this time, I can recall to memory no single feature of her face nor the colour of her hair. Yet I remember the exact quality of that lack. 'Oh, yes,' she said.

'She's hurt, she's bleeding.' I touched Laura's face, dabbing at the blood that ran from under the aid. The child stared up at me incuriously, seemed to be in a state of shock. 'What are we going to do?'

'Nothing,' Mrs Calder said, and made a sign to Laura who turned at once and began to tidy spilled blocks into a carton.

Listening, Walsh kept the buttery grin with which he'd glanced up from his desk smeared in place. What had I expected? That he would rush outraged from the room and drag Mrs Calder from her class?

'She's a very experienced teacher,' he said.

I heard the words. Watching his mouth move, I thought this must be what it is like to be deaf.

Walsh said, 'You won't forget your first class, not ever, I expect. I never have. Half of them on probation. I still see the names of one or two of them, regulars at the Old Bailey. You don't forget the names. Every Friday I used to take them for a game of football. And I'd join in! Gave some of them ideas about getting smart with me. *Not* a good idea. I'd put in the weight,' a meaty shoulder twitched, 'or a dig with the elbow or whip the feet from under them.' All innocence and good nature, he melted without shame. 'And those lads worshipped me.'

'I want the Cruelty Man in here!' That's exactly what I said. The phrase out of my own mouth, as soon as I heard it, sounded ridiculous. 'I— Will you call him?'

'Call? The . . . "cruel" man?'

'"Cruelty".'

When I was a child at school in Scotland, it was the name some of the children gave to the inspector from the RSSPCC. The Cruelty Man. It had no meaning here.

'I told you what she did.' At the thought of it, I reached out my hand towards the phone. 'If you won't call him, I will.'

'You won't, you know! Not a good idea!' When he shouted, his teeth showed yellow. The thick meat of his fingers made a cage for the blackness of the phone. 'Not from my office, not from here, you won't!'

And if then I had forced his hand up, who would I have phoned? Christ, I was so young!

'You shouldn't be out of your class,' Walsh said more quietly. 'You have the wrong idea of what you're here for.'

It was the heavy weight of a sort of authority I was in the habit of offering obedience. My father having died when I was a child, I had no gift for rebellion.

I even started to go back to Mrs Calder's class, but that was impossible. Instead I went to the staffroom in search of help and, opening the door, was startled by a thundering crash. Huddled in the farthest corner, Turner nodded sardonically over a cup of tea.

A square smiling man was picking himself up off the floor. 'You're new to this madhouse,' he said. 'I'm Fitzy. I've been off ill. Full of beans now though, thank God.' And he held out his hand, which I shook, not seeming to have much choice.

'Speaking of God,' Turner said, 'nothing serious, I trust?' At the blankness of my stare, he shuffled the lace-up boots with his thin old ankles in an impatient two-step. 'I told you he wanted to see you. You did go?'

A thousand years ago. I had to think what he meant. 'He told me I'd got a First. He saw it in the morning paper.'

'You're pleased. Naturally . . .' He studied me gloomily. 'I was a headmaster. Did you know that? . . . I thought someone might have mentioned it.'

But now the square man, Fitzy, was pacing back with a soft padding of black gym shoes. He posed with the intent stare of an athlete gathering concentration, rocked his weight from foot to foot in preparation, then with a muffled cry launched himself at the wall. As he mounted it, he turned his body, reaching up to bang a foot over his head, seemed to hang for an anguished instant and surrendering to gravity fell with a crash that made the cups on the table chime and jangle.

In a heap on the floor, he stared up at me hopefully.

'Did I do it?'

'What?'

He sprang up and looked at the wall; went up closer and put his nose against it and peered up. He was quite a small man. The scuff marks were above him.

'You can't tell,' he said disgustedly. 'Not unless you get a mark. Did you think I got above that one?' He stretched to touch the highest.

'With your foot, you mean?'

He shook his head in reproach.

'You're not sure. Even if you said I'd done it, it wouldn't mean a thing unless you were sure. That's what people don't understand. There wouldn't be any satisfaction. It's not just about winning.'

He sat down; I had made him lose heart. If he hadn't been there, I would have told Turner, I'm sure I would. I sat trying to think of some way to begin. The silence stretched.

'Mr Turner . . .'

'Campbell,' he said, very brisk and sharp; and went on as if I'd pressed a button: 'Get your PhD.'

'What?'

'I've given the same advice before, plenty of times. I was headmaster of quite a large school, you know. You're a very different fellow as doctor from plain mister. That's what I told the brightest ones. Oh, yes, particularly in this profession.'

I was leaving the building when Walsh caught up with me. The grin was back wider and creamier than ever.

'Off are we? That's all right. Wouldn't allow it normally, but this is by way of being a special day, am I right? Mrs Calder will manage by herself.' Hot blue eyes stared above the grin. 'Very experienced woman. She's devoted her life to these kids – retires next year.' He pushed the morning paper under my arm, and went on quickly as if clinching an argument, 'Go off, have a celebration – or, what I'd do, go home and share what you've achieved with your mother. The joys as well as the sorrows, eh?'

Or did he really say that last bit? Perhaps it's a stray from memory, something I've read framed under glass, or like a text burned into wood with a poker, hanging on the wall of an abandoned house. SHE MAKES EACH SORROW ALL HER OWN; AND, ALONE IN ALL THE WORLD, HAS NO ENVY OF YOUR JOY. YOUR MOTHER.

Only when I got back she wasn't there, as it happened, my mother. I sat at the bedroom window, not thinking at all just listening to the noise the traffic made spilling down from New Cross into Queen's Road. It was muted like being in the middle of an island, where the sea noise doesn't ever stop though you only remember to hear it again when you lick your lips and taste the salt. After a while I got cold and lit the fire in the grate downstairs, using the newspaper Walsh had given me. It had begun to burn before I remembered the notice of the exam results.

Paper goes quickly, writhes in the fist of the heat, turns brown and yellow then black. Somewhere among the flames, George Campbell, my name was burning.

I waited until it was finished then went out to buy another copy of that paper so mother wouldn't be disappointed. I can't remember if I got one; it's a long time ago. It must have been the afternoon by then, but perhaps I wasn't too late.

BOOK ONE
BREAKING

ONE

His name was George Campbell and he was afraid.

'Just this,' he went on, 'that part of being a good teacher is the ability to turn a subject round, let light reflect from each facet, so that you discover how many possibilities there are.'

He was over fifty, with red hair, a colour he regretted, inherited from forgotten ancestors. There was a time in the past when he had enjoyed listening to his own voice; whether that had ever been a part of being a good teacher, it had not occurred to him to consider.

'Let's say you're doing a project on Red Indians. What kind of images come to mind? Squaw, papoose, war-bonnet . . . cowboys? Naturally, cowboys. All those simplifications from films and children's books. Oh, we can't ignore them – they're *one* part of the truth. But don't let children think that's how the people we call Red Indians live now. The past affects the present, but it isn't the present. We have to keep the two separate. Little Black Sambo walks in and takes the wrong seat on a bus in Alabama, and the world changes a little.'

They stared back at him blank-faced. He should have been able, by this time in the session, to attach a name and a history to each of them. He knew the names as they recurred on a class list or a sheet of marks. He knew the knock and edge of their individuality as they confronted him daily. It was the connection between the two which escaped him. In desperation, he looked towards a girl who sat by the window, a mild creature, who would laugh when he made a joke. Consciously, after a moment, she raised her gaze from her clasped hands and returned his look with the curiosity of a stranger.

'It does change. Start with the past, the real past. Indians of the forest, the fisher folk of the lakes. The Plains Indian to whom the horse came like a gift of freedom. On its back, they voyaged the empty land, and that unbounded space made them mystics, so that even when the white men came and they were defeated and

11

hopeless, they invented hope and danced a great dance which was to bring all their dead to life and drive the newcomers into the sea.' He could still appreciate the sound of that, mechanically, like the memory of a savour. It was a project he had done more than once. 'As for today, do you know that there's a tribe of Indians who work in New York as high-construction men? The men of the tribe specialise in that work. Can you imagine them, pacing with a free step along the narrow metals of a skyscraper? A job, you see, one hundred per cent modern, but with the accent on courage, the ancestral bravura. And I can't believe there isn't some of the old mysticism too, high up there over the city. Over the city . . .' What would it be like for them when they came to earth in those violent streets? 'And – and the Cheyenne were marched, marched for a thousand miles, dying, women, old men, children herded along by troops of the United States. Or take the Aborigines in Australia. They're not blackboys mating for ever with their humpies in some timeless limbo. Not now— '

Terribly, then, they sniggered his thoughts slithering from him. He didn't lack the vocabulary; he wasn't slow; he knew that hump meant screw; screw meant winding hard flesh into soft flesh. He had read some of the paperbacks which had instructed them. Hump meant boss-backed and Hugo's poor cripple and the English king dying with his fingers poked out like horns and crying in the scraich Olivier invented for him. Did they know it meant those things too? And it meant the humpbacked stationmaster when he and Sylvia had searched for Chris. Chris eleven years old and three hours late from school. He had run to the station and a child had been there and was gone. With Sylvia in the car searching the dark streets. It was hopeless. Human shapes passed like panthers or beaked birds of prey. She'll be cold, Sylvia said. That's another thing! he burst out, clenching the wheel, Those short skirts! Oh, God, she cried, near hysterics, that's you, expect the worst. He tried to pull himself together – she'll remember this; how I collapsed – I wasn't any good. Oh, God, he stammered in idiot repetition, placatingly, we're not in the middle of the Brazilian jungle; of course, she'll be safe. Chris had gone into town with a friend, using her rail pass, to share in the buying of a birthday present. His daughter was safe. He had thought his heart would stop, and what had it been but only the shadow of grief?

'Do you know the British settlers used to leave clothes for them to find? Clothes that had been worn by cholera victims, so that the disease would be transmitted to the Aborigines. They wanted to exterminate them, you see, as troublesome pests.'

And the same thing was happening in South America now, he wanted to tell them; and had other examples pressing upon him, when a bulky coarse-voiced woman cried in what appeared to be anger, 'Oh, yes, teach them how bad the white man is. We've heard it – the wicked white man!'

The strangeness, the unexpectedness of other people; her question, the strangeness of her passion, drove him out of himself to take account of that. If he had been able to foresee an objection, it would have been methodological: could children take in such concepts? how would you put them across?

'But I didn't – I didn't intend "the wicked white man".' There was a pause. He avoided their eyes. 'Black men in Africa . . . I remember a film of a police action – they beat them with their truncheons. Black police beating, beating, villagers, their own people, squatting in the dust. Beat some to death. *Le ratissage*, they called it.' He hesitated, struggling to think. '*Raking out*, that means.' He forced himself to look at them and felt a smile, horrible and misplaced, move his lips. Half his lifetime ago, bright threads of scarlet blood ran from the deaf girl's ears. A fraud, afraid, he sat there pretending to have authority. 'Yellow men. Brown . . . they all commit great crimes given the power.' Bright threads of blood. 'Men are not different – given the chance. Not in that.' If he allowed himself, he would break down. He was on the edge of a desperate situation. 'I didn't mean the white man was wicked. I just meant don't trust people to have absolute power over one another. That's no good, you see. Not between cultures, if the gap is too wide. Not in homes for the mentally sick. Not in prisons. Not even parents with children.' Why had he said that? What would he find in answer if they challenged him – parents, *parents?*

'I know,' the bulky woman cried out, inspired, 'like the principal of the college here.'

They brayed laughter, perhaps only in relief.

As he stared at them, trying to understand, Peters rocked the door open, balancing its arrest in his meaty hand until he had gathered every eye. For the group, as students of teaching, it was in itself an object lesson.

'A phone call, Mr Campbell. In the Department base.'

In the corridor, he protested feebly, 'You should have told her I had a class. I could have rung her back.'

'Oh,' Peters said neutrally, 'I think she wants you quite urgently.' Hard not to admire the way he let the last word trail a shade, another behind it swallowed just in time – urgently . . . again.

They did not like one another, but they had worked together for ten years. If a colleague fell dead, you were upset; a heart attack, sad; a lingering cancer, horrified. So some careful neutrality when Sylvia phoned was par for the course.

From the phone as it lay on its side on the desk, there piped a distant brittleness. Sylvia was talking. He waited until the sound stopped and then took up the phone cautiously. There came the echo of a buzzing emptiness and he listened to that.

'If I stop— Everything falls on me. Why should I bother? Bother bother bother bother. Stupid word.' Her voice came more faintly.

'Sylvia?'

'He's given up. He'd give up if I let him be there be that all our lives stuck and here too stuck stuck.'

Gently, he knocked the mouthpiece upon the blond gleaming wood of the desk.

'George?' The single word blared in challenge. She had taken the phone up again from where it must have been laid down, perhaps in her lap.

'Hello? Sylvia?'

And this a little breathlessly; a man who has been hurrying.

'At last.'

'Yes. I'm sorry. I was with a class. I had to leave a class.'

'I've been waiting such a long time.'

'I'm sorry you had to wait.' He had practised patience.

'You don't care about Chris. I told you it would happen again.'

Sweet God! a voice in his head wept, spare me this. A confused shameful image of himself crucified horrified him and he wiped it away – physically with his hand brushed at the air – while the shameless unstoppable voice cried, Spare me this!

'George? I know you're there.'

14

'Have you been in her room? We said we wouldn't, you know that. We said— We promised.'

'To trust her. That was your idea.'

'No. Dr Nicholas – you were there when he spoke to us.'

'Dr Nicholas – a GP. What does he know? Trust! You would trust her into her grave. Don't you think I've eyes in my head to know she's been – doing that, doing . . . *that* again. If you had eyes, you would have known.'

Sick, he lay against the wall. With the phone at the full length of his arm, there was no way of making sense of the little noises that came from it. He was the one who had refused to know. As if cowardice could save Chris.

'. . . those vile things. Oh, she'd hidden the stuff – hidden – under tights in a drawer. Anybody who'd looked— Not hidden. I don't call that hidden. She doesn't care.'

She wanted us to find what was there. It's the part of her that wants to be saved. There is a part of her that wants to be saved, but it wasn't me who looked.

'I'll come home.'

'Whatever for?'

'We need to do something.'

'There's nothing to be done now. She's out. I don't know where. That's what happens when you trust her. How will neglecting your work help? That won't help, not if you're to be what you are – are now – for the rest of your life.'

If I stop, she had said that morning, all – all fall down. All fall down.

'If my work's so important, then why did you— ' he started to ask; stopped himself.

'What? Why did I what?'

'Nothing.' She had phoned as quickly as possible to tell him what hope there was in trust. 'Try not to worry,' he said. And before she could respond to that, 'I've got to go. I must. That class— I'm being called. I'll be home soon. As soon as I can.'

When the little voice finally was silent, he replaced the phone gently.

He stood outside the tutorial room, listening; the section was very quiet. But when he went in, they had gone. It was only twenty to the hour, with another ten minutes still before the end of the

period. He should be angry, he told himself, and did feel slighted
and then instead an unmanning relief.

'For the rest of my life,' he said aloud.

Once, for him to be in this place had been an achievement.

He had been teaching in a school in Wandsworth when his head
of department pointed out the advertisement in the *T.E.S.* 'For
College. Have a go, Campbell. Why not you as soon as the next
chap? You've got the experience.' A big florid man overflowing with
temporary goodwill since he had just been appointed to the
Inspectorate. It would have been ungrateful not to apply, and he
had got an interview and done well. A week later the letter came
and he took it to the headmaster who read it and read it again.
Looked up at last and, sighing, shook his head, 'Yes, yes. So you're
off, Campbell, to be a lecturer. A College of Education . . . You
came into teaching at the right time.'

Oh, success then. Even the headmaster envious, who kept a
bottle of gin in the drawer of his desk and was dying of cancer;
though that was a secret, even from the headmaster, then. It was
the second winter of his time at college before the letter came: '. . .
feel you would welcome the opportunity to contribute to a memorial
fund'; a circular to whom it might concern out of a man's working
life. He had put it aside and neglected to answer; it was a call from
a past he had put behind him, and, anyway, he had never liked the
man. He should have answered. How could he look for mercy now?

Chances taken and missed. His whole life a series of accidents.
At that, he had a sudden appalling vision of the car crash in which
his wife had been injured. He saw the jagged glass and the blood
upon her cheek.

How could he teach who had so much to learn?

The window of the lecture room framed a corner of lawn and a
rising curve of steps. As he watched, a student came down the
curving flight, a young girl, brushing long hair back over one
shoulder. The years rolled back, and he stood, young, on a corner
waiting for Sylvia. The river of girls flowing from offices thinned to
a stream and then a trickle, and he was sure that he had missed her
and was full of unreasonable anger, but waited, and she came at
last, walking alone. 'George!' and her face lit up and it was for him;
and with one hand she put back her hair from her shoulder, long
brown hair falling almost to her waist. The night before they had

16

quarrelled, but now at that chance gesture of her hand something in him moved to a decision. Soon they were married. Later they had a child.

'Oh, Chris,' a voice groaned, and when he realised that he was crying he scrubbed at his cheeks with the palms of his hands to dry them, but the silent tears flowed too quickly and it seemed to him that he could never in his life again face a class of students.

TWO

Because of Sylvia's call, he cut short his contribution to a meeting of the committee which concerned itself with student discipline, pretending to be unconscious of the principal's disapproving glance as he left early. If he had been going home by car, corners, lights, streets would have been hastened away by his anxiety. The train, indifferent, moved to its own time. This was the way he travelled every working day. Sitting by the window watching the markers of the journey being overtaken, he understood how commuting by train was one of the endless trivial options which had come to make up the sum of his existence. Each morning he took a train which got him in earlier than need be for his first class. The one that would have suited him best, however, meant arriving for his students five minutes late; and so he preferred to get up before seven and breakfast alone rather than bend the rules.

Everyone was getting off the train. Coming to with a start, he realised something must be wrong. Following them, he bundled out on to a platform bleaker than he had ever noticed from the security of the train. Crazed tiled walls, dirty and chipped, under an arch of grey concrete. It smelled of the city and being alone in a crowd. A morose man shabbily uniformed edged his brush's gathering of scraps along by a wall. On the line opposite, a train came and went; windows of faces so blank and indifferent they seemed hostile; time passed. They had been waiting almost an hour when a railwayman came calling through the crowd.

'What is he saying? It's like a foreign language. I don't understand.'

But he had spoken aloud, and a pale girl shied, swivelled hare eyes at him and edged away.

'There's an accident somewhere up the line,' a man explained. 'A bad one by the sound of it. There won't be anything this way, mate – not for a bit.'

18

He followed the grumbling crowd up into the street. At the entrance they dispersed with extraordinary speed until he was left by himself. Derailed, he wondered what to do. There would be buses, but the district was strange to him.

Sanctuary! he screamed – meaning it as a kind of joke; yelling inside himself in silence, as he stood there in his dull tweeds looking about calmly as if coming to a decision.

He had turned left, intending to examine the route numbers on a bus shelter about twenty yards away, when a blow struck him just under the shoulder. He fell heavily, instinctively throwing out a hand but it was the one which clutched his briefcase. The awkward fist smashed down and that pain was followed immediately by the length of the pavement beating sickeningly along his body.

In the bruised and dazzling sky of shock a moon face swam.

'Are you all right?' An arm like a clamp of beef tugged him upright. 'What an awful thing to happen! You turned so suddenly. I— Sure you're all right?'

At the indignity of the unwanted touch, he scrambled and lurched and came to his feet blinking and sick in the midst of a huddle of people.

'I'm all right. Thank you. Thank you.'

He forced his legs to move, blundering through a gap in the circle.

A hand caught him by the sleeve. Moon Face muttered, 'Have a drink. Really, I should. Give you a chance to pull yourself together.'

'I'm all right.'

To escape, he stepped out into the roar and snarl of the road. On the opposite pavement, he realised that he had crossed away from the bus shelter. He walked to the corner carefully as if something had broken inside him. A sign swung over his head: 'The Restless Servant.'

Inside it was noisy. Plates and axes, the faces of the drinkers hung in the air. In the corner there was a door labelled Gents and he went there because he could not push through to the bar and in a loud voice ask for a drink. He washed his hands, splashed water on his face and found there was no towel. With wads of toilet paper, he dried himself and rubbed at the dirty marks where he had fallen. All the time, a fat man leaked slowly into one of the stalls, groaning, with his head resting against the cement wall.

19

Through a passage, there was a lounge bar where the light was dimmer and the noise from next door subdued to a muttering as background to the voices of a couple in an alcove, gentle and occasional. It seemed a very safe place.

Patiently, he stood at the bar until a man appeared, holding a white cloth, apologising, 'Sorry. Rushed off our feet through there.' He found it comforting to be spoken to in that way; he ordered a double whisky and sipped it slowly. The pain in his knuckles gathered and travelled into a white pressure at the back of his wrist. He contemplated seriously the possibility that he had broken a bone. When he ordered another whisky, the barman without having been asked made it another double.

A long time ago, a man he had worked beside said to him one night, Take care. You're not a social drinker. The phrase had seemed to him then, almost a teetotaller, to carry a mysterious warning.

At some later time the barman refused to serve him again and he was angry, but when he came out on to the pavement a group of people came with him and he decided that probably the place was closing for the night. The knot of people unwound with uncanny rapidity. He stood yawning alone on the pavement. The speed of it reminded him how the crowd outside the railway station had rushed away in every direction; and he had begun to smile at that, when suddenly, irreparably, he understood the enormity of what he had done.

Sylvia would think he had been in an accident. She would think he was dead. Nothing else could have prevented him from rushing to her side. A light wind sprinkled the streets with rain. Going home seemed hopeless.

The solution came to him as he began to walk, as if the movement stirred his brain. He would go to Jan's and pretend to believe Chris was there. Having been told she was not, he could go home with that as his excuse for being late. Confirmation of his shrewdness came at the first bus stop, when, as he paused to check the indicator board, the right bus slid to a halt beside him.

Sylvia's younger sister was blonde and largely made. From their first meeting, she had made fun of him. She had been part of his fantasy life for a long time until, shamed and resolute, he had expelled her from his dreams with all her works.

20

'George!' Her pale brows rose. She was all astonishment; and yet, as she stared, an unconscious grin took the line of her cheek.

What she said, however, was serious enough. A touch, even, of panic: 'It's not Sylvia? Never Syl?'

'Certainly not.' He shook his head and to reassure her shook it again. 'Nothing like that. Not at all.'

'You're drunk!' she cried and the grin popped out, full grown.

She drew him into the hall. 'Out of sight with you or the neighbours will get up a petition. They're dead keen on those.' Her long fingers prodded, turning him into the front room.

'Charlie!' she called. 'God! You've been falling down. Don't deny it.'

'It's not George! You have a twin brother, George?' And good-natured Charlie, unbuttoned and yawning from before his television, gently shook his belly with laughter. 'It's him here, eh? Never you.'

The tiredness began at his toes and crept up, a slow death. While they discussed him, he felt the numbing ache.

'What about when he goes home? Phew? Sylvia's doghouse, eh? There's a thought.'

'Can that, Charlie,' Jan said. 'You know better than that.'

Charlie looked shame-faced, but perfunctorily like an old habit he was in the process of breaking. Then, amicable, they discussed him.

He had to speak before the numbness reached his heart. If I fall asleep in this chair, I could die, he thought, dimly hoping for panic to drive him out of his weariness.

'I wanted a word with Chris.'

'Chris?' Charlie handled the name, passed it to Jan.

'Chris?' she said. 'You don't think she's here? Why ever should you think she's here?'

But looking up, he caught their sudden glitter of suspicion, yet blundered on with the childish deception he had prepared. 'She's with Trish, isn't she? I thought – that is, we thought – ' Blundered to a stop, betrayer of his daughter, flesh of his flesh, to these strangers.

It was Charlie who went to the door. 'Trish!'

Chris's cousin appeared with a towel wrapped round her head. 'I'm trying to get my hair washed.'

'You seen Chris? Your uncle's here looking for her.'

'Ow – oh – ow,' she understood.

'It's all right,' he said. 'I made a mistake. Really.'

'She told her father she was staying with you,' Jan said.

'Naow. Not with me.'

'I don't think she said that.' He was trying to explain it was all a mistake.

'I don't see why you should call me a liar,' Trish said. An end of the towel sprang loose as she shied and snorted. 'It's not me that's the liar. You want to look a bit nearer home for the liar.'

He had always thought of Trish and Chris as friends and allies. Suddenly he understood how she was corroded in her plainness by envy of his daughter.

'She wouldn't say that about you, Trish.' He was on his feet, trying to escape. 'Even when you failed – when you didn't get in to art college – I know she thinks of you as her closest friend.'

Trish paled venomously.

'Don't think I'm sorry not to have gone. It would be better for her if she hadn't.'

Then he knew that his petty attempt to hurt her was going to be disproportionately punished. She trembled on the verge of some hateful disclosure.

'She'd no right to say she was here. It makes me look bad with Mum and Dad.'

'I know. It was wrong of her.'

'I mean they might think she'd arranged it with me. I mean . . .'

Charlie and Jan, however, were self-effacingly silent, intent on what was coming next.

Unexpectedly, he was sick with anger against the stupid vulnerability of his daughter who had put herself into hands like those of Trish.

'She's with her friend, I expect. A man friend. I mean a man friend.'

'"A man friend",' he mimicked, hating her ugly lack of beauty. Hadn't there been someone like her full of humourless malice in every class he had ever taught, even when he'd become too practised to care?

She might have read the words on his forehead, trembling with

22

anger, giving one fierce nod, running from the room. They heard her feet on the stairs, but said nothing, waited.

She came back holding out a crumpled sheet of notepaper.

'Here! Take it!'

It tore between them as he snatched it from her. The sharp noise of separation drove him forward past her 'I mean *now* call me a liar!', running from Jan's shrill surprise: 'Here, where are you off to? You're being ridiculous. Charlie'll give you a run home. George!' and fled from the thought of being restrained by Charlie – physically ran, left the front door swinging, through a hail of open-handed blows from the night wind into the unseasonable street. Night air or emotion, he was drunker than he had been in his life. He walked the tilting pavements like planks.

Under a street lamp, he unfolded the paper he had clenched in his fist. He had to smooth it flat before he could read it, under the livid light scrawled as if in dried blood. It was an instruction. The writer gave an address where he could be found 'sometime'. It made him uneasy. He rubbed his eyes trying to concentrate, then held the crumpled scrap closer to find what was wrong. 'The flat's on the eighth floor. Don't worry if the lift isn't working. Walk up. Keep walking up. Keep knocking. You'll get lucky. Sometime'. It was signed 'Lolly'.

Yes, that was it. The command was arbitrary, made no sense, had no purpose. He leaned his head against the gritty concrete of the lamp base. When he was a child at school, just after his mother had brought him to London, a teacher had taken a group of them to see a dog-training class. They had been supposed to feel a pleasurable excitement at those long heads resting on paws, the eager tongues, the brown intent eyes, so much obedience. He had remembered them later, when he was taken to the circus, where animals walked baring their obscene bellies on command.

Lights from a car swung across the face of the buildings and stopped. People got out, doors banged; only with the hesitation that meant payment did he realise it was a taxi. He ran forward, shouting Stop! clutching the sheet of paper with the address. The car had begun to move but came almost to rest. The driver twisted in his seat to look at him and then, as he lurched half over trying to get the door open, cursed, 'Not in my cab, mate. Find somewhere else to vomit.' With a great pull, the door whirled him off his feet.

As he flung out a hand to save himself, the nearside rear wheel ran over it. The pain was like the end of the world.

Later he would have no memory of the journey to the block of flats.

The taxi driver had come back.

'You've bleedin' well done it now.' They looked together at his hand. Three of the fingers had been burst open. 'That's a hospital job. Get in the cab and I'll take you.'

'No. I'll be all right. I'll go home.'

'Where's home then?' sharply, with a withdrawing suspicion.

And he had given the address of the flats, which fortunately must have been near since the taxi took him there although he could remember nothing of the journey.

The entry hall was undressed concrete; through a glass door he saw the paired gates of the lifts. The flat number was 83, which meant, he supposed, the eighth floor. He pressed the button; the doors closed; his stomach told him the box moved. Almost at once it stopped. The indicator lit 'Basement'. The doors sighed open. Long avenues of pillars, no colour but grey, hard light and straight drawn shadows. Without realising he had moved, he was pressed against the back wall. From somewhere out of sight, footsteps tapped. The doors closed and the lift began to rise.

Flat 83 was marked as one door of a series on the left side of a grey corridor; through windows on the right the lights of Bermondsey shone far below. It was cold and still. His watch had been smashed when he fell; it might be midnight; it might be much later. He had lost all sense of time. In the taxi he had wrapped a handkerchief round his hand. Cradled against him under his coat, it was a drum pain beat. There seemed no reason to be here. He listened for the sound of voices inside. They might be asleep.

He pressed the bell.

He thought it was a boy who opened the door, and then his own shadow swayed from the face and he saw it was old and corrupt. A moment later he saw that there was an internal stair running down into the flat and the figure was standing on a step below his own level; with that alteration, it was a man, neither young nor old, who answered him in a high Cockney whine, 'Chris? Jesus!' He plucked him in with his left hand, drew him down. The rake of the stairs was frighteningly steep, as threatening as ice, but the figure

24

descending turned its head, red lips in a white face, 'Chris – Jesus. Jesus Christ! do you see the joke?'

At the bottom of the stairs, there was a room narrow as a passage. The only light came from a table lamp that had been knocked over and lay on its side against the wall. There was a mattress under a tangle of blankets beside a couch. As he hesitated, the sweet unexpected stench of human dirt brought bile into the back of his mouth.

'Is she here?'

'Here and everywhere,' the man said. He fell on the blankets. It seemed unwilled, yet he kept his composure in falling. He giggled, his face made indeterminate by shadows. 'Didn't you know She rose on the third day?'

Beyond an archway, there were kitchen shapes of cupboards and work surfaces. In the light of the fallen lamp from the other room, he saw that it was empty. He drifted past the dim shapes to the sink by the window. As he stood, toy roads tracing the dark night below, the acrid smell of spilled urine came up at him from the sink. It was inconceivable that his fastidious daughter could be in this place.

As he came out of the kitchen, he found the man had got up from the mattress and was at the top of a second flight of internal stairs.

'I'm going to look down there too.'

'Not entitled, ducky.' He was slightly built and swayed as if it was a struggle to stay awake, yet gave despite that the impression of a compact and dangerous tension. He giggled on the same note as before. 'I hope you're not one of those violent types.'

'Come with me if you want. I have to see.' His voice disgusted him; in his own ears, pleading and tearful. I will go past, he thought. I have to. He pulled the injured hand free of his coat and it hung in the parody of a fist.

'Oh, so much blood!' the man said. 'I haven't seen so much blood since I slept with Lolly. He thought he'd taken my cherry – absurd boy.' He leaned closer. 'I feel I can trust you. Piles – nothing more romantic.'

In disgust and something like fear, he thrust him aside. Pain exploded at the contact with his mangled hand. As he stumbled down the steps, the high complaining voice followed him.

'Isn't it sad to grow old?'

25

Beyond the fire door, there was a landing with a lavatory and a bathroom. Both were empty. At the bottom, there were another two doors, the last of so much choosing. There was no way of preferring one to the other. He opened the door on the left.

There was a woman lying on a bed. Her skirt was bundled round her waist and she was naked under it. He looked between her parted legs. As he came closer, he saw an outlying arm with the insect stings of the drug like eyes in its soft flesh.

He had not known that he was so strong or so cruel. He half carried, half forced her up the flight of steps. The man was sprawled over the mattress. The figure lay so still it was like death rather than sleep. He let Chris go and she fell at the bottom of the exit stairs. Going into the kitchen, he was surrounded by dim shapes. The table tipped over, he kicked at stools and chairs, with one of them he shattered the soft gleaming of glass cupboards, a door fell open and pale light spilled out and he went behind it and heaved and the cabinet tumbled, gobbling its light in a tipping smash of jars and bottles: ice cubes sprang out like dice. In the next room, the man lay deaf, still. One hand was in the pool of light from the lamp. He looked down at the hand. The wrist was thin, a gleam of white bone. With his heel, he stamped down. The man screamed and convulsed. The movement carried him over the lamp and with its breaking, black darkness fell on them. He crouched in the dark and felt his way across the floor to Chris. The dark was full of moaning and cries. His outstretched hand touched flesh. It shrank under his fingers and Chris's voice screamed, hot against his lips, 'Oh, Lolly, please, no. Please!' and the man fell silent, then in sea echo out of the dark cavern whispered, 'Lolly? Is that you? Oh, you bastard, you mad bastard.'

'Please, don't hurt me,' Chris cried, turning her head on the pillow.

It had happened so suddenly. Sylvia had been holding Chris and then had shuddered and thrust her away and begun to beat her with closed fists. And his daughter let her arms hang helplessly before the blows, which were real blows, punches, a dozen of them landed (so many? what anger of his had held him as witness to so many?) before he wrapped his arms round Sylvia and swung her off, wrestling her down into the chair. Chris stood in front of them

26

where they sprawled, still embraced, panting; the punches had gone into her belly and fallen on her breasts, from one blow on the lips bright red blood ran down her chin. Given by a man, such a beating might have killed her.

'For God's sake, Chris!' he wept in his distress. 'She didn't mean it. She wouldn't hurt you. She's taken her tablets – I made her – she's asleep. She didn't know what she was doing.'

'Please, don't hurt me, Lolly,' Chris pleaded in the hasty breathy whisper of a child and what was horrible to him, the father, was that her eyes were wide open and fixed upon him.

When she was little and wakeful in the night, he had lulled her with stories of beanstalks and bears and dwarfs, scraps from pantomimes and Disney, and then, as he realised how poor his stock was and turned to Andersen, tales of the princess and the pea and the unclothed emperor which made her laugh, though as it turned out what she liked most was to be sad for the match-girl and for Kay in the house of the Snow Queen. Sad stories: it must have seemed natural to offer her another one, although he could not remember how he had slipped into making a tale of the leaving of Breagda or, running through it now in his head, how much he had given it then a shape borrowed from the Brothers Grimm.

—*There was an island once upon a time and still, since islands mostly don't go away. It sat in the wild sea and the calm sea out in the west where the world ended. It would have seemed a bare place to you, without a tree and with all its edges made of cliffs. But men and women lived there and boys and little girls too, and they wouldn't have couldn't have dreamed of living anywhere else. There was no money on the island and no shops. No one told anyone else what to do. Instead they met every morning in the village street and decided what job had to be done that day. I suppose sometimes it would be to build a house or repair one, and there must have been other things as well, but mostly they lived by hunting the sea birds and their eggs. To do that they had to swing down the cliffs on ropes. Oh, those cliffs. They started half way to the sky and went straight down like the side of a tree into the waves. The truth is no one was ever able to climb so well or so bravely as the men of Breagda. They lived like that for a long time, hundreds of years hundreds and hundreds of years, until one day . . .* Until one day, Chris, the fairy-tale was over. The bother is deciding just when;

27

not all at once, I suppose. Not with the sailing ship that anchored in the bay and brought the smallpox that saw off most of the two hundred people who lived on the island then; there were never to be so many again. Not with the infant tetanus that killed two out of three babies in the nineteenth century. Not even with the Reverend Malcolm who came to the island when the babies were dying and called that God's judgement on wickedness; he was the one who forbade the children to play games, but made the rule that they should carry a Bible under their arm wherever they went. And after all isn't that part of a fairy-tale still? – a black one? When this same Reverend Malcolm was an old man, he looked at his watch one morning and said to himself, I think it is time I was leaving them now: and off he went into retirement back to the mainland to the town where he had been born; by then he had been on Breagda for twenty-five years and his watch had stopped long since. And isn't that like something out of a fairy-tale too? A black one. And anyway wasn't that what the nineteenth century was about: mills and steam, missionaries in jungles, soldiers in deserts, traders everywhere: everything changing into something else, flicker flicker quicker, black and white pictures, the first movie unwinding out of the dark? The fairy-tale came to a stop when there were only seventy people left and they were sick a lot of the time and partial to taking gifts from the tourists who came in the summer. The men could still climb those impossible cliffs, but the strange thing is they didn't have accidents any more; they had become too cautious. A nurse came to help them, this was after the First World War, and decided it was too wretched a place for people to stay; and so one summer day when the sea was kind the Government sent a boat and took them all away. When the sun came up the next morning, for the first time in a thousand years no one lived on the island. Not even the dogs. They had drowned all the dogs the morning the boat came.

A groan from Chris brought him out of his thoughts. She was always fond of dogs, he told himself wryly.

Holding a book out of the school library, she had come to him one time. She had been eight, maybe nine. It's a real place, she said, Breagda, the island you told me about when I was little. Oh, yes, he'd admitted, it's a real place all right – and my father, your grandfather, lived there when he was younger than you are now with *his* father: they were among the people who were taken away from the island when the boat came that day.

A place you could go to, really go to . . . looking up at him, her brows pulled together in a frown. An island off the west coast of Scotland, he had said. In the North Sea? No, he told her, other side – far out in the Atlantic. Where America is! she decided.

That had made him laugh. Have you read this? she'd asked, holding out the book. He'd explained that he had never read *anything* about Breagda. It had struck him how appropriate that was. He was a bookish man, who found it hard to learn things unless he saw them in print; but this knowledge had come to him as an oral tradition, passed on in stories from his grandfather. He had an image of hands linking and though some of that endless chain of people closed their eyes or strained away, still the connection was made: the unbroken chain of the generations: back from his grandfather through all his ancestors on Breagda and forward again to himself, a Londoner, and the child his daughter. Moved, he had reached out and touched her on the cheek. But Chris had been angry. He had never been quite clear why she had been so angry. You told me it was a story, she had said; I didn't believe it – not as a real place. Perhaps if he had been able to understand, find the right thing to say to her at that moment; but he hadn't understood; he still didn't. She had never mentioned Breagda again.

He saw that she was wiping at her lips with her tongue. The wound at the side of her mouth had reopened and from the split crust a bright bead of blood welled out and soaked the tissue he held to it. Eyes closed, she lay unprotestingly still and after a while the bleeding stopped and he laid the tissue like a red flower among the clutter of jars on the bedside table.

She said something over and over again, but too quietly for him to hear until he bent over close. 'I want to be sick,' she whispered.

Next day, however, he was the one who was ill. While she was cared for in her own bedroom at home, he endured a hospital waiting room and afterwards had his hand cut and drained and stitched. The shapeless torn flesh was only recognisable as his because of the pain.

THREE

'There's a kind of summer's day when sunlight calms the spirits and settled weather offers a magical assurance that things will go well.'

I've read too many nineteenth-century essayists, he decided, and laid down his pen. Yet he was, in whatever style, happy. Through the window he could see Chris. Around her on the grass there was a scatter of paperbacks, suntan lotion, glass and jug of orange. The night he had rescued her came from another planet – at least was alien to this clean and settled neighbourhood.

As he put his diary into the drawer of the desk and made his way outside, he lingered on the notion of 'rescued'. Father in off-white armour; knight of the absurd; oh, all of that . . . but he had done it.

The hedge by the back lawn had sprouted a fringe like the wild hair of a violinist. Pulling the leaves in little bunches, he stood for an idle moment smiling at the blue peaked cap Chris wore to keep the glare from her eyes.

Quickly he crossed the lawn and, leaning over, laid a hand on her shoulder, 'Hi, daughter.'

But even the feel of that shoulder, a tooth of bone, told him his error. It was Sylvia who swung her face to him with a grimace of annoyance.

'Don't do that.'

'Sorry. I thought— '

'I know. You wouldn't be here if you'd known it was me.'

'Not true,' he said, and sat on the grass beside her. 'Where is Chris, anyway?'

She looked at him without replying.

'She shouldn't be moping indoors on a day like this.' A sharp twist of apprehension squeezed his gut. 'I'll call her.'

'Must you?'

'It's not good for her – with the sun shining like this.' Beyond the arch in the hedge, roses made plump splashes of colour against the brown earth. A bee clung to the yellow stripe of the empty deckchair, refusing to be disturbed as the canvas flapped in a puff of wind. 'Such a beautiful day. I thought she would be out sitting in the garden.'

'Where you could keep an eye on her.'

They stared at one another until he glanced away. If marriage was a duel, they had met at dawn once too often. He was tired of being wounded, tired of being patched up, tired of their endless encounters.

'You were the one who said we must trust her,' Sylvia reminded him. 'So that she could find faith in herself.'

'I do trust her.'

'You think she's better . . .'

'What are you talking about? Of course, she's "better". My God, have you forgotten the state she was in that night I brought her home?'

'Forgotten?' Her face spasmed in what resembled disgust, though it might have been remorse. 'I wish I didn't have to remember.'

Did Chris? he wondered. Did Chris remember her mother's fists?

'Sometimes it's better to forget,' he said.

'The calls too?'

The first one had come just after he returned from the hospital and, as he listened, his stitched and bandaged hand had lain in his lap like a thing discarded. The pattern had always been the same: a man's voice asking for Chris followed by silence.

'They've stopped,' he said. 'Can't you be glad I brought her home?'

'Home? When did you bring her home?'

He did not understand.

'That night. From the flat I told you about.'

She lay back and pulled the peak of the cap forward so that he couldn't see her eyes.

'That's all right then,' she said.

'I don't know what you're getting at.'

'That's all right then.'

He waited, knowing she would not resist the temptation to continue.

'I wasn't sure whether you meant that time – or the one before.'

31

'That's vile!'

She tilted her head to where she could peer at him from under the peaked cap. After a look that seemed no more than curious, she settled back until her eyes were hidden again.

'Oh, *trust*,' she said.

'What?'

'It's simple enough. You're afraid even to remember the last time – not to speak of the one before.'

'There wasn't a time before,' he said violently.

'There was, you know.'

'We weren't sure – it was different. An illness.'

'Oh, God. Of course, we weren't sure. How could such an idea have entered our heads then?'

Thick tears blocked his throat. He turned away in case she saw his weakness. Beside the hut, there was a low terrace of earth with roses. The stones that made up the retaining wall came from the house on the corner. When it was being taken down out of the way of the new ring road, he had seen his chance and had a quiet word with two of the workmen. He was proud of that piece of enterprise. Somehow it always added to his pleasure in the roses.

'This time,' he said, 'I know it's going to be all right.'

'You're always so sure,' she said ironically. 'So certain of yourself.'

The grey voice chilled him. He waited for the blow to fall.

'How much did your visit to the precious flat cost us?' she asked, so softly she might have been thinking aloud.

He had gone back to the flat on the second day after he had rescued Chris. All the night before, he had been unable to sleep, tormented by images of her humiliation. No man; no mysterious Lolly; no vengeance; instead he had found the owner, ignorant of all of them, back from a three months' business trip, raging among the ruins. For Chris's sake, he had bought his silence.

'I don't understand,' the man had said, looking about in something like despair, 'why should anyone hate me as much as this?'

Sylvia scratched the air with thin fingers.

'Now,' she said, 'we can be sure.'

'Please. You sound too much as though you – disliked her.'

'Sure of the first time – sure of the second – sure— '

'This time it's different,' he tried to promise.

'I can't imagine why.'

32

He hated her for that.

'You want her to fail again. Is that the only company you want? Just the two of you, hiding out of sight,' he said.

She put her hand to her cheek. His own words appalled him. 'Sylvia?'

She raised her arms and folded them across her face. The action was horrible to him in the bright garden. As he tried to think of what he could say that might reach her, a breath on the air turned him to see Chris under the rowan tree, without motion, half-shielded by the hedge. The fabric of silence ripped; tore into outcry and ragged anger.

Pushing past her, he clambered on to the low terrace so that he could look over the wall. One glimpse showed him a boy in the gutter. Bright red mantled his head. The rear wheel of the push-bike beside him was still spinning. Two men were walking from a car. A second boy was shouting, his voice high and trembling. 'Bastards, bastards. Oh, you bastards,' he sobbed. Bulky and authoritative, hair grey and expensively styled, the taller of the men spread out his hands: 'Now,' he said firmly, 'no need for that. No need for that,' bearing down upon the boy.

'It's an accident,' he explained, jumping back down on to the path. 'Don't look!'

Sylvia shrank away, putting up her hand as he passed to hide the scar upon her cheek. From the house, he phoned and then went out, dreading the sight of the boy in the gutter; but the ambulance was there and the motionless shape under the blankets was being tidied away.

Spectators had appeared from nowhere. A policeman spoke to a hand radio which muttered throatily back. The authoritative man was telling a plump sergeant, 'My friend had no chance. Not the slightest. The boy came from the siding there, wobbled out in front of us – with this fellow holding on behind him,' and he nodded towards the second boy, quietened now and standing apart.

Drawn out of himself, Campbell stared at the man with the attentive sharpness of dislike. As if he felt that look, the man's gaze flicked across at him, but then slid beyond, turning greedy, apprehensive, speculative.

Chris was huddled against the wall. She held her hands to her breasts.

33

'Go back,' he said. 'You shouldn't be here.'

Her lips moved soundlessly.

'Chris!' He shielded her with his body from the man's eyes. 'Please,' he said. He was afraid that she would make a scene. 'The boy's not badly hurt. They're taking care of him. The ambulance men know what to do.'

Later, someone would come and hose the blood out of the gutter. He did not know who would be responsible for that, but surely they couldn't just leave it there.

'Anything wrong?' It was the younger of the policemen. 'Miss?'

'She's my daughter,' Campbell said defensively.

At the sight of the uniform, Chris straightened up. She even attempted what must have been meant to be a smile. With an odd sidling movement, back to the wall, she went crab-fashion until, clear of them, she half ran back to the shelter of the house.

'We live in there,' Campbell said. 'She's young. She was upset.'

'Did she see it happen?'

'No, no. We were in the garden. Heard, we heard it. But just noises. We couldn't say what happened.'

'I see.' The policeman's radio dribbled noise. 'She looked upset.'

'She's sensitive.'

'You get used to it,' the sergeant said, joining them. 'I've seen them with their brains knocked out – you could've emptied what was left with a teaspoon.'

Walking back, he was sickened by the ugly image. The police car was parked at the gate, but he assumed it was there because of the accident until he went through to the garden and found a young constable talking to Sylvia. His first reaction was anger: police marching through his property, coming to pester them with enquiries. Next moment, he was afraid – was it about Chris? – and yet his automaton body carried him unhesitatingly forward.

'This is my husband.'

The policeman was raw and uncomfortable. He glanced at Sylvia as if he expected her to explain. When it became evident she had no intention of doing so, he said, 'It's about a Mrs Margaret Campbell,' and, stumblingly, read out the familiar address. From him, as he bent his head over the notebook, there came a mingling of sweet and sourness, rank sweat and the cloying taint of a hair spray.

34

'My mother.'

'Yes. That's right, sir. We had a message.' He was not much more than a boy, hot and uneasy. Perhaps, it occurred to Campbell, it is the first time he has had to do this. 'She died suddenly. Apparently, they've been trying to phone you . . .'

'It's been out of order.' He heard himself explaining and wondered if the constable knew that he was not telling the truth. They were ex-directory and of the kind that would not accept even a caller's name via the operator. The mysterious Lolly had forced that upon them.

'That would be it. If you could get in touch. That was the message, sir.'

'She's never been ill.'

'Well . . .'

'Thank you,' Sylvia said. 'Thank you for telling us.'

To his astonishment, she wanted to come with him; and then Chris declared she too would go to her grandmother's funeral. 'Are you sure?' Sylvia asked. 'It's a very long journey to Glasgow.'

The funeral was set for Thursday. The day before, early in the morning, he got them into the car, and was locking the front door when the ringing of the phone summoned him back into the house. He spoke his number and waited. There was no reply although he could hear that the line was open. 'Hello?' He listened to the silence sighing; a continent of silence with the sea at its edge, like the shells he had held to his ear as a child. 'This isn't doing you any good,' he said. 'You're not going to get near Chris again. I took her away from you.' Someone opposed him and that opposition was boundless and without restraint. He read the silence like the eyes of an enemy and cried, 'I hope you rot in hell!' But for him that was an excess, and, sobered, he remembered that the line had been made ex-directory. No one was there. Yet whispered, 'Don't you know when you're beaten?'

In the clear light that promised heat later, he set out with his wife and daughter on the motorway from London to the north. As he drove, his thoughts kept turning back to what had happened. It was like a bad omen.

Someone had put the phone down at the other end.

35

FOUR

The house smelled of cats.

'I'm your father's Uncle Benny,' the man said to Chris and took Campbell's hand in both of his. Campbell gave it and then tried to pull away but the man held on, squeezing sympathy. 'We haven't seen much of you this while, George. Your mother though was aye talking about you . . . how well you were getting on. She was the last of ma sisters – after your Aunt Jess passed away. I'll miss her.' Campbell was surprised to see his eyes were red as if with weeping. He turned away and blew his nose.

'It's an auld truth,' he said, blinking and patting his nose with the handkerchief, 'blood's thicker than water. Nothing like a family at a time of sorrow.'

Over his uncle's shoulder Campbell saw a black cat stalk from the kitchen. Gently his stomach heaved, as it prowled under the sideboard and settled itself in what seemed to be a box of sand. Over the rim, from one surviving eye it widened on him a malevolent gaze. Under his stare, the eye watered and squirmed shut. As it dipped its head, he saw a patch of sores where the fur had been scraped from between its ears.

'You'll be ready for something to eat,' Uncle Benny said, 'but you'll want to see your mother first.'

At his side, Campbell felt Chris jerk unbelief. Almost at once he understood, yet his own heart knocked for there was just the papery edge of a second's part in which he too thought he would see his mother alive again.

'She's upstairs,' Benny said. 'I don't know if . . .' He looked at the two women.

'No,' Campbell said firmly.

'Yes,' Chris said.

Sylvia sat down and turned her face from them.

In one of the upstairs rooms, beside a pillowless bed with a smooth drawn cover, the coffin had been set on trestles. He looked at what had been his mother's face. 'A peaceful end,' Benny said, coming nearer after a discreet pause. 'You can see she just slipped away. An easy end – when it came to the bit.'

Campbell went to the window: a slope of shabby grass, shops at the bottom with boarded windows, ugly houses identical in rough-cast like prisoners in a line. 'Don't be afraid,' Benny counselled behind him. 'You'll see, love. She's at peace.' Chris was standing where he had been, looking down into the coffin. He tried to find something in her expression. She seemed calm.

Downstairs, they refused a meal and drank tea. His uncle's wife, querulous and faded, besieged them: 'Well, a sandwich then? Just a sandwich? You can't have come all that way without needing something. Did you stop to eat on the road? A sandwich then? You'll surely take a sandwich?'

'I'd like to go and have a look at Mother's house,' he told Benny.

'Now?' His uncle looked reluctant, then was overtaken by a need to adhere to the fitness of things. 'If you like. I'll come with you.'

'No need.'

'It's no bother.'

'I want to go by myself!' He spoke with an uncalculated sharpness, and added, 'I just want to sit quietly and— '

'I'll come with you,' Chris said.

'No, you won't.'

He knew that tone was wrong, but he was in the grip of an inexplicable passion. Any reason he could give would sound in his own ears like a pretext. When Chris followed him to the door, putting on her coat, he had no energy to refuse her a second time.

'You'll find everything's in order,' his uncle grumbled. 'Nothing's been touched. Nothing's been moved.'

As they left, his aunt's voice pursued him like a bad conscience.

'But you're not away without a bite to eat? . . . He's not away without a sandwich?'

The name on the brass plate was almost worn away. Chris came silently to his side. He rubbed the plate with the edge of his hand.

'"Campbell".' He felt the faint warmth the plate gave back to him. 'My grandfather.'

'The one who told you all the stories when you were a kid,' she muttered, surprising him.

Behind the door, there was an envelope addressed in his own writing. He took it up and walked about the flat with it in his hand. The place was small: a lavatory, no bath; a dark hall and a box in the corner, waist high, which he found to be half full of coalite; a kitchen with butter in a dish, staining the air with its rancid odour. There was only one other room, with the empty bed and the sheets folded back. Chris was standing by the window. Joining her, he was freshly struck by the clean buildings and the prospect of grass.

'I remember the time my mother brought me here to visit.' He remembered the train, crowded, and shabby the way everything seemed to be after the war. He remembered how much he had hated having to share this room with his grandfather, even if it was only for a week. He remembered the smell of Sunday morning bacon and standing at this window while his grandfather's voice droned on from the bed behind him. 'Black tenements and broken windows. You wouldn't believe how much it's changed.'

'For the better?' she asked. 'Look at that wall over there.'

He angled his gaze down towards a gable end set at the edge of a stretch of open space where there had once been a building. Some time in the last decade or so they had got round to tearing down that dereliction, which was something surely; even if, as he now saw, the boys with the paint sprays had turned the gable into a palimpsest – DERRY/UVF/FUCK THE POPE/AND THE QUEEN – testing as if to see how freshly those glowing stones would soak up their never-never land echo of someone else's reality.

'When I was very young,' he said, 'I lived in a flat like this. Just the same size. I remember sleeping in a bed in the kitchen and wakening to see the firelight on the walls and my mother and father sitting talking together. I don't remember anything more about him.' The words didn't convey to her – how could they? – how safe it had been. He had been in the safest place in the world.

'The war came and I was evacuated.'

Exiled from Paradise.

She would know what it meant – to be evacuated. He had sent her to good schools. She was well educated. Somewhere along the way, she had come to him and asked about how it was organised, where he had been sent, things like that; and in her turn showed him a fat packet of notes and pictures, grainy copies of old newspaper clippings describing how well villagers had coped, cheerful vicars and organising colonels (ret'd) and home-made jam and fresh air and coos! and cors! at grass and cows; a platform of children by a train with luggage labels round their necks – to be collected. All the stuff that had been dished out to her class for their project in history. Ancient history.

What could any of that mean to Chris? Should he say, People of my age were made by the war. (Which war? she might say. You talk as if there was only one.) That's right. The Nazi War, Churchill's and Hitler's. Only one for my generation – the roots of memory. We were children and our lives were ripped up, torn up by the roots. After that for some of us no place would ever be home again. (Poor you! she would mock; and remind him of the people who really suffered – in death camps then; later in Vietnam; and now in South America, South Africa, the Middle East. When she cared, she had her causes off pat: a child of her generation.) That doesn't matter, he would say to her. What is real is real. Real for me. Real for people like me. Reality isn't something you trade in for a more valid model, a later model.

'Those stories about Breagda,' he said abruptly. She turned to stare, raising her eyebrows at him. 'I didn't hear them when I was a child. My grandfather crammed them into that week. The one I spent here with my mother – when I was eighteen.'

'He must have been in his dotage.'

He thought about that; said, surprised, 'He wasn't much older than I am now. Maybe he wanted to tell them to someone and there wasn't anybody else. Maybe he felt that was all the time he had.' Thought about that, 'And he wasn't wrong. I didn't come here again – not until years later.'

There was an old rocking-chair with one broken arm; it had been his mother's favourite seat, by the side of the window where she could watch the life of the street. Chris sat down now in this chair, as if she too wanted nothing more than to share at a distance what went on down there below them. Seeing her like that, he recognised what people had said to him – that Chris was beautiful. Normally, he was aware, because she was his daughter, only of her familiarity or the changes which flawed it. She was wearing a skirt

39

and a tailored jacket with a white blouse; the colours of the costume were dark and Sylvia had picked it out for her as being most suitable for the funeral. In those clothes, she was like a stranger to him, a familiar stranger. It seemed to him that when she was young they had been close. He had carried her in his arms. He had listened, even if only with half an ear, while she chattered. Certainly, however he had been at fault, his heart had been unbarred to her more than anyone in the world.

'It's small and mean and *nasty*,' Chris said, not looking at him but continuing to stare out of the window. '*You* didn't come back. I don't see why you let Grandmother stay here.'

'She could have stayed with us – there was a home for her. But when the old man left her the house, she wanted to come back to Glasgow. I never understood why.'

He was still holding the letter he had found lying behind the door. By the time it came, she was dead. A neighbour had become suspicious and then Benny had come and taken her to hospital and afterwards to his home. But she would not let them get in touch with her son – 'in case he worried'.

'I didn't even know she was ill,' he said, and ripped his letter across and kept on tearing until the fragments were scattered on the rug at their feet.

It had been a cruel trick to play on himself, imagining until it was too late that he had grown indifferent to her.

In the car on the way to the cemetery, he looked past Chris at the bright morning. They were taking the slip road from the motorway, descending in the clear air.

'I can hardly credit it,' his Uncle Benny mused with a sigh. 'Sitting here with you both – going where we're going. I've been this road too many times. I was at your grandfather's funeral here – your father's father that is . . . Your mother and I were only children when *our* father died. In those days you walked behind the hearse. I can still see the big horses, matched blacks, fine beasts, with the feathers, you know . . .'

'Plumes.'

'Aye. With the plumes. Wouldnae fancy walking on this road.'

'No.' In the fast lane, one swaying lorry chased another.

'No respect now . . . Maryhill Road was full of people. And the sun was shining, I mind that. And I couldnae get over it – all those folk rushing about on the pavements. Do they not know my father's dead? I was wondering. I was just a boy and I felt it was wrong. It's funny, isn't it?'

'I don't remember my own father, not really.'

'Do you tell me that?' The question came with a touch of sharpness as if examining a fault. Campbell felt Chris stir at his side and wished he could explain that the impression of criticism was an accident of the unfamiliarity of the rhythms and accent of his uncle's speech. Yet it pleased him to imagine that she might have wanted to protest and take his part. 'He was called up early, right enough – or did your father volunteer? It's too long ago.' He sighed and drew a rectangle of pasteboard from his pocket. 'I've asked your cousin James to take a cord and Bart, of course, and . . .' As the names were listed, Campbell puzzled over what might be meant, but understood when he was handed the card. There was the dark outline of a coffin with numbers grouped around it – the numeral 1, which stood at the head of the coffin, had been circled. 'I would've discussed it with you last night,' his uncle said as they passed between the cemetery gates, 'but you came back so late.'

When the minister spoke and the men each took one of the cords and began to lower the box into the grave, Campbell saw them as if from above making the shape of the outline on the card. He felt calm and was afraid that it might seem he did not care, but as the coffin went down he noticed how smoothly cut the sides of the hole were and the muscles of his cheeks jumped and trembled as he thought of her being left in such a cold place; and so that was a sign to them that he had the feelings of a son.

From the cemetery, they went back to a restaurant in the city. 'Changed a bit, eh?' Uncle Benny remarked, looking around as they got out of the car. Across the way reared the ugly concrete legs of a fly-over with glimpses of high-rise flats between them. He knew this must be a great change, but had no memories from childhood of what had been there before. Not wanting to offend his uncle, he nodded; then shook his head as if there was something to regret.

It was a Co-operative restaurant. Of course, he thought, and the management of the funeral too would have been given to them. All the mourners came to the meal; soup, steak pie, salad; most people seemed to choose the steak pie; tall gaunt men with plump white-haired wives; over the sudden release of noise, the man beside him, some prosperous cousin with a broken-veined drinker's nose, asked, '. . . and in your own line? How would you say business was doing down south?' Those of the women who had not gone to the cemetery reappeared here; Sylvia sat beside him with Chris on her other side. There were more people than he had expected – a gathering of the clan. He found he believed in a ritual for dying and, to his surprise, something in him responded to the day's arrangements as decorous.

Afterwards only some went back to the house; 'just the close family like,' Benny explained. Even so, the dull little house banged with people. He knew some of them by name, but even they were more strangers than the most casual of his colleagues at work. They made a point of personally offering sympathy; he struggled to proffer an acceptable response. 'She didn't always have it easy? . . . No, that's true. My mother spoke of you, of course. I've often heard her speaking . . . about you.' He became obsessed with the need to see Chris. His aunt offered him tea insistently. As he watched, it struck him that most of them were as strange with one another as with him: a clan that existed only to bury its dead.

An elderly man, white-haired, upright, with the brick complexion of outdoor work, looked seriously into his face. 'Aye,' he said slowly, offering the single word as if with a burden of meaning. Campbell searched hopelessly to remember his name. 'Aye.' He patted Campbell on the shoulder. 'We're all poor creatures.'

It seemed funny – Campbell was sure he had used these words before; these would be the words he kept to be spoken at funerals, and just in that way, to be begun as if upon a sigh and carried to the end with a weighed solemnity. Yet, they were true. Faced by death the unreasoner, what was left to be said? As if a film had been cleared from his eyes, he saw the essential goodness of the man who had said those words – how much kindliness motivated them, and from how much simplicity and deprivation they rose. Tears he was ashamed of stung his eyes.

'It's later's the hard time,' the man said. 'It hits you hardest when you're left alone. Once everyone's gone . . .'

Campbell realised the man was describing a grief of his own; and

42

at the same time the speaker seemed to feel that also for he smiled apologetically and cast about for something else to say.

'Your father and me were close. We were always friendly like, but after he came out of hospital we were close.'

Campbell knew that his father had been killed near a place called Bardia in the Libyan desert. He thought whenever he remembered that of his father's body in the back of a lorry with the sand drifted upon it; but that was only an image from some film he must have seen as a child. His father had been buried out there. He looked sceptically upon the man.

'A long time ago and— ' No longer listening, Campbell searched over the man's shoulder for Chris. And for Sylvia. Where was Sylvia? In his anxiety about Chris, he had forgotten his wife. A cold knot cramped his stomach. Where was she? Had someone said something to set her off?

'Your father – I was saying about your father.'

'Sorry?'

'I'm saying he would have been pleased at the way you've got on. He believed in education. He was a fine man. Too ready with his fists maybe. But fair fighting you understand – not like these young animals nowadays. Not that there was any fight in him when he came out of the asylum. He was dazed, like, from what they did to him there. I'll tell you a thing I've kept to myself. We were sitting, your mother and him and me – I made a point of looking in most nights at that time – and I said something and then I could have bitten my tongue out. "Care a damn whether it's Baldwin or MacDonald," I said, "you'd have to be a right loonie— " And I got fankled on that – "loonie", you see. Lunatic. But your father gave me a right black look and knocked out his pipe on the grate. "If I am," he said, "I've more to worry about than hearing the word. Since I'm not, I'll need to see it means no more to me than other folk." I thought that was awful good. He told me afterwards, "That was the night I knew I was going to get better. I'll never look back." Poor George! With the war he didn't get long. Not long to look back or forward.'

In all his life any hint against his father's sanity had been kept from Campbell. Suddenly trembling with anger, he said, 'We're all poor creatures,' parodying the man's accent.

'Aye,' the man said and, to his confusion, patted him on the shoulder.

'I have to find my wife,' Campbell said desperately, 'if you'd excuse me.'

'Of course.' Then confidentially, 'She was brave to come. She shouldn't let it bother her so much,' and ran a finger lightly down from his cheekbone to the jaw. It seemed to Campbell a dreadfully observant tracing of the line of Sylvia's scar. 'Tell her if she can just accept it and be herself, other folk'll not worry about it. It's not easy but you always have to remember it never means as much to other people as it does to yourself. I'm real glad she managed to come – knowing it troubles her so much.'

This stranger talked of his father's madness. Now he discussed their nightmare years since the crash as if he had a right to share in them from his great distance.

'Excuse me – I have to find my wife.'

'Don't worry. She'll be having a rest upstairs.' And, as he tried to move away, caught him by the arm. 'Before you go, tell me, are you a sailor? At all, I mean. Do you sail at all?'

To exorcise anarchy, Campbell answered, 'Yes. I sail. Not recently, but it used to be a hobby of mine.'

The burnished old face split in a gape of satisfaction.

'It's in the blood, I knew it. You're your father's son. Maybe he wasn't in his right mind, but it was still a great bit of sailor work that got your father across to Breagda. He said to me it was cowardice made him run there. But I said it took a hero to run to Breagda. In winter? Over those waters? In that apology for a boat?' He smiled as if at a joke Campbell was fitted to share. 'A hero to run to Breagda in any case, eh? Just a bare rock, though you'd never believe it if you heard them singing about it at the Mod or at a ceilidh with the tears stottan off their ankles. I'll tell ye why folk lived there for a thousand years – because they didnae ken any better! Take them away from it, and who would go back?'

The bedroom they had been given was in darkness. He crossed to the window and jerked the curtains apart. The sunlight was painfully, startlingly bright. Don't they know my mother's dead? the words came into his mind, and then he turned and saw his wife sitting in the chair by the bed.

'There was an awful man,' Sylvia said in the whisper he hated

44

and had been afraid to hear. 'It didn't do to worry too much, he said. I'd never seen him in my life before. The surgeons nowadays did such wonders. No one who didn't know would see – see— ' She gave a gasp like the beginning of a laugh or a scream. 'Not like the war, he said. The poor burned pilots, he said. Sweet Christ, I'd never seen him before!'

'He's an old man. I've just been talking to him.' But as she turned her face away to hide the scarred cheek, he knew it was going to be no good. 'It was ridiculous – with me too. He talked about my father.' The words about his father, however, stuck in his throat. 'It comes as a shock to us. We don't understand how he can know so much, but he means no harm. He thinks of us as family.'

He took her hand. It lay in his clenched like a stone.

'Don't spoil Mother's funeral,' he heard himself pleading. 'You know she liked you. Isn't that why you came? You've done so well, so very well.'

She put up her hand to cover the cheek she had hidden. The crazy hope of getting her to go back downstairs disappeared. How would he get her home to London? He saw her beside him on the motorway, threshing across the seat, hysterical because she imagined an overtaking driver had seen her face. That had happened once.

'Is something wrong?'

Uncle Benny hovered in the doorway. He laid Sylvia's hand gently in her lap and stood up from where he had knelt at her side. With a finger to his lips, he led the way into the corridor.

'She's not well then? I knew something was wrong. I'll get the wife to sit with her.'

'No!' The word burst from Campbell's throat. At his uncle's look of offence, he struggled to get his voice under control. 'I'm sorry, it wouldn't help. We shouldn't have come.'

'Not come?' His uncle stared as if he had spoken Chinese. 'To your mother's funeral?'

'I don't know how I'll get her home,' Campbell said dully.

'I'll fetch the doctor,' Benny said. 'There's a surgery at five. I'll go myself. It'll be better then – everyone will have gone by then. No need for them to know.'

A face from below widened its wise relative's eyes on them and descended. The living-room door opened on sorrowful animation, rattle of cups, tang of smoke; as they waited, they heard it close.

'Look, it doesn't matter what any of them think. She'll get worse if she has time. Can't we go now?'

'To the doctor? Well, it's just that the surgery isn't till five. Maybe the wife'll have a number for him.'

'If we could be quick.' He forced himself to quieten. How shameful it would be, after all, for them to see the completeness of his panic. 'We've been through this before. Too often. It was a stupid mistake for her to come. She can't go outside.'

'Like claustrophobia,' Benny said.

'She can't bear anyone to see her.'

'Because of the accident. Aye, we'd heard that.'

Of course. Eyes from so far away; how could he – how could Sylvia – have lived their torment and never had a sense of those eyes?

'But it's not so bad. Not what we thought it might look like – with what we'd heard from your mother. The wife said to me last night it wasn't as bad as we expected.'

'It is to her.'

'Are you sure you wouldn't like the wife to sit with her?' his uncle asked.

He tried to think.

'Chris would sit with her. She wouldn't mind Chris.'

His uncle stopped on the stair so abruptly that Campbell blundered into him.

'But didn't you know? She's gone off with her friend.'

'Her friend? Chris doesn't have a friend here.'

'Oh, she knew him all right. No doubt of that. They were carrying on like right good friends,' his uncle said with a touch of scandal; but then, basically kindly and well-intentioned, went on, 'though he was a bit annoyed she was hurrying him away for I think he wanted to offer you his condolences. He struck me as a nice lad. Very well-spoken.'

'But who was he?' Campbell asked.

'It was a silly name. She called him . . . Lolly. Maybe it was a joke. Anyway, I gave them the keys of your mother's house. Chris wanted to go back there, just for a last visit. She must have got something out of going there with you.'

46

'Lolly.' He had been so sure she was over all that. He had been so stupidly triumphantly sure.

Looking up at him, his uncle faltered, 'I mean that seemed natural enough. I didn't see any harm in it.'

Sylvia stirred and turned her scarred cheek on to the pillow.

'She'll sleep now,' the doctor said. 'You'll see, she'll feel more like herself in the morning.'

'It's not like that.' He despaired of ever being able to explain. 'She won't go out. She just can't. Not since the accident.'

The doctor turned her face to the light. He was a heavy old man and the bed sagged as he shifted his weight from one buttock to the other. She slept now too deeply to be wakened, but despite the sedative she struggled feebly to hide her face. Campbell saw not the record of her injury but the black shadows and the lines around her eyes their time together had sliced more deeply than any scar.

'No point in pretending it isn't there,' the doctor said. 'But it's a neat job. I can't see it should be a barrier to an ordinary life. I have a patient with a birthmark that covers half her face. Marvellous sense of humour. She works in a paper shop. I tried to get her a job at the check-out in the supermarket, but the manager wasn't keen. More fool you, I told him. She gets on splendidly with people. It's all in the mind, you see.'

Campbell tried to follow the old man's argument, but sluggish misery slowed his wits.

'I'll look in on her in the morning. That'll be the time for a chat. I tell the young men a good GP can teach the psychiatrists a trick or two – not theory, practical psychology.' Twinkling, he settled more comfortably on the edge of the bed. 'I mind fine once being called out to a farm not that far away from here – there are fields on the far side of these houses though you'd hardly credit it – and what a night! The back end of November and I'm driving along cursing the weather and wondering what made me stupid enough to be a doctor in the first place. I arrived to find the daughter had tried to commit suicide. There was my problem. I wonder, do you see it? She'd made a hash of the first attempt and she was just waiting for me to leave to try again. Pregnant, of course. I knew she was just biding her time, waiting for her chance. Suicide's like everything

47

else – you improve with practice. Never believe that tale about them not being serious if they don't manage it the first time.

'So there was my problem. What was I to do? I doubt if you'd guess my answer. I got her out of bed – told her mother and father to stay put – he was a big brute of a man – and got her to the front door. I took her along by the elbow and she came like an empty sack. Anything to get rid of me. Look up there, lass, I said to her – and, oh, but it was a cruel sky, a terrible sky. *I* wouldn't like to be going up there tonight, lass, would you? And the look on her face told me plainer than words that I'd won.'

With his white hair and blue eyes, so unhurriedly, heavily, there on the edge of the bed, to Campbell it seemed this doctor should be wise.

'I have a daughter Chris – that's why I wasn't here when you arrived.'

'Yes?' But he had risen from the bed and taken up his bag to go.

'Please!' Campbell put out his hand to hold him and then, realising what he was doing, stopped in time. 'I know it's not why you came – but if you would only listen.'

The old man waited, poised.

'My daughter Chris.' His brain was numb with misery. Terrified that the doctor would become impatient, he drove himself on. 'I was too proud of her. God forgive me, I used to boast to neighbours of how well she had done – you're boring them, Sylvia would say. When we found out, when we found out, she was much more ill than I realised. She got better but it happened again. I'm sorry.' He was not a man who cried. Stupid, stupid. 'She was a clever girl at school. But not a bookworm, she was good at tennis— '

'What exactly's wrong with her?'

The question astonished Campbell. 'She takes drugs. Didn't I say?'

Something altered in the old doctor's expression. 'Oh, drugs. I thought— '

What? Cancer? Was that what he had thought? Something all sorrow; unmixed with disgrace.

'I was told she'd gone off – to my mother's flat. My mother's dead. They had no right to be there. I knocked but they wouldn't answer. I couldn't hear a sound from inside.'

But he had known they were there. His fists still ached from pounding upon the closed door. He had beaten upon the door until he was in pain and then he had tried to kick it in. He had punched at it with the flat of his foot, as near the lock as he could; but there was a fat brass handle and all he got for his effort was a jarring that drove up to the base of his skull. As he had rubbed his head in pain, a whisper of sound in the sudden silence made him look up. The spider tracery of iron rail winding overhead stirred some memory and his mother was peering down from high above and changed at once into a stranger, an old woman leaning out over the banister, trembling and threatening to call a policeman; and that was the inexplicable thing – that though she was a stranger yet she still threatened to punish him.

'They?' the doctor asked.

Campbell shook his head. He could not betray Chris. He wanted to put his arm round her and hide her from all of them.

'Drugs?' the doctor asked. 'Hard drugs? And for how long?'

He tried to calculate the eternity since her sixteenth birthday. By Christmas they had known something was wrong. After that, a year more, was it almost two?

'A settled addiction then?'

'And how many relapses?'

Campbell was not himself a man who suffered much in the way of illness, and so this succession of questions gave him confidence. It was so reassuringly medical.

'I'll come in the morning and talk to your wife. But your daughter . . . that's a different business altogether. There really isn't much I can suggest there. She's too young, relapsed too often. Too sick and that's the truth of it.'

'Hope,' Campbell asked quietly. 'What about hope?'

'As for hope, we never give up hope. Where medicine stops, some of us find a place for faith. But as for hope, there wouldn't be much cause for it – not in the literature.'

'Not even for a child.'

The doctor surrounded him with sad authority.

'I couldn't promise she'd be alive this time next year.'

'No one has said that to me,' Campbell whispered in fear and anger.

'You must understand I offer an opinion – only based on what you tell me – because you insisted.'

49

'They told us it was serious. We never doubted it was serious.'

'As serious as cancer. As serious as the plague. If it were just the body, we'd be in an easier case. Oh, the body gets addicted – I could explain that process to you. Why do they go back after a cure, knowing it's death? That's the question. Mind and body like two hands tugging – and everything over the edge after them.'

'Hope. You mustn't take hope from me.'

'I've simply tried to give you an honest answer. It's not one I'd have forced on you. Addiction patterns like your daughter's are suicide. Your daughter is trying to die – I wouldn't have any confidence about stopping her.'

'The girl on the farm. You stopped her. Why not Chris?'

The old man avoided his eye.

'I'm sorry. I have to go.' But held by Campbell's look said hastily, in irritation, 'I've simply been honest with you. What do you want me to say to you? You've punished her and you've loved her – you've tried those ways, I know. Hope? The world's too much for her. Man, how can I tell you why? This daughter of yours wants to kill herself. You want to stop her – well, hit her over the head – drag her off to a desert island. The world or her, one has to go.'

But stopped at the look on Campbell's face.

'I'll call back in the morning,' the doctor said. 'Let your wife sleep. She'll see things differently in the morning.'

FIVE

Half a dozen times he had stopped the car to check that Sylvia was breathing. He swung the car on to the hard shoulder and stopped. Breath snored in her throat. Just ahead two men were changing a wheel on a black Ford. As he bent over her, she sighed and muttered in her sleep as if trying to pass on some secret. Bent over her body, he became conscious of the two men in front who had straightened up and, staring in, were speaking uneasily one to the other. As hastily as if he had been guilty, he pulled out on to the slow lane.

For miles he watched the mirror, but if the Ford passed him he missed it.

When he arrived at her sister's, all three of them were at home. Charlie helped him carry Sylvia into the house.

'Could we take her straight upstairs?' He struggled for breath.

'She can go into Trish's bed,' Charlie grunted, but Jan blocked the way shaking with rage.

'What did you do to her?'

The dead weight began to slide in Campbell's arms. He jittered between the task of holding her and the blonde fury of his sister-in-law.

'The doctor gave her something so she'd sleep. She's really all right.'

'All right?' For a moment he thought she was going to hit him. 'Look at the colour she is! Are you trying to kill her?'

'Let us get through, for God's sake!' Charlie said. 'My arms are coming off.'

Against his better judgement, Campbell felt a brief warmth of affection for Charlie who, lurching forward, got them on course for Trish's room.

Jan trod their heels as they half-dropped Sylvia on the bed. 'Get out. Both of you. I'll take care of her.'

Trish was in the front room, legs tucked under her, reading a book with dramatic nonchalance.

'You'd better help your mother,' Campbell told her. The physical effort had left him feeling sick. Black spots dabbled the room as it rocked slowly round, a suburban carousel. He tried to remember when he had last eaten. 'She's undressing Sylvia.'

Without looking up, Trish turned a page then yawned. Charlie gave her a quick look. Campbell had heard him rage at her for less. Now, he said nothing; turned to the drinks cabinet: 'Whisky?'

Campbell's legs gave way and he half fell into the chair. The mellow fire from the little glass spread in his chest as he sipped.

'Better?' Charlie grinned. He had emptied his own glass and refilled it. With the bottle, he gestured a question. Campbell shook his head in refusal.

'You've had a time,' Charlie said and splashed more into his glass.

'Is that wise?' Trish asked from behind her book.

'Little cow,' Charlie said without heat. 'Big turn-out, was there? At the funeral?'

'Relatives. I was surprised – there were so many relatives.'

'Better after you're dead than coming round beforehand to tap you for a quid.' He laughed at his own humour and emptied his glass again in a quick movement.

'Christ!' Trish said.

'What put Sylvia over the top?' Charlie asked.

Campbell stared at him.

'I mean – upset her. She hasn't been that way for a bit.'

'Travelling. We should never have gone.'

'And what about your bloody uncle or whatever he was?' Jan appeared abruptly, blonde, big, an avenger strayed out of Norse mythology. 'Sylvia started on about him when she was half awake. Bloody savages your relatives – don't they know anything about how to behave?'

'I don't suppose,' Campbell groped after the right words, 'he said something . . . very . . . dreadful. It wouldn't have taken much. She hasn't been out among people for such a long time.' Words lengthened like burdens in his weariness . . . such a long time.

'Much? He was going on at her about her face. Said her scar wasn't too bad. I never heard anything like it.'

The fine jut of her breasts dominated his view of her; that it was so didn't alter the reality of her anger or his unreasonable guilt, but his response was not within his choice.

'I had to leave Chris.'

'Don't tell me about Chris!' Jan's anger swept her close. He wondered what would happen if he laid his face into the silence of her breasts. 'What's she made of, letting her mother go off alone in a state like this? Where is she? I wouldn't let Barty go off sick without I was with him.'

It took him a moment to remember Barty was the dog. Like an untidy wig, it crouched between her feet showing its yellow teeth in sympathy.

'She's not well either. I had to bring Sylvia, but I'll have to go back.'

'What do you mean not well?'

Before he could answer her, Charlie spoke, shaking his head mournfully, 'I'm sorry to hear that, George. I was speaking to an ex-C.I.D. friend who explained it all to me. They get hooked, you see. Use the lavatory water – right out of the pan. When they're hooked that is. Out of the public conveniences— '

'Shut up, Charlie!' Jan said. 'Is she like that again?'

She made it an accusation.

'I don't know,' he said, and that was a lie, although he had only listened to the silence behind a door.

'This C.I.D. bloke,' Charlie said, 'he claims there's boozers in the East End where they don't sell nothing but soft drinks. Charge a bomb for them, mind – but still, soft drinks! You have all these hard faces sitting around with lemonades. Something sweet. Because they're shooting it up with the needle, see, and so they don't— '

'Shut up, Charlie!' Jan said.

'Not that I believe it,' her husband grumbled. 'I reckon he was trying to wind me up.'

'Is she like that again?' Jan asked, coming close to Campbell. 'Why isn't she come back with you?'

Trish put down her book and looked at him directly for the first time. 'She gone off with a fellow?'

He felt their eyes on him, as if truth were a print-out from a machine that they held in their possession.

'Thought so,' Trish said, and went back to her book.

'Don't you see, I have to go back to fetch her? And then I'll bring her home.'

The car engine had started, when Trish came running from the house. He leaned across and wound down the window on the pavement side.

'You're a real marvel with your women, Uncle,' she whispered, pale and venomous. 'Lunatics and scrubbers. You really do things for them.'

He slammed the car in gear and swung out. Light exploded in his mirror. A window full of mouthing masks swerved past him.

Cow! He rubbed his face as if she had actually spat upon him, scrubbing away her spittle. Over and over, he smashed his fist into her mouth. Again, again, blood burst from her mouth. His fists ached on the wheel.

'Cut your losses,' Charlie had said. 'It's happened too often, isn't that true? You'll only give yourself more grief going back up there.'

'You go now and leave Sylvia in that state,' Jan cried, 'and you needn't come back.'

But in Glasgow he had settled that choice when he had left his wife, sick and in hiding from the world, and gone to look for Chris.

After a sleepless night, he locked up the house and drove under a cloudless sky to the college. The principal qualified humane noises with administrative detail, '. . . a letter about your wife's condition from her doctor', worried over creating a precedent, admitted the exams were over, finally released him. He had a brief leave of absence to care for Sylvia.

He had done that properly, he had been cautious, he had taken care not to burn his bridges there. Yet he went from the principal's office recklessly, without pretence, to Ron Peters, who spent each summer sailing off the west coast of Scotland. 'Doc Blair's your man,' Peters said. 'He can't use it himself. Odd you asking now – I had a letter from him only this morning – moaning about having to go to a conference on geriatrics in Madrid. He'll fix you up. I reckon this is your lucky day.'

Next he lifted the greater part of their savings from the bank, and even felt compelled to invent an explanation for the indifferent clerk.

After that, there was only one thing left to do. He sat in the car until he saw Jan come out with a shopping basket, then rang the

bell with their old signal, hoping that Sylvia would come. It was
Trish, however, who opened the door to him.

'No!' She moved to shut it with what seemed a reflex movement.

'Stop it, Trish.' He held it against her pressure and then forced
her back. In the hall, he searched her expression for some sign of
shame but found only a leaden composure like hopelessness.

A wave of dark sound from the living room beat after him as he
climbed the stairs. Against the record player, it would have been
pointless to knock. Even when he had gone in and closed the door
behind him, the music wept, demanded, though Sylvia clenched
her eyes in sleep.

He pressed her shoulder. Her head rolled on the pillow away
from the touch of his hand; there was no other response. With a
stab of panic, he wondered whether she had wakened since the day
before.

'Sylvia?' he whispered. 'I'm going back for Chris. It's not true
what they say, that it's hopeless. What right have any of them to
say that? She's our daughter, not theirs.' A faintness of warm breath
stirred against his cheek like an abandoned promise. 'Jan will look
after you – till I come back. I will come back.' Why had he said
that? 'I'm sorry, I'm so sorry.' But even as he was saying that, what
he wanted to tell her was that he was not the only one who had
failed Chris, they had both failed her, both of them, not one more
than the other. 'I won't let them take hope away. I'm going back to
find Chris. And when I do, I'm going to take her somewhere safe.
I'm going to make her come with me to Breagda.' It was said aloud,
spoken at last. 'Even to me, it seems mad— But, Sylvia, what else
can I do?'

He turned his head, thinking to kiss her, but straightening
instead laid his hand softly like a benediction on her poor scarred
face. At the door, some instinct made him look back. Eyes open,
she was watching him.

Going north again, he travelled alone. It came to him as if for the
first time that his mother was dead. Retracing his journey, the past
like a distant landmass fell behind and Breagda, which he had never
seen, rose up resistant out of the sea . . .

. . . cliffs . . . and the wind rushing down swooshing from the
North Pole to blow across it, Chris, but the people who lived there
knew it was the best place in all the world. Far out in the sea.

55

Where America is, Daddy? Before America was, and past where the sun sets, Tir na n-og, the western land, the land of the young where there is no death. No death, Chris.

Until one day at the end of time, are you listening? not too sleepy? a beautiful princess came to the island and asked everyone to go with her to visit her father's kingdom. *But I'll bet they didn't go, Daddy! You said they liked Breagda better than anywhere in the whole world.* Well, some of them perhaps wanted to go by then and maybe some of them were for staying, but the thing is, my darling, they were terribly keen on being polite and the truth of it is that none of them could think of a way of refusing her invitation. When the morning came, all of them, even the old men and the children, went off with the foreign princess. But not the dogs – they had to kill the dogs before they got on the boat. It was a fine thing to be at sea in the morning, the sun shining and the boat rushing across the sparkling waves, no wonder if the children cried out for the fun of it. Only afterwards, wanting to go home, when they tried to go back, the island had floated away. Every one of them searched and searched, but no one ever found Breagda again.

He wished that Chris was beside him so that he could make a different ending for the story he had begun for her. It wasn't true that he was the only one who had failed her; they had both failed her, both of them. During the long months of misery after the crash, hadn't they locked their daughter out? Who could doubt that must have been when the hurting of Chris began? He should have told Sylvia that; and warned her the search for any other reason for what had happened would only destroy them both. But he had never been able to tell Sylvia any of the things that most mattered to him.

Never been able to tell her about the deaf girl and Mrs Calder. Never been able to tell her about being a child during the war; about the estate; never been able to tell her about the Migdales. Not able to share any of it; and wasn't that how he had failed her?

Not ever been able to talk with her about the day his grandfather came home on leave from the sea, and how he might have learned from him the names of the trees but there wasn't time; no time since that was the very same day the telegram came. His father was lying dead impossibly small in the middle of a splash of yellow that meant a far off desert on Mr Migdale's map. It was not strange he

56

had never told Sylvia any of it; when had he ever talked out to himself what had happened on the day that changed his life? In that, as in everything, a failure.

Until now. Until now.

Hours and the road flowing under his wheels, retracing a journey. And then for a time it frightened him that he could not recall his mother's face clearly. Stories, it seemed, were harder to forget than people.

BOOK TWO
BETWEEN

SIX

'It's only a wee boy!'

That's what she shouted. Why should I remember that?

Big girls, three of them, standing behind the war memorial; suddenly there in front of me as I ran up over the hill and out of the trees. It was the fat girl from the sweetie shop who cried out, swinging her red moon face from me in fright.

I wanted to shout back at them, I'm not so wee! What do you think you're doing hiding there?

Instead I ran past them and round the tall stone block covered with names, the kilted soldier with the moustaches standing guard on top, and swung with the curve of the grass away from the path and down through the park. It was a long narrow park, just a strip really, with the railway on one side and the cemetery on the other behind a wire fence. I passed a woman with a dog on a leash pulling her arm out to full stretch, and then two old men – I'm sure they were there that day, they were always there – on a bench just out of the shadow of the hut where the gardener kept his spades. From their pipes blacky-grey puffs went up straight in the air. There couldn't have been any wind.

It was awful hot with there being no wind and me running, watching all the time for enemies, and wondering: What were they doing those girls up there? I knew more than they imagined. If they were doing things . . . Whatever they were doing. Oh, but it was hot; my face was on fire.

'Mammy! Mammy! Mammy!'

I thought she was gone. The black range sat abandoned in the afternoon light. I was forbidden to run into the room where my mother slept, but I did and it was empty. And that left only my own room, so small my bed filled it and I had to squeeze in the door.

Aah, my breath sighed, aah.

'Gone off and left you?' my mother said. 'Don't be a blether. I'll never go off and leave you.'

So that was all right. Everything changed. Coals hopped in the fire and the clock chattered to itself.

Or was that another day?

My mother stood over the black range. Potatoes knocked at the lid of the pot. When she turned, her face was fiery from the heat and drops of sweat clung to the soft line of her cheek like tears.

'Mummy! How often have I told you? Mummy – not *Mammy*!' She lifted the wave of hair from her forehead, brushing it up with the back of her hand. 'Do you want folk to think you were dragged up?'

'What difference does it make?' I asked. 'They'll just cry me a Glasgow keelie anyway. Doesnae matter how Ah talk.'

'*I* not *Ah*,' she said, but her attention had been caught elsewhere. 'Who calls you a keelie?'

'The boys at school.'

'What boys?'

'All of them . . .'

I reached over the table for a slice of bread but she was too quick for me and I pulled back my hand stinging.

'Who then? Honestly, it's like pulling teeth getting something out of you.'

'Peter Macdonald and Jock Martin and his wee brother Sammy. Ach, the lot of them.'

I wanted to tell her how much I hated all of them, but it was like a secret that was too dangerous to give away. Standing alone in the corner of the playground, I would watch them writhing and falling the machine gun jumping in my hand as I battered them down.

'That lot!' his mother cried contemptuously. 'Country scruff! Cannae even talk English properly.' She lifted the big iron pot across the hob. It took both her hands and she gasped a little with the effort. 'Peter Macdonald? Is that the wee boy wi the withered arm?'

'Aye.'

'Well,' she shook her head, too indignant to tell me to say *yes*. 'What are you dreaming about? Taking snash from a wee cripple. What would your father say?'

Tears came into my eyes. My father was a soldier so he must be brave. I couldn't bear the thought of being touched by that pink hand loose at the end of Peter Macdonald's withered arm. Would my father have understood, if I had been able to tell him that?

'Oh, here now,' my mother said, 'don't cry. Come here and stop being such a softie.' She pushed my hair up the wrong way. 'Ye'll need to learn to take a stoot hert tae a stey brae.' She pointed at the kitchen range. 'Imagine having to cook on a thing like that in this day and age.'

When she smiled, she was young. She seemed to me younger and bonnier and cleverer than any other mother in the world.

'One day soon we'll all be home again,' she said. 'This war won't go on for ever.'

'I don't mind it here,' I said. 'Don't like school. But here at home, just us, that's all right.'

She put me away from her and straightened up.

'Do you remember your grandpa?'

The question took me by surprise. I shook my head: no.

'Do you remember all the sweeties he would feed you? I used to be sure he was going to ruin your teeth. And the stories? Every time he was home, telling you about all the countries his boat had taken him to.'

'Does he have a beard?'

'No! He'll be upset if you don't remember him. He's awful fond of you.'

An unpleasant suspicion struck me. 'He isn't here?'

'Oh, but he is.'

I looked at the two closed doors. It would be awful cheeky if he was in my room; and surely my mother wouldn't allow him into her room?

'Where is he?'

'Gone to the Migdales to look for you. When I said you might be there, he was neither tae hold nor tae bind. He was that anxious to see you.'

Like us, the Migdales had a cottage on the estate, but we were evacuated from Glasgow and had been put into this place by a billeting officer. Mr Migdale worked for the BBC and he had a big map on his wall to show where all the armies were and they had rented their cottage and they talked about the Family at the Big

House as if they knew them real well. It was not the same thing at all.

'Is he going to sleep at Mr Migdale's house?' We had no room for him.

'Of course he isn't. He'll sleep in here.'

And then I noticed the iron frame stacked behind the couch and the dirty black screws spread on a paper on the table.

'That's the pins for the bed. I got it from Mrs Maclean. Her Sim fetched it over. Only he forgot the key to tighten it up, so you'll have to go down and ask for it.'

The chauffeur-man that lived in the lodge was out on the bit gravel at the front of it, washing one of the Family's cars. The local boys said the Family didn't usually live in the Big House much, but since London had been bombed the old lady, who was about eighty, and the son and his foreign wife were all there. The car was black with big mudguards, and the man with the hump on his back was so wee he had to stand on the running board to wash the roof. Sprinting up through the woods to the Migdales' cottage, I crouched from tree to tree like a commando looking for a throat to slit. All the real men were away at the war, my mother said.

The heavy clock noises plopped one at a time into the quiet of the kitchen. I felt like a burglar though they had told me just to walk in if no one answered. That's the country way, Mrs Migdale said. I went back to the outside door that was still lying open and knocked on the inside as loud as I could. I closed the door and then I opened it, but that did not seem right either so I put it over until it was almost shut but without catching the lock.

I was so busy trying to make up my mind that the noise made me jump out of my skin.

'What are you laughing at?'

'Oh, little George Campbell,' Joan said, 'I didn't know you had a temper.'

Having a temper seemed better than getting a fright. 'Just shows ye don't know everything.'

'Ah wouldn't be too sur-r-re o that,' she mimicked me. It seemed unfair that she made me sound like Peter Macdonald, while he and all the other boys in the village laughed at me because I came from Glasgow and didn't talk like them at all. 'Come here, darling little George, till I tell you something,' she said in her ordinary voice.

She sat up on the edge of the table and grinned at me. Getting up had pulled back her skirt and I could see the inside of her leg.

'Give me your hand,' she said. I stood dumb, not a word in my head, trying not to look where her legs went up to some meeting place in the dark. 'You must.'

Her hand over mine was warm and dry.

'Mummy's gone to the village to make sure they aren't making too much of a mess of things for tonight. You'll be down in the audience, George, and when you look up you'll see me, high up there on the stage. And it doesn't matter if I whisper, you'll hear every word. Mummy taught me how to speak on the stage.'

And she laid my hand against her.

'Feel the breaths I'm taking – little breaths. You take them like this, quickly, quickly.'

Over her shoulder, I saw Diana watching from the open door into the passage. When I tried to step back, Joan held on to my hand. Her eyes were closed. Diana's face sharpened to a long nose like a finger pointing.

'Silly boy,' Joan said in the whispery singing voice. 'Feel how I'm breathing. Like this, silly, silly, silly.'

Under the rough wool, I felt her breast like a little bird you would not squeeze no matter how gently for fear of hurting.

'What the hell's going on here?' Mr Migdale shouted from where he had appeared behind Diana. He had turned into one of the flags he stuck on his map to be the British. His forehead and round his eyes was red but underneath he had gone a funny white.

Joan let go my hand and I jumped back but she only smiled at her father and said, 'I was teaching George about breath control.'

'That's a new bloody name for it,' Mr Migdale said, but the red and white in his face began to change to the usual in between colour all over. From his height in the air he drew back his upper lips and showed his teeth at me in a kind of smile. 'Well, young haggis,' he asked, 'would you like to see the latest development on my map? I've put a black flag in where Hamilton is.'

Maybe it was because he worked for the BBC in Glasgow he had a map on his wall. A map with all kind of wee flags – the British were white with a red cross; the Russians had a red flag; and there was one for the Italians and there had been one for the Finns. The black flags were for the Germans.

'Oh, Mr Migdale,' I whispered, 'have the Germans landed? Are we invaded?'

He shouted at me, 'Who do we know who knows Rudolph Hess, eh?' and then gave a big wink and waited, bending over me.

I could not understand why he was so pleased that the Germans had invaded Scotland. After all, the English were on the same side as us.

'You're frightening George,' Joan said.

'Nonsense! George Campbell is not so easily frightened. He has the blood of chieftains in his veins.'

'Really, Daddy,' Joan said in a weary voice, shaking her head at him, 'I sometimes think you're quite mad.'

'Like Ireland,' Mr Migdale said, 'they all have the blood of the ould kings. One part blue blood to three parts Guinness.'

'You *are* mad.' Diana put her arm round his waist. 'Could that be why we love you so much?'

I loved both the girls, as far as a small boy can love, but until that afternoon I'd thought Diana was the nicer. Before then, I'd felt that Joan was somehow always ready to laugh at me.

'When are we going to eat?' Mr Migdale asked loudly. He gave himself a kind of shake and Diana took her arm away. 'I suppose we are going to eat?'

The way they ate it was like a picnic. I had asked my mother: Why don't we just have our dinner on our knees by the fire? Because we're not tinks, she said; your dinner's ready, have you washed your hands? But when I told her that the Migdales didn't call that meal dinner they called it lunch, she said never mind, and put another potato on my plate even though I hadn't asked for one.

Diana said to me, 'Is it not time you were going home?'

'Not until he's seen the map,' Mr Migdale said. 'Can't let a cell member of the Scotch fifth column go home before he's seen the map.'

As we went along the corridor, Joan squeezed my arm gently.

Diana put her tongue out at her. When she put it in, she said, 'Cow!' in a loud clear voice.

Ahead of us Mr Migdale jumped round. His face was red again, and he shouted, 'What was that?'

His mouth made ugly jerking shapes as he came towards us.

66

'Don't you bloody dare!' he said, and he hit Joan's face with his hand.

'It wasn't bloody me!' Joan screamed and started to cry. 'It was her.'

As he glared, we heard the front door open and Mrs Migdale's voice called, 'Coo-ee!'

'It's Marmee,' he said in his ordinary voice.

Joan stopped crying, and all three of them looked as if nothing had happened.

'I've just met the most extraordinary creature,' Mrs Migdale said coming into the corridor. 'He's some kind of foreigner and I can't make out a word he's saying. Come and speak to him, Jack. He's at the front door.'

When we went through, the front door was open and I thought she must have forgotten that for she said quite loudly, 'He must be from the camp. He'll have wandered off and be trying to find his way back.'

There were foreign people at the camp: Polish people; Germans too, some of the boys said, but I didn't believe them.

The man had a heavy woollen jersey that rolled up right over his neck and when he smiled you could see that some of his top teeth were missing. I knew who he must be even before he leaned forward, blinking out of the sunlight, and asked, 'George? Is that you, George?' He reached out and took hold of my face and, after a moment, each hard hand patted my cheeks with a funny little stroking movement. He did it as if we were alone. He did it as if the Migdales weren't even there. It was terrible.

'It's my grandfather,' I told them.

Outside we walked without speaking. He was not a very tall man but he was broad, with a heavy hand that laid upon your shoulder kept you to a pace that had no hurrying in it.

'Fine trees,' he said as if to himself, and then more briskly: 'What about that one, George? Can you tell me its name?'

'No.'

'And that one?' He was pointing, and I looked around afraid the Migdales might still be in sight and watching us. 'Would you know the name of that tall fellow there?'

I shook my head.

'Do you think a sailor shouldn't know about the trees? Right

67

enough, you don't see many trees out at sea. And when I was a boy
your size, I was on Breagda and trees have little enough chance
with the winds that blow over that place. But this last trip when
the boat was sunk under us, I kept thinking about trees, oh, forests
of them. Isn't that a strange thing? I've always been fond of trees.'

'I don't know the names of any of them,' I said, angry and asking
myself what did it matter.

It was quiet on the path that climbed up through the wood and I
could hear the breath blow from my grandfather's lips. He walked
as if he were tired.

'That will never do at all, not at all.' But the big hand squeezed
my shoulder gently. 'We'll walk every day and you'll learn. You'll
give your father a fine surprise when he comes home.'

'But you said— '

'What? I'm always saying something.'

'You said you wouldn't be here long. That's what you said to Mrs
Migdale.'

'Was that what I told her now? When she said to me, Come and
see us when we have more time.' He laughed without any noise,
wrinkling up his cheeks. 'I doubt I exaggerated a wee bit there,'
and he winked down at me.

But then, not laughing at all, he said, 'Don't worry, George, I'll
be here. After what happened on the last trip, I'm due a rest. And
who but me would teach you the names of all those tall fellows?'

And all I could think was: Is he going to be there in the mornings
when I get up and go into the kitchen? Will he be there when I
come home from school? Will I never have my mother to myself? I
was thinking about those things when a boy on a bike came swoosh
from the side path almost running into us.

'There's a rascal in a hurry.'

'He doesnae have any right to be here. None of them have.' By
that I meant the people of the village.

'You know him then?'

'It's Peter Macdonald's big brother. He'll have a telegram. He
works at the post office.

My grandfather stopped walking and turned me towards him. 'Is
there another house up there, apart from where you live?'

'Just the Big House. Right over on the other side of the hill.'

He began walking again, but came to a halt after a step or two.

'I don't think you should go home just yet, George.' I listened to his breath sigh in and out. 'It's a fine day. Go and play with your friends while the sun's shining.'

What right had he to tell me what to do? I wriggled trying to escape the weight of his hand on my shoulder. I didn't know what to do. I didn't want to tell him I had no friends. Suddenly I remembered there was after all something I was supposed to be doing.

'I've to go to Mrs Maclean's. To get the key for the bed.'

I don't imagine he understood what I was talking about, but he let me go as if it didn't matter.

The bright sun slanted yellow and shone green through the leaves and I ran with my head back until I was dizzy and the noise I was hearing grew until outside the Macleans it roared so loud it was a miracle the windows stayed in. The room was full and everyone had a glass and Mr Maclean crossed with a bottle in his hand and an enormous woman was falling down into a chair and there was a baldie man stretching an accordion. And all of them, even the fat woman falling, seemed to be singing.

'Here's a burglar, missis, a wee thief come tae see whit he can steal frae ye,' bawled the big man with the red face, still holding me by the shoulder. 'He was keekan in the windae when Ah went outside for a breath o air.'

'Away, Willie Christie, don't be any softer than God made ye.' Mrs Maclean shook all over when she laughed. 'It's the wee Campbell boy – the evacuees, ken, in the orra man's auld hoose.'

'Oh, aye. Yon braw lassie. Here, maybe Ah'll see the boy home. She'll be missing her man tae gie her memory a bit jog, like.'

Mrs Maclean leaning over was so big I was afraid she would overbalance and squash me.

'Pay no heed to Willie,' she said, and the heat of her came over me like an oven. 'That's just the drink talking. A respectable woman like your mother would frighten the wits oot a blather-skite like him.'

'Jessie, dear.' A little woman in a red dress was clapping Mrs Maclean on her enormous arm to get her attention and so before she could interrupt us I said, 'I've to see if you've a key that would tighten up the bed for my grandfather.'

'Just a bit get-together for oor Tam,' she was explaining to the woman in the red dress. She looked at that as if she was about to cry, but then said briskly, 'His faither says once Tam's joined up the Germans'll have no chance.' And then vaguely to me, 'You could ask Tommy.'

Mr Maclean had bow legs and he wasn't much taller than I was. He worked as a gardener on the estate.

'The key, the key.' He pushed his thumbs under his braces and thought about it. 'For tightening up an auld bed . . . I could lay my hands on one o those for ye.'

'And surely at the closing of your day Dee-da-dee-dee dee-dee deedle-deedle dee dee And deedle deedle dee tae Galway Bay,' Mr Maclean sang going ahead of me through the lobby. Even with the door shut behind us, we could still hear the noise of the party. Another song had been started.

'Could you guess who that is?' he asked pointing to a picture on the table beside the bed. It was in a frame but the cardboard around the photo had faded yellow. A soldier in a kilt stood with his arms folded in front of a painted tree.

'That was me,' Mr Maclean said, his voice muffled as he bent forward to rummage in the press. 'Do you think I'm a liar?' ·

He straightened up red-faced holding a shoebox without a lid.

'Cheer up! I was a fine figure of a man, right enough – but it's not yesterday or the day before.' He sighed. 'I was in the Black Watch.'

'Is that it?' It was a little bar with a square hole in one end. It looked nothing like a key.

'That's it all right.' He lifted up a corner of the mattress and fitted the hole over a screw that stuck up on the frame. 'See? A couple of pulls like that to tighten it. Put it in your pocket and you'll not lose it.'

It was time to go back home. I remember for some reason I took the long way round, walking slowly by the estate wall where it was catching the last of the sun. Maybe I was hoping my grandfather would be gone by the time I got back.

He was still there though. He held out his hand to me and I think I had a notion he was offering me a sweetie the way my mother had said he did when I was small. His face frightened me, white under a thatch of black hair, the bristles round his mouth where he hadn't shaved rough and grey. My mother was hidden in the corner in the big chair with her back to the window. All I could see was her hand on her lap open on top of a bit of paper with printed words stuck on it.

My mother hated the twilight, but the room darkened and darkened. It was past time the light was on; I didn't want to do it without being told. It seemed to me my mother should want me beside her, but she didn't say anything. To punish her I sat on the floor near my grandfather's chair. He called me Iain, but I didn't answer him for that was my father's name.

After a while, my mother said, 'I'll take George and go to my sister in London.'

My grandfather reached out and took hold of me by the shoulder.

'No need for that surely. To take him away from his own people.'

My mother said something that sounded angry, her voice loud in the dark, and my grandfather made a little noise and his hand loosened from me. Looking up I saw that he had covered his eyes, and I moved away, sliding on my bottom from where I sat near his chair. A little at a time I kept moving until I rested with my back against the wall by the door.

My mother said again, 'What is there for us here?'

When my grandfather started to talk in a foreign language, I was afraid; his voice was quiet like Joan's whispery voice when I held her by the breast and then less like that than anything in the world. The language he spoke rose and fell and had the sound of the sea in it; and perhaps my fear was mixed with anger for I knew fine my mother couldn't make it out any more than I could. It wasn't a tongue I heard again for years; I had left university, I was teaching; I overheard two men talking at the corner of a London street and followed them like a fool until I found what they spoke was Gaelic – and as late as that understood the old man wasn't talking that afternoon to my mother or to me but to his son, my dead father.

I felt I was too big to cry and would if I stayed there.

'I'll away to Mrs Maclean's,' I said, and had the door open and was off without either of them saying a word, but maybe they didn't hear me.

I had never been out so late on my own. In fact I didn't want to go near the Macleans. I hated the memory of the fat woman and how she had never stopped singing even when she was falling down into her chair. I went with my hands held out in front of me among

71

the trees and the path twisted about until I wondered if it was a path at all or if I had found one and lost it again.

Like blind man's buff, I had been spun round. Where the trees ended, there was a house with a white half moon above it. It had a chimney as pointed as a witch's hat against the glimmering sky and the other side raised up as if to be a hump on its back. Downstairs a single window shone with a yellow light. The moon kept its one eye on me as I crept across the grass to peer inside.

They were all there: Mr Migdale slumped down in his chair studying along the length of his legs as if he had a tiny map stuck on each shoe; Mrs Migdale at the table with her hand covering her eyes; and Joan was there and Diana, at opposite ends of the couch, like two dolls that had been laid down and overlooked.

If I ever saw them again, I don't remember.

Trying to go home, I came among bushes of brambles. A curling branch whipped across my bare knees, another tore at my hand as I fell. I found myself lying at the foot of a grey cliff. I sat up and sucked at my hand. In a moment, buttons black in the silvery light came out along the line of the scratch. When they fattened and ran together, I smeared them, then licked and spat splashing against the mossed stone. Stone on grey stone climbed into the air above me, a castle, one of those old castles with a deep moat of water round it to keep out every enemy. Touching it, I felt the last warmth of the day pass out of the stone.

Far in the air above me, stuck into the cement, necks and bases of broken bottles would be glittering like spear-points under the moon. I began to tramp along and Mr Maclean in his Black Watch kilt marched beside me and ahead of us Tam was going off to defend my mother and Joan Migdale and the old lady in the Big House and all of us who lived in safety behind the high wall of the estate.

BOOK THREE
BREAGDA

SEVEN

He had calculated the times and distances and fallen into the irretrievable sleep of exhaustion, escaping from his uncertainty. When he wakened groaning out of a bad dream, the lamp had grown pale. A shock like ice ran through his stomach and arms. He had gone astray again; in mindless reaction, he struggled out into the cockpit.

At the first step, he fell and on his knees gaped at the calm unending undulation. The ocean was being drawn from under the boat by an immense winding engine. Had he slept? Was he awake now? The uncommitted light spilled from the horizon into his outthrown arms. The island had been passed during the night. He had to put about. Entirely astray, he was taking them north into the emptiness. With a shuddering effort, he drove himself to his feet.

Dead ahead, water boiled and a grey rock glanced in the smother. Not astray— The sun shone a red eye beside the ancient wall of the island, from whose giant shadow white congregations of gulls spilled across the morning. Even in the instant of that astonishing enormous presence, old habit hurried his body to save himself. He brought about and the boat plunged and trembled back from the open jaw of white water.

He knew the place; although he had never seen it before, there was no room for mistake. This was Breagda. The cliff rose sheer from the sea. Even on this gentle morning, great waves beat axe blows against the oldest tree in the world.

To lie clear was a necessity, but he took the boat back further than he need have done until it might have seemed as if he was in retreat, as though it had been enough to come this far. The rock wall dwindled upon the single spread of sea and sky. He came back across the flow of waves, smacking white water past on either side. He would have made this time last for ever. The cliff came already

75

to a turning edge and so he went out farther than he needed for the joy of seeing it again as if for the first time. In all his life, he had never seen anything so clearly as the cliff and the light changing down the lengths of the beating waves and suddenly a gash of green high on the face that meant grass and the land behind.

It was a game to go further out each time; to find Breagda each time as real in the morning light as the knuckles of his fist on the tiller. At the northern end the profile of the island fell and there was sand and a showing of green turf, and then on his next return he saw, almost missing it as he went about, a hook of land beyond the beach putting a protective arm round still water.

At the entrance a hidden brutal current swung the boat lurching, and then he was through into smooth water, so clear that he could see the sand wrinkled on the sea floor and judge his distance as he drifted towards the shore.

The anchor split the mirror; air and water shimmered then resettled into smoothness and silence. In the hot light, he stripped off his shirt and stretched for the victory of being well and alive. Little birds bobbed like corks in the shallows and clockworked across the dark ribbed sand at the water's edge. The air smelled salt and uninhabited, blown from the top of the globe.

He sat on the deck against the coach-roof dangling his legs over the side. As steadily as a cradle, the boat rocked and he rehearsed the things he would do: unlash the dinghy, row to the beach, pull it up on to the sand, explore. There had been a community on this island – as a boy his father had watched the boat come that ended it. As an old man, his grandfather had spoken of the necessity – 'there was no more living on the place at all' – but if that was so why had the man sounded angry and sorrowful, the anger could only be unreasonable and how had sorrow survived so many years? The people had walked out of their houses as if on a Sunday morning going to church and they had gone down to the boat and been taken away. All that they brought with them was what they were able to carry, and that meant most of their things had to be left behind; but nothing had been destroyed. To survive they had learned to preserve; nothing in their way of life for a thousand years had taught them to destroy. The community of crofts where his father's people had lived from beyond the reach of folk memory would be there still . . . however broken by weather and time.

Food would have to be taken ashore. A storage place would have to be found for it. There was plenty to do that should be done before dark. He dangled bare feet above the tamed sea. The clarity of the water was something to marvel at in the brilliant light. Vague images of crowded pools, of chlorine stinging the eyes, of children yelling . . . he tried to remember the last time he had gone swimming. Standing up, he stripped off his trousers and had begun to drag off his underpants when a thought made him pull them on again. In a clumsy landing, the water punched into his belly. Thinking he was surfaced, he swung his right arm in the crawl and, under water, beat stroke on stroke with dream slowness until, in the moment of panic, he broke free, sucked air, dancing specks of black and gold a tunnel he swam into, cold, cold, then that passed and he felt the power of his arms and little waves splashed salt in his mouth with the suck and spit of his breath.

Only when his legs went dead, the cold came back and with it suddenly the fear of drowning. But then at once after that his left leg trailing rubbed its toes upon sand. The water came just over his waist and he began to laugh and throw it up over his head and shoulders and beat down with hands grinning like an idiot as it spouted.

The boat was only fifty yards away and he settled forward, reaching for it with the long slow pulls of the breast stroke. In the silence, he heard his breath gasp at each pull, ah, ah. The letters of the *Lazy Charlotte* rose and fell and he swam towards her name across a saucer of light.

On deck after a moment of hesitation he stripped off his pants and wrung them out over the side till the last drops drew a line of stitches where blue darkened to green in the shadow.

He woke up unsure whether hours or minutes had passed. The wood of the deck was warm under his nakedness. He yawned and like a cat stretched out his cramp. He felt as if he had slept for the first time in many years, this waking felt so different. Next moment he placed another feeling – that sharp sensation was hunger; not punctual expectation but the thing itself, rare and poignant. He delayed for the deliberate pleasure of that recognition, pulling on shirt and trousers with the leisure of ritual. Not hunger, he decided peaceably, chiding himself with the sad posters of children – appetite.

He had brought coffee bags in a jar as a luxury. Using one of them fitted his mood of celebration. With a spoon he turned it in the cup of boiling water. The coffee smell tickled the air. As he fished out the bag, he pressed it against the side of the cup and the darkest of the infusion streamed out. The dark brown went white as he poured sweet milk wastefully out of the tin. Holding the cup, he reached out his other hand to the curtain that divided the cabin. He held a pinch of it in his fingers, hesitated, let his hand fall. He went through the whole sequence again and then, as if absent-mindedly, took a sip from the cup. The warmth unfolded inside him.

He belched.

The bread came wholesome from the heavy wrapping of foil. He cut two slices, thick slices, *doorstep* slices, he thought grinning, and buttered them and built a pile of pickles on one from the only jar and sliced cheese on to the other; the two faces married, and not a pickle spilled, he climbed out into the cockpit again.

Open sky and a glittering privacy of water; salt sea smell and coffee; giant gobbets of bread and filling that bulged his jaws. *Doorstep* slices. The last of the coffee – how well he had judged everything – was just enough to swill and wash the last mouthful down.

'Dear God,' he asked aloud, 'what the hell's happening?'

In the pause which followed, the stillness was broken up like refracting light into the changing cry of birds, the sea's constancy and, near as breathing, the subtle smack and suck of calm water along the hull, yet had the mood, resettling, of silence until something alien, a noise from the cabin, turned his head alertly.

She was lying on the port bunk. He stared in disbelief for she lay face down and her hands were lashed behind her with a white cloth that looked like a handkerchief.

'Get up!' he said harshly. There was a smell in the air he almost recognised. When she lay still, he bent over her. The cloth at her wrists was slack. 'Did you tie it with your teeth?' With finger and thumb he tugged very lightly and it came undone. 'Did you step through to get it behind you?' The white cloth hung in his hand.

With her face in the pillow she said, 'I called and you didn't come. You left me like this.'

'No. I didn't.'

78

Her hands nested as if bound at the separation of her buttocks. He tried to control his anger at the idiocy of her play-acting. 'Stay like that if you want!'; but in the middle of saying that his voice trembled and he could have wept for her.

She heaved up in a flurry. There was a stain on the bunk and his eyes went to the wet patch at the crotch of her jeans. The sharp tang filled the cabin.

'I called,' she said slyly, 'and you didn't come.'

EIGHT

The dinghy skittered as he pulled too hard. It was the foolish
thought that Chris might have taken the boat and left him abandoned: foolish since he could see the *Lazy Charlotte* drawing
nearer. Foolish anyway to imagine Chris able, or willing, to take
the boat out to sea. The idea was ridiculous but there on the bright
water it chilled him as if a cloud had gone over the sun. The island
seemed very small on the wide ocean and the dinghy spun as he
pulled too hard but then in the tussle to compensate, two beats
with one oar and catching the rhythm together on the next,
thankfully the thought was lost.

It was the same foolishness that made him imagine she had
vanished because she was nowhere to be seen. He would look on
the deck, on either side of the coach roof where she might be lying
asleep as he had slept, then below and there would be no place big
enough to hide her; and he would rush out and stare round the
whole empty impossible circle of the horizon; no hiding place and
slowly, slowly, he would lean out and see her lying on a quilt of
sand looking up at him through the clear water.

He held the dinghy to the side of the boat, and called softly,
'Chris!'

She would be eating, sitting on the bunk scattering crumbs, or
reading. Perhaps she would simply be sitting quietly, thinking,
trying to make sense of all that had happened.

She lay where he had left her, on her belly, face down into the
pillow. The urine smell still faintly soiled the air. Instead of being
relieved to see her, anger and disappointment knotted his stomach.

'I found houses,' he said. 'A street of them – all of them empty.
One must have been the meeting hall, a kind of church. I kept
imagining a door would open and someone would come out and call
me. Your grandfather . . . if things had been different, I might have
been born here and he would have come to the door and called

80

me.' They had looked more entire than he had thought possible: but, of course, there had been a commune settled on the island. He remembered his mother writing of them in a letter – she had read of it in a newspaper and sent him the clipping roughly torn out. Young people in search of a dream; beards, sandals, free love and money too – enough at least to survive a winter or two on Breagda. 'I didn't go into any of the houses. I thought we'd look together. I couldn't explain to you what it's like. You would have to come and see. It's strange . . . but it's— ' He wanted to say *marvellous*. 'I kept thinking someone would appear at a window or a door would open.'

He took her by the shoulder, but there was something peculiarly unpleasant in feeling her body shudder from him. His temper began to slip.

'This place stinks. My God, you stink. How could you do that to yourself?'

She mumbled with her face in the pillow.

'What? How can I make sense of that? Turn round and talk to me.'

'I'm not going anywhere.' She spoke to the side of the boat, enunciating carefully, a pad of silence round each word. 'It doesn't matter if I stink since I'm – not – going – anywhere. Satisfied?'

He was willing to think it a concession that her hands lay by her head removed from their parody of bondage.

'I'm going, you know. Either come or you stay on the boat.'

He stopped and realised he was waiting for her to catch him up on the silliness of what he had just said – evidently, if she didn't come, she stayed. He could hear her say it – 'evidently'. It was the kind of thing she was very sharp about spotting. She was like him in that.

'I don't know if you'd want to risk being left alone on the boat.' He felt quite calm. 'You've never been alone on a boat,' he continued reasonably. 'I doubt if you've ever slept alone.' Half way through that he stumbled, since it seemed to mean more than he had intended. 'Not having been alone on a boat, I don't know how you'd feel about going up on deck in the morning and there being nothing in sight but gulls. Just you alone in the middle of the North Sea.'

As a lie, it was the kind of unfair pressure of which he disapproved. Yet an earthquake might tear up the anchor. Anything was theoretically possible. She lay, indifferent to solitude.

'At least get up. Get washed. Change your clothes. It's disgusting to wallow in your own dirt.'

Very tired and contemptuous, but quite clearly, her voice said, 'Oh, piss off! Please?'

He changed what was a blow into a grab at her. His fist clenched on the waist of her jeans and when he felt them tear he began to haul them down over her thighs.

'If you won't do it,' he gasped, 'I will. I'll make you decent.'

But she exploded, threshing so violently his grip broke. Crouched in the corner of the bunk with her jeans down round her knees, she mouthed at him, 'You dirty bastard!' Her face was squashed and pulpy with loathing. 'I know what you want. You dirty old bastard!'

Too suddenly for her to resist, he picked her up.

As they came outside, she started to kick but he held her tight against him as he got to the side.

'Chris,' he said, 'you're a lapsed human being. But I'm not going to let it happen.'

With a flex of his arms, he dropped her into the sea.

As she fell, he took account of how easily he had lifted her. His arms retained an impression of lightness and at once he was afraid for her. When he had gone to his mother's flat, the door hung open and he had found her inside, drugged, confused, vulnerable to any intruder. She had encountered him like a figure in a dream and gone with him in that condition. Only on the dock, boarding the *Lazy Charlotte*, she had begun to struggle and he had caught her up, crushing her in his panic for fear she might cry out. Thin-armed and fragile, she had beat against him in silence. Now, as she fell, he anticipated her heart stopped by the water's murderous attack.

She slid under. The water sprang up and hung like a fountain of ice. He could see nothing.

Arms flailing, she beat up blue-lipped in veils of white. Her fight for breath ululated screams but her eyes never left him. The water sleeked her head. She held up her arms to him and he clutched her by a wrist and elbow and dragged her out and into the boat. She had lost her jeans in the water and he lay across the seat watching them dance in slow motion to the bottom.

'I'm sorry,' he said as she sprawled at his feet.

That was something on which he prided himself. It was important to apologise when you were in the wrong. He had never believed in the omniscience of parents.

She stammered what might have been an answer.

'What?' he asked; but then saw how badly she was trembling. The shaking of her legs reminded him unpleasantly of fish he had seen landed and gasping for air.

'Come below,' he said.

She rolled away from his glance.

'Stay then. The sun will warm you.'

In the cabin, he found a towel and in the case he had brought from London a pair of jeans, a shirt and pants. No bra. Should there be? He had no idea if she wore one. He looked at the stuff in the case. At last, he pulled out a cotton vest.

'Here,' he said, sticking his head through the hatch and throwing the bundle on to the seat. 'You can dress there. The sun's out. You'll soon be warm again. I swam this morning. Feel how hot it is.'

She looked at him without any expression he could read in the shuddering muscles of her face. Her body seemed to tremble more violently.

'Please,' he said. 'Do it now. I'll make a hot drink.'

In front of the calor-gas cooker, he waited listening with the half-filled pan in his hand. After a long time, he heard movement. He interpreted the sounds. A heavy sigh told him he had been holding his breath. When the water poppled and steamed, he poured it over the coffee. With the two cups held before him, he called from below, 'Is it all right?'

There was no answer.

There was an incommunicable satisfaction in taking command. Since his mother's death, the world he lived in had become one in which he made decisions. The dinghy went to and fro because he had decided to gather some of their stuff on the beach before they set off to find a place of shelter. Strictly, they would need little that day; that did not matter. The thing was to choose a shape for each day, and so he made a number of crossings and the sun settled down the sky.

He hauled the dinghy free of the water and had got the box half lifted when a twang of pain knocked him to his knees. He peered round at Chris. She had her back to him, sitting in the same place she had occupied since he brought her to the beach. Her chin resting on her knees she seemed to be looking out at the open sea on the far side of the sickle of rocks.

Gingerly he eased up until he was crouching and then came to his feet. The pain settled to a steady throb. He dropped again to his knees and pushed the box, but at the first pressure pain burned the same place. He rested and then, leaning against it with his back, nudged the box clear. When he had let it go, it had fallen against the side of the dinghy. He was astonishingly relieved to find no damage had been done.

'That's enough,' he said, speaking across the stretch that separated him from Chris.

As he stood up, the pain sharpened.

'Enough! I've brought enough. We'll look for a place to spend the night.'

She stayed stubbornly turned away. Anger jetted black in him. He stumbled towards her.

'I'm finished,' he yelled above her. 'Finished!'

She twisted as if at an electric shock. Her white glance terrified him, then he understood she had heard nothing until he towered over her. His ears were opened and what he had thought was silence beat like drums.

'We've brought enough,' he said quietly. 'Time's not something we'll run short of – let's go and look at the houses.'

The beach ended gradually in grass. A long swell of the ground like a sea wave lifted them to where the houses came in sight.

Relieved to be off the sand and on to the cropped firm turf, he had walked a little down the slope before he realised Chris was still standing on the rise above.

'That's it?' she asked.

It was as though she had come awake.

'One of them must have belonged to your great-grandfather,' he said. 'My father was born on the island.'

'Oh, my God!'

The houses curved away from them, made of undressed stone.

They could see the nearest one had no windows. Chris came to his side and they walked until they came to a place from which the whole front of the house could be seen.

'The roof's fallen in,' she said.

'Some of it.'

About half of the roof had caved in. A timber hung awry like a tooth half punched out.

'Is that the one?' she asked.

'What?'

'The one your father chose to be born in.'

'Your grandfather,' he said. 'Come on.' She moved obediently with him.

'Anyway,' he said, 'you don't choose to be born.'

She made an odd noise. 'That's true,' she said.

'Are you all right?' He stopped and turned to look at her, but she walked on.

'What's wrong?' he asked, limping to join her.

Now it was her turn to stop. She looked in pantomime at everything round them. He thought: that's her Against Face. When had he christened it that – before she was ten, before she went to school? Once it had been a joke to him.

'What's wrong?' she mimicked. 'I can't imagine. What is there that could possibly be wrong?'

And she made the same little noise that hurt him to hear.

In front of the houses there were narrow fields of high grass full of yellow-headed flowers.

'That one,' he said.

The grass ran steeply up to a house that had added one storey to the basic ground plan of the others they had passed. The roof seemed to be whole. The important thing was to make a choice. He stepped over the ruined fence. He warned himself not to look round but heard her following him. In the days of the village, all this would have been cut to feed animals. Would there be any left on the island? It rustled past his waist as he waded upwards. If the roof is all right, he prayed, then I have done the right thing. If it is all right, Chris will be cured here.

He reached out and took the handle and the handle moved down and the door under the gentlest of touches opened.

'What are we doing?' He turned at the note in Chris's voice. She was pale and agitated. 'You can't walk in to someone's house.'

He stared at her blankly.

'Someone's house? This is Breagda. The last people were taken off when your grandfather was a child. The whole island is empty except for me and you.'

NINE

'It's peat,' he explained, and felt triumphant.

He was surprised to see how close the croft village appeared. It had taken them more than three hours to cross the little valley and climb the first hill.

'Pete who?'

For a moment, he thought she was trying to be funny but she seemed simply puzzled. He was stabbed by an old affection – something from the time before his love had brooded over her, fierce, angry and protective.

'You're a real little Cockney.'

'Christ!'

'It's peat,' he said, holding his temper. 'They cut it in turves. There were special spades for cutting it.'

The hollow had been peeled like an apple. He stepped down and walked on the brown pelt, turning to follow the tracks of the cutting.

'What for?' Chris called.

'What?'

'What for?'

He grinned at her. She had crossed the trenched ground direct and stood on a raised welt of green turf that made her level with him. The wind blew colour into her face.

'What for what?' he asked in serious parody.

He was afraid she had taken offence, but then she repeated simply, 'What for – the peat – what use can it possibly be?'

'They burned it.'

She bent down and touched the brown side of the gash. The vertical surfaces of each trench were layered with cuts.

'It's fuel,' he explained. 'If it weren't for the peat life wouldn't have been possible on this island – or on most of them, I expect. I don't think it's really good for burning but there's no end of it.'

'But wouldn't it be wet?'

'They piled it in stacks to dry.'

Chris straightened and looked across the hollow in the direction they'd come.

'How did they get it down to their houses? I didn't see any road.'

He thought about that. What he knew about such things was magpie plunder.

'They carried it. In baskets – créels, I think they called them. The women did it – I seem to remember the women carried them down. And then they made these stacks so they dried in the wind. Or perhaps they dried them first up here and then took them down to the houses. They made a store of them at the end of each house – I'm sure that's right.'

'Oh, God,' Chris said with a groan, 'what a place.'

It was their second day on the island and the second day the sun had shone on it and them. Under the sough of the wind, a faint gathering of notes he recognised suddenly as sheep bleating somewhere on the far side of the hill.

'You think so,' he said pleasantly.

'It's miles from here to the houses. The women must have been killed by it.'

'Oh, no, I shouldn't think so. Being used to it, you see.'

'I wouldn't ever be used to it.'

She sounded younger than he had thought she possibly could again.

'If you'd been born here,' he started reasonably.

'No way,' she said. 'That's not possible.'

Indulgence went over like an oiled switch into irritation.

'Don't be stupid. Of course, it's possible.'

She shook her head.

'That really is,' he said, 'particularly stupid or very arrogant. What's so extraordinary about you that means you couldn't have been born here?'

'No way,' she said again with her head down.

'Is there in heaven some divine ordinance against Chris Campbell being born on Breagda?'

She looked up at him.

'There must have been,' she said, not sounding at all like a child.

'My fault for bringing theology into it. I didn't realise you were a

88

good Calvinist determinist.' He smiled malevolently. 'There may be more of Breagda in you than you know.'

'I don't *know* what you're on about.'

It was his turn to look down, not sulking naturally but containing his unrighteous anger.

'We'll have time. I'll explain the doctrine of unfree will to you.'

'That'll be nice.'

She walked away on the path of the raised turf. He kept a step or two behind, following along the brown floor of peat.

'Still,' he said, unable to let it go, 'you might have been born here.'

'Not me,' she said without looking back. 'It wouldn't have been me.'

'From Calvin to Freud. There's no end to your resources.'

'Mr Nelson used to say that.'

She increased her pace so abruptly he was taken by surprise. He watched her neat progress along the baulk of turf. In the jeans and shirt, from the back where you couldn't see the yellow under the tan she had got in those last weeks in the garden at home, she looked graceful and in control.

'Who's Mr Nelson?'

'A teacher I had at school.' She spoke without looking round. 'He said things like that – "Did you produce such wisdom out of your own resources, Miss Campbell?"'

The drawn rhythms of it reconstituted for him some timorous sadist guddling up a jeer of sycophants.

'In just that tone, of course,' he said.

'What?'

But they had come to the crest from which the crofts could be seen spread out like toys in the clear air. He sat down.

'I need to rest.'

She walked on. As he watched, she faltered to a stop, and sank to the grass not far off. He lay back and closed his eyes. Though there was a wind, the sun was warm.

'I had a teacher,' he reflected aloud. 'Miss Darnaway. She used to make the bad boys stand in the waste-paper basket and say, I'm rubbish.'

A long time ago, in Clapham, when his mother and he had come to live with Aunt Jess.

'Didn't the parents object?'

He wouldn't have been able to hear her voice in a city street. It muttered across the cropped grass and scatter of grey stones. He felt ridiculous pleasure. They were having a conversation.

'I don't suppose they knew. Children don't tell, or make a muddle of it when they try.'

'Perhaps she picked her victims,' Chris said.

He lifted his head. For a moment, he thought she was asleep but then she put an arm across her eyes shading them from the light.

After a pause, he began again, 'If you imagine she was odd, what about this? My mother came from Glasgow. Born and brought up there. All her people were. They weren't too keen on her marrying my father. He was what they called "a wild Highlandman". He used his mother's pronunciation – 'a wild Heelanman'. 'One of her uncles in particular took against him. Before the wedding he met her in the street and the first thing he said to her was, "Don't talk tae me aboot Heelanmen. They're aa half daft." And then he told her how his firm had sent him to one of the islands – they had a contract with the council and one of the jobs took them to the village school. Fifteen kids and a teacher, a man called Maclean, a fat red-headed man, smelling of drink. Apparently, according to my mother's uncle, every morning when he appeared – he was always late – the whole squad of kids jumped up, gave the Nazi salute and chorused, Heil Mr Maclean! Heil Mr Maclean! Heil Mr Maclean! He'd taught them to do that. Every morning!' He shook his head smiling.

He had thought she would laugh. It had always seemed funny to him. His mother had made a sing-song of it: Heil Mr Maclean. They had used it sometimes as a private joke. Yet, thinking of it now, he wondered at her fondness for the story, since his father had been a Highlander and killed in that war.

'Bloody, bloody hell,' Chris said.

'What?'

'It's disgusting. Bleeding savages!'

'I don't think that's true or fair.' Half closing his eyes, he followed a white cloud like plucked wool trail across the high blue sky. 'I always had an affection for the story. Maybe it shows how tolerant those people were. Perhaps he was a good teacher and the parents put up with his eccentricities.'

'Eccentricities!'

'I suppose I always imagined him as a local man, one of the islanders. It seemed very tolerant.'

'More likely they were over-awed because he was "the teacher". Peasants.'

'Bugger you!' he said, but on a breath so mild it died on his lips. She muttered something too softly for him to hear.

'Your friend Lolly or whatever his real name was.' He reared up on one elbow so that he could watch her. 'You soiled my mother's home with him. If he'd been there when I came, I'd have given him a hiding.'

She gave an audible snort.

'What's that supposed to mean?' It didn't matter that he knew he was being childish. 'If he was anything like his little poncey friend.'

She took her arm from her face and laid it by her side, at the same time replacing it with the other arm. In mid-exchange, she said on a note of disbelief, 'Poncey?'

He thought of the night in London when he had rescued her, of the stinking flat and the obscene little man.

'Can't you recognise the signs? I thought no one of your generation was naïve. Limp-wristed, I mean. Little Mr Half and Half.'

'Oh, well, poncey. Yes,' she said and laughed to herself.

'Not that they're all obvious. I didn't say that. I once taught beside a man called Bennett. Six foot two with a moustache like Wyatt Earp. Only, you see, he struck up with E.P. Atkinson – Head of Geography – and E.P. was like your Lolly's friend, a bit obvious. Though funnily enough it was the boys who got on to them before I'd noticed anything. Next thing he and E.P. had a tiff, wouldn't speak to each other. Funny thing to see Wyatt Earp flouncing.'

It was his turn to laugh. He had talked himself back into a good humour.

'Funny lot altogether, teachers. I remember when I'd just started – not started properly really – there was a fellow in the staffroom used to see how far up the wall he could run. He had marks on the wall and kept trying to beat his record.' He had never forgotten that man and had often told the story. He put on his Cockney charlady's voice. '"Ee, is that the sort of geezer wot's teaching the kids fings? Blimey!"' And added reflectively in his own voice, 'Blimey.'

But when he opened his eyes, she was far down the hill, her body slim as a boy's, jaunty in movement – though who could know better than he the unkindness of that deception?

He did not catch up with her until they were back in the village. As she tired, she had gone more slowly, resting often, yet he had dallied to be even with her like a lout in a country courtship.

She was standing by the fallen gate. Her shoulders slumped and she was looking up towards the house as if trying to gather energy for the climb. She seemed so exhausted that he was ashamed.

'Not much but it's home,' he said as he joined her. Immediately then would have eaten the words washed down with vinegar at the look of contemptuous misery she turned on him; but then distressed him more by wiping it, blinking, away. She's afraid of me – not afraid, not afraid . . . He followed miserably wading the tall grass to the house.

For supper he served slices of bread unwrapped from the foil, and eggs fried in vegetable oil. She ate without interest, like a lesson recapitulated after being forgotten and painfully relearned.

He had sluiced out the floor with water from the burn that morning so at least it was clean. There was a sideboard with a broken door and a table he had found in one of the neighbouring crofts and carried across. On the wall there was a picture of George V, heavy and Hanoverian.

'I'm surprised they left that behind,' he said, pointing with his knife. 'I'd have thought they'd be mad keen on royalty.'

'Why?'

Carefully she cut the corners from a slice of bread and carried each of the little fragments to her mouth in turn.

'I don't know.' He chewed reflectively. 'Further from Buck House the more seriously you take them – some idea like that?'

'Buck House,' she repeated neutrally.

'Yet I wonder if that's true?' He took a green plastic box from the rucksack. It held two slabs of cheese and he sliced a piece from one and sat it on a fresh piece of bread. 'I remember at the Coronation – or her wedding? – one of those enormous East End women, pearly queen type, you know, or at least pearly duchess, yelling at the coach as Elizabeth passed, "God bless yer griecious young Majesty!"' He smiled at the memory. 'Unless, of course, you want to argue that the East End working class are on a different planet from your actual royals – which is after all a fair distance, and nothing to do with geography.'

'Christ!' she said.

'What now?'

'"Or at least pearly duchess". Christ!'

'Don't swear,' he said childishly.

'Fucking Christ!'

'Blasphemy won't help.'

'What will?'

'You shouldn't feel like that.' Her helplessness angered him.

'Nobody should feel like this.'

'Cancer?' he asked, loading the single word with a world of sensible reproach.

'Fucking schoolmasters,' she groaned. 'It's not a competition. Haven't you ever been sick?'

'I brought chocolates.'

'The expert,' she said, putting her hands to her face.

'You made us experts.'

'Haven't you got that the wrong way round?' she asked into her hands.

'I don't see how you can be that sick. From the day of my mother's funeral until I came back to Glasgow – there wasn't time to get sick. You were cured before we left home.'

'"Cured". The expert.'

'So eat your chocolate. That helps, doesn't it?'

It was a detail that had always disgusted him. Cramming down sweetness as a substitute typified the whole weak corruption.

'What am I doing here? You bastard bastard this fucking Christ place oh you you.' Motionless, she stood one arm bent rigid before her. He scrambled up from where he had been sitting with his back against the wall. Her voice rose word by word until all distinction was lost in a single noise of animal despair.

'Please. Please. Chris? Please.'

As he came closer, she screamed, neck corded, mouth torn rubber, until he was terrified she would die of it. He hit her in the face very hard. The scream choked but he hit her again before he realised it was over.

She sighed.

'Chris? Are you all right? I'm sorry.'

She shook her head – no. He tried to find something to do or say. Before he could speak, she went out and he heard the outer door close.

He went to the window. His legs felt stiff as if he had been running. This window looked out on to the back of the house. A low wall of stones bounded what might once have been the kitchen garden. He listened to the silence. At home the sirens of police cars screamed past the garden walls: Co—ming Co—ming Co—ming. Along the uneven top of stones a shape flickered too quickly for him to identify it. Uneasily, he turned to find that Chris had come back inside.

'There's nothing out there,' she said. 'I don't like it out there.'

From the entrance lobby stairs ran up to a tiny landing with one door and beside it a drawn curtain. In the little room behind the door there was a wooden base of a bed and he had put Chris's sleeping bag on it. The curtain covered a cubby-hole with a sloping roof and a skylight with half a pane missing. In the morning he had swept up the sharded glass and bird droppings and laid his own sleeping bag by the wall.

'It's dark,' Chris said.

'It is, isn't it?'

She had stopped on the landing just above him. He saw her as a shape against the dark.

'Wait, I'll find the door for you.'

There was in this room a single sheet of glass set into the roof, but webbed and smeared the light lost itself in corners.

'I don't much want to sleep here,' Chris said in a small voice.

'I'll clean the window in the morning,' he said. 'I'll be through there.' He twitched back the curtain. The box room flooded with unexpected light. Through the broken pane the clear northern sky glowed high and pale. 'See. Nothing to worry about.'

'Could we go down again? Please. Just for a little. Then I'll go to bed. I am tired.'

He nodded fiercely and ran down ahead of her. Treacherous tears blocked his throat. He worked with his back to her, fussy and intent, but poured water on the coffee too soon. Lukewarm it formed a layer like grease.

'It's all right,' Chris said. 'No, really.'

Like a polite schoolgirl, he thought, practising to be the perfect guest. Sylvia would have been proud of her.

'There have been people here,' he said. 'Since the islanders left. I checked it up.' In Glasgow, before he came for her. 'The army used it for a time, and then there was a commune that landed without anyone's permission. Not long ago, someone tried to set up a holiday village.' And failed. Like the commune. 'All failures. Except the army, of course. I expect they'll come back one day, plus a missile or two.'

'There isn't anyone here now?'

He shook his head. It was deserted. Crusoe's island.

'I did bring chocolate,' he offered hesitantly, afraid she would break down again. 'If you wanted some . . .' She was holding the cup between both hands as if warming herself on a winter night. The coffee in his mouth tasted bitter and cold. 'Why not? I'd enjoy a little myself. A piece of chocolate.'

'Why not?' she wondered, head bent over the cup.

To get at the chocolate in the front pocket of the rucksack, he tugged at stiff tongues of canvas.

'Can't remember what I brought. There's even more on the boat if—'

Heart stopped, he crouched listening.

It was like leaves dry blowing on an autumn road; it was nails on a kettledrum. It was like nothing but itself. His skin crawled. Behind the wooden boards of the wall, rats were running.

'Oh, Daddy,' Chris whimpered.

'It's all right.'

He forced himself up and, on the place, banged with his fists. Instantly there was silence. He bent close, his head almost touching the paper flaking in shards from the wall. In spate just then feet ran as if scampering across his flesh. He beat on the wall crawling forward as he struck to drive, to herd them, out of the house.

'Stop!' He heard her whisper but his fists walked the wall forcing them, forcing them. Unclean! 'You must stop. You'll go mad or I will.'

In the corner, he listened panting.

'They've gone, Chris.'

Her eyes were wide and black. All the time afraid she would scream, he persuaded her with meaningless noises made of words that said, rest, I am here, like the soothing that settles a frightened bird into stillness. Slowly they climbed the stairs, the big torch making a tunnel of light they ascended. She sat on the edge of the bed and he unlaced her shoes and took them off. 'Lie down. You must sleep.' He unzipped the sleeping bag and began to coax it round her. But she came alive in a spasm of terror and caught his hand.

'I can't be alone.'

'It's all right. No need to be alone. Who's talking about being alone?'

He rubbed the shoes from his feet and, still held, lay awkwardly beside her. The window glass was pale with evening; but later when he tried to get up and she held him, a star glittered in the circle he had made with spittle and a finger in the dirt. He was cold and eased into the warmth by her side and fell asleep.

Wakening was agony. He was tucked half under Chris. The bag had worked down to her waist. She was asleep. Sunlight slanted from the skylight to the floor by the bed. He dropped an arm into it like a swimmer into a pool, and at the movement knots and cramps squeezed his legs and neck and head. Cautiously he rolled off the boards and stood up; just under the skylight he stretched his neck in the gathered heat. When he tried to pull up the sleeping bag to cover her, she said in a clear complaining voice, 'Don't, Daddy.' She was asleep.

With his shoes in his hand, he padded downstairs. In the bright morning, the room looked more desolate than before. 'It's well swept,' he said aloud to himself. 'That was a good job well done.'

He had begun to make breakfast before he noticed the green plastic box. It had a yellow lid that clipped tight to keep things fresh. When he saw what had happened, he took off the lid and lifted out the two lumps of cheese. After a moment's thought, from his rucksack he brought a tin that held candles; he emptied them on to the table, wrapped the cheese in paper and put it inside. He pressed the lid on hard.

Outside the air was like spring water. He carried the empty cheese box in both hands and as he walked looked about as if searching for something. At the back of the house there was a lean-to shed and beyond that half doors. The upper one was splintered and peering through he saw it was a byre with round stones set in the earth as a floor. The yellow lid of the cheese box had been chewed, one corner gnawed away. He squeezed the box through the sagged gap in the half door and let it fall out of sight.

TEN

He despaired of making her feel the idea of an island. A cluster of words and images rose in him, each sharp and clear, but it was the pattern of all of them that mattered and he was not able to explain any of it.

'Where?' she asked again.

'We'll see when we get there.' He was impatient to be off. 'All we've seen is the beach and the bit from here to the hill.'

She was sitting on a stone, huddled although it was so hot. Her nose was running.

'I won't sleep in that house another night,' she said.

'Let's go then. We'll find another one.'

To his relief, she got up. He started down the steep field from the house, bracing himself, feeling the muscles of his thighs tighten and release at each step. Near the bottom he let the slope run him down the last dozen yards so that he came with a jump against the last piece of fence. Wire tore from the rotted posts.

'All the houses will be the same,' Chris said behind him. 'Why should one be different?'

He thought that she was complaining, but when he looked at her face he saw she was frightened.

'It's really not a problem,' he tried to reassure her. 'They have funny preferences – I'm sure we'll find a house they've never been near.'

'They?'

He was reluctant to name them. What they had heard last night was a dream distance from the bright morning and the sound of the sea just beyond the ridge. He walked away along what he thought of as the village street. Houses were set back on either side.

'Oh, Jesus, I hate them,' Chris said coming up by his side. She shuddered. 'When I was . . . bad, you know. One of the worst times. I woke up in a flat somewhere. I'd flaked out in a chair and

98

fallen out of it – or somebody had taken me out of it. I was on the floor and the electric light was on. This thing was sitting up looking at me. And I couldn't move. It ran up on me.' She pressed her hand under her breast. 'It was as if it understood how afraid I was. It touched me.'

As they went on, she rubbed her hand over the place under her breast. He tried to push away the image of her lying naked and helpless. He remembered the flat in London. The stinking smell of urine corrupted the salt morning.

'This way.'

He caught the offending hand by the wrist and pulled her after him. The path angled towards the hills where they had discovered the peat workings.

'I heard sheep yesterday,' he said panting a little as they climbed. 'We could eat a sheep.'

He waited for her to say something.

'Or a lamb,' he said. 'We could be self-supporting.'

He waved an arm possessively, embracing the whole island.

'We've got the tins,' Chris said, 'and packets of things.'

'That's capital. You don't want to eat your capital.'

'You have enough for days. And there's more on the boat. You said so.'

'Won't last for ever.'

She fell on her knees; perhaps her foot had caught on a tangle of grass. Without rising, she looked up at him.

'But it doesn't have to, does it? How long does it take to punish me?'

'Punish?'

She leapt up, however, and with a burst of unreal speed scrambled ahead of him. Heart-sick at the word, he took a moment to recover and follow her but already she had begun to stumble and lag. It wasn't difficult to catch up.

'Punish?' he asked. 'You should know better than that. To *help*. Just to help. And not for a day longer than it stops helping. This is a breathing space – think of it like that.'

His own words made him draw a deep breath as if persuasively. A drift of heavy sweetness on the air made him think of a flower someone had called honeysuckle on a walk a long time ago.

'There!' Chris said and pointed. The track ended at a house. That disappointed him.

'Could we look there?' Chris asked in a small voice.

At first he didn't understand, then objected, 'It's rather far up. We'd have to cart all the stuff up to here.'

'I'll help.'

He was touched.

'No harm in looking.'

But as they began, as if by agreement, to walk towards the house some perversity put a word in his head he could not resist saying aloud.

'Gralloch.'

She looked at him enquiringly.

'It's the word they used for skinning a deer – or disembowelling it, I'm not sure. Anyway, I daresay it would apply to a sheep as well. It's rather splendid. Gralloch,' and he rolled it in his mouth.

'Have you ever skinned anything? I mean, really, in real life.'

'Oh . . . sausages,' he said, and made a slitting gesture with his thumb. 'Down from its sausage throat . . . A firm cut – the beginner doesn't put weight behind it – it's tough stuff, skin.' Unluckily then he remembered Carroll's story.

'John Carroll,' he explained to her silence. 'Isn't it funny? You never seem to forget the names of people in your first job – like boys you were at school with.' He was quiet for a moment trying to remember; he remembered the faces of two boys, neither of them friends; their names were gone. 'We shared a staffroom – Carroll and Tanner and Jacobs and Hubbard – he was Welsh.' How glibly they rolled from his tongue. 'He'd been reading a medical textbook. Don't know why – he taught classics. It had a chapter on suicides, the ones who try to do it by cutting their throats.'

They had arrived at the front of the house.

'Can we look inside?' Chris asked.

'Not yet. Let me finish first.'

The dry stones of the garden wall were tumbled and scattered.

'It's not so easy apparently. Skin's tougher than you'd think. With the first cut, they only trace a line. So, you see, you get three or four of these superficial cuts. I expect a lot of them give up at that. But if they don't, they start sawing away. Some of them almost cut their heads off.'

'Could we go inside, please?' she asked.

'One chap,' he said conversationally, following her, 'had enough

100

energy left to kick the St John's Ambulance man downstairs. Rushed out of his room with his throat sawed open and kicked him downstairs. He was one of the ones who meant it.'

'Yes.' She had her hand on the latch of the door. 'Thank you for telling me.'

It was so unexpected he thought she was making fun of him; but surely, if so, she would open the door and go into the house. Instead she waited with bent head, her hand resting on the latch. A terrible uneasiness prevented him from thinking. He pushed past her.

As the door opened, something sprang at him. A claw or an extended finger rubbed him from cheek to chin. He flung up an arm and knocked it away.

'Oh, God,' he said. 'It's a fishing rod.'

A black whip slanted trembling from the opposite wall.

'Careful!'

Clumsily, Chris brushed it as she went in past his stupid immobility. He picked up the rod and gathered the line. It hung down in loops from his fist.

'Fishing line rots fairly quickly,' he said into the darkness of the house. 'I wonder who left it here and when.'

In his other life he had lacked patience. Now attentively he unpicked the knots and strays of the line. There was a twist that needed unwinding as he went. Gradually the line went down scribbling its to and fro on the grass. When he had unswirled the path from hook to reel, he said aloud, 'I've unfankled it,' and the word from his childhood surprised him. The reel jammed and freed several times but finally he had wound to the last turn and sat on one of the tumbled stones of the wall holding the rod angled out over the dry turf. With a glow of pioneer satisfaction, he called, 'Chris! Come out! We're going fishing!'

As he looked up, a little brown bird with a blunt clown's head wavered in through the open door and vanished.

'Chris!' he called again in warning. He waited amused for her to be chased out by this new intruder. The blank house made no response. After a time, the bird came out quickly in a changing flickering like a man blinking at the light.

'Chris?'

He got up and walked as many paces as cleared the front of the house. Bare country stretched to the hills behind without even a tree to make cover. Separate from the rhythm of his heart, he felt another pulse under it as if an alien heart had begun to beat inside him.

With the hook in its throat, he took the rod over his shoulder and walked away. Looking back from the top of the first rise, the house seemed already distant. The second time he turned some twist of the land hid it altogether. After an hour's walking, he came on a narrow stream deep cut between rocks. He sat on the edge of it and made a cast that snagged in a bush on the other side. He tugged gently one way and the other until it came free carrying an unripe bait of dull-pink summer berries. Not daring to cast again, he swung the line over and let it dapple beneath the racing surface. No sooner had it been caught by the stream than a quiver passed along the whole connection of line and rod into his clasped hands. He jerked in surprise and the reel sang as the line ran out. Next moment with an unskilful fury, the tip of the rod curving near the surface, he tore threshing from the stream a fish that looked large, then small, and neither one nor the other as it convulsed on the bank at his feet.

He did not touch it until it had stopped moving, but when he tried to take the hook from its mouth the resistance made him squeamish and he retraced his steps carrying it with the line still attached. The fish that had come so vivid from the water grew dull in his hand.

When he came in sight of the house, Chris was climbing the track from the village with a loose bundle clasped in her arms. As he watched she disappeared inside, reappeared at once and had gone some way down again before he caught up with her.

'What were those?' he asked. 'Was it the sleeping bags?'

She nodded. 'I couldn't spend another night in that house.'

'Why should you?'

They followed the darker stripe of turf downwards. She glanced sideways at his burden.

'It's not likely to get away, is it?'

He was offended.

'There's a way of doing these things,' he said grimly. 'You have to cut the hook out.'

102

'You should have taken a knife with you – one of the ones with the things for taking stones out of horses' hooves.'

She seemed ready to laugh. He knew that should make him glad, but after a struggle managed only to say, 'I'll remember that next time.' The light went out of her face and they went on in miserable silence.

At the house, in fact, while she gathered things to be carried up to their new resting place, he found a knife and went outside. The excuse, if he had felt one had to be spoken, was that it was too dark indoors, but Chris followed him outside and with her watching he forced himself to lever the mouth open. To get at the hook he pressed wider and with a tiny clear crack the jaw broke. He cut the hook out in a messy lump. With relief he laid the fish on a stone.

'You have to gut them,' she said. 'Otherwise it taints the flesh. Make you sick.'

The knife was very sharp and sliced butter-easy down the belly. By accident, he did it right and a gush of intestines dropped out of the slit.

'Our first fish,' he said looking up at her, 'we could live off the land.'

ELEVEN

Perhaps the people of the commune had discovered, among whatever else as they carried their search as far from Gomorrah as Breagda, that, like Chris, they were terrified by rats. In any case, it seemed that they too had chosen this house high on the hill to occupy. It was in repair. Its roof had been patched, though another winter would begin its second dilapidation. The amount of furniture suggested other houses had been looted to supply this one. The best evidence of the commune's presence, however, was the sentence painted in red across the fireplace wall. With the night warmth of his body lapping him to the chin, hands pressed between his knees, he tested his memory.

DRIVE YOUR CART AND YOUR PLOUGH OVER THE BONES OF THE DEAD.

He remembered it too well, too quickly. Disturbed, he opened his eyes. Chris on tip-toe was hanging a picture on a nail so that it hid part of the painted sentence. He wriggled half out of the bag and sat up so he could see. In an unshadowed noon light it imaged a lake, mountains, and across them the legend: 'My grace is sufficient for thee, 2 Cor. 12: 9.'

'What are you doing in your finite wisdom?' he asked softly.

She startled at his voice, and then with a deliberate movement straightened the picture. With her back to him, as if studying it, she said, 'I found them hidden away in a cupboard. They must have belonged to the people who lived here. Those old relatives of yours.' Looking down, he saw a fat stack of picture frames against the wall by her feet.

Wincing at the chill linoleum on his bare feet, he padded over and gathered up the three on the outside of the stack. He shuffled them: a windmill; a tangle of wayside hedge, greens and browns; an Italianate house flooded with unreal sunlight on the edge of a lake. – Across each of them, a rhyme that jingled together with a

104

biblical citation. John 14, 15. Proverbs 3, 6. Musty with childhood
and misery, a genteel Scots voice in his ear chanted nasally – John
Fourteen *and* Fifteen Proverbs Three *and* Six; wood brown gleam
from the lovingly polished pulpit; later, radio bells tolling Monday,
Monday.

'Going to hang up all of these?' and when she didn't answer, 'Is
it your intention to hang every last one?'

'I do want to.'

'Let's have a look before it goes up. Oh, yes . . .' He took from
her the picture she had lifted. 'Extraordinary. Here, let me.' A full-
rigged sailing ship, all labelled, beating north under a cargo of
metaphor.

Time of Sailing—Second Corinthians six *and* two—Behold now
is the accepted time.

Reluctantly she gave it up and with a parody of ceremony, he
suspended it from a nail and stood back to admire.

'Corinthians . . . Colossians . . . Thessalonians . . . Galatians.'
He moved his finger across the glass. 'All the way to Revelations
Ten *and* Six. Strange.' His lips twisted unconsciously as he reflected
on its strangeness. 'Did you know the ancient Hebrews believed
the world was supported on pillars? With a roof over it stuck with
stars. And the roof had windows in it and, when they opened, the
waters that God had divided to be above the firmament were let
through. Do you know what that was, Chris? That was the rain –
that's why it rains. Did you know that, Chris?'

When she didn't answer, he stared and, giving up, began to
dress. As he made a breakfast, he watched from the corner of his
eye her stubborn progress round the room. He spoke only once
when, having run out of nails and ledges, she began to stand the
frames in the recesses of the windows. With a grimace, he said,
'Light. Let there be – please?'

The stack used up she turned about in the middle of the room.

'Not a bit like home,' he said.

She continued to turn, satisfied, absorbed.

'And, lo!' he said, 'she surveyed the place and her works were
good.'

'Shouldn't that just be "saw"?'

'If it isn't, why, yes it should be. What lover of English prose
would use "surveyed" when he could chip "saw" out on a stone?'

'I don't see the point of being blasphemous.'

He was genuinely astonished.

'You mean that wasn't just literary criticism? Have you been reading the Bible behind my back?'

'I've read the Bible.'

'Stranger and stranger. How odd the world is on this side of the looking-glass.'

She seemed as if she would weep. Abruptly then her unhappiness became more real to him than his own; and not long after they went out together.

'Why did you make so many sandwiches to bring?'

'This is an expedition not a walk. We're going,' he thought quickly, 'to the end of the island,' and at once, choice made, banners and trumpets invisible went ahead of him as they turned towards the first hills.

His plan of campaign was simple. 'If we keep the sun on our left, we'll be walking back down the island. Do you remember the cliffs, Chris?' The great wall of the island rising out of the sea that first morning: for a moment, he expected her to share his excitement – and then remembered why she had not seen the cliffs of Breagda.

At first it was comfortable walking but then they began to climb. They followed sheep paths and he tried without much success to pick out the easiest ways, sweating in the hot sun. He took off his shirt and, knotting the arms, let it hang down his back. The rucksack straps cut into his shoulders and he kept easing it with his thumbs as he leant into the steepness of the hill. Ridge succeeded ridge deceptively. Unaware, they came to what lay ahead of them.

A squat mountain stood up across a plain from them in a series of profiles, like a man shrugging in slow motion. Sun on water struck up signals of light from the broken ground below.

'We could bear left to go round it,' he said, standing with hands on his hips, opening his chest to the freshening wind, 'or we could go over. Not to the top, of course, I don't mean to the top. But if we just kept straight ahead – over the first shoulder, we could manage that, don't you see?'

But, as if not to see, she declined to the grass.

'What's wrong now?'

'I'm tired of walking.' Her voice came muffled from behind the two arms that shielded her face.

'We're walking to the end of the island,' he said quietly, clenching his will above her like a fist. 'I won't take excuses. It will do you good.'

After an uncomfortably long pause, she said to his relief, 'Give me a moment to rest.'

'A moment,' he said heavily, and settled himself beside her, who had decided, it seemed, to be his accomplice.

Yesterday's trick of the slope worked again, giving shelter. Under the wind he lay in still air watching an insect the colour of grass cling to a ruffling stem.

'This would be a terrible day to die,' Chris said.

'Are there good days?'

'Dying came into my mind. I'm very tired.'

'We're walking to the end of the island.'

'Have you never thought of dying?'

'Not till I get to the end of the island.' He took pleasure in the harshness of his humour. 'The sun's shining. Don't be boring. You have your life in front of you.'

The heat was heavy like a weight. It would have been easy to give in and sleep, but he thought of Chris on tip-toe hanging the dusty texts. Those old Hebrews who believed the world rested on pillars (above what nothingness? what chaos?) spent a lot of time thinking about death. They had created in thought a place scooped out of the hollow fruit of the earth to be a home for the dead – only at first, wandering their desert, they had not believed in an after-life, knowing the dead were shadows. He would not lose Chris to death. On the blackboard shadowed at the far end of the empty lecture room he had gone into last summer someone had printed – AIMS. With a piece of chalk he had written 'sex' beside it as a joke, and then rubbed it out in case anyone saw. As he worked correcting papers at a desk, he kept looking up at the blank single word that was left. At last, he wrote under it a list – Elevation Autonomy Triumph Happiness. Above them he printed in first – Desire, thinking of his initial joke; then replaced it with – Dreams, which didn't seem quite right either; dreamless, dreamlessness . . . Id est, DEATH whose dominion extended over Breagda as over the world.

A gull squealed like chalk on the blue board of the sky.

He wrenched himself up from the grass. At the sudden movement, Chris uncovered her eyes. 'Yes,' he said as if she had questioned him. 'Oh, yes,' he repeated implacably and began to scramble down without looking back.

Coming off the hill was easy enough, dropping over the turf, and for a little on the flat it was like that but then white-headed flowers signalled from among more vivid green and they had to circle patches of wet bog. Still the squat mountain drew him. They settled to a steady pace, his health matched against the mysterious resilience of being young. Things began to go badly. It was hard to keep a line when the land flexed, gullies that had been invisible from above opened; he had the illusion they were struggling to cross the fingers of a hand unclenching under the mountain's chin.

'Last year I was in one of the lecture rooms by myself,' he said, talking at the ground as he picked his steps. He had started intending to tell her about the AIMS, but then for some reason changed his mind. 'Just by myself and I'd been sitting, just sitting not even thinking, and I suddenly got up and scrawled in big letters on the board – THIS DAY MARCH THE FOURTH I ALTERED MY LIFE. All sprawled out in big letters.' Yet this story was also true. He had tried to get a message through in so many empty rooms.

An awkward jolt as they struggled down the knuckle of a last monstrous finger knocked the breath into his throat.

'All sprawled out,' he insisted breathlessly, but she made no response. They set themselves to the rising incline in silence.

Had he been trying to impress her? He hadn't been conscious of that as an intention. Perhaps he had been trying to interest her. He would admit to trying to interest her.

Doggerel from one of the texts ran together in his head – only one life 'twill soon be past only what's done for Jesus will last.

'Manchester sainted!' he burst out. 'Protestant variety though. Those awful pictures and the verses— In curly letters, for God's sake, against a background of leaves.'

'For God's sake,' she repeated quietly with a changed emphasis.

'And I suppose that's quite clever?' His breath failed, however, so that he had to fight to speak without stammering. Irony fell short of what he needed. 'Only it's not – it's childish, stupid, irrelevant.' His head rang in the brazen air. The sun leaned on him from its noon height. 'Don't you see my point?' he gasped.

Common sense advised his slack body that the mountain was to be gone round. Instead, though at an angle to the impossible central absurdity, he led her towards it. Like a creeping thing, in the knowledge she was following, he set himself to cross a pleat of the mountain's shoulder.

At her endurance he directed a chant drawn from the soiled impedimenta of his unsought childhood. Breathless, he made breath:

> 'Yield not to temptation
> For yielding is sin,
> Each victory will help you
> Some other to win.'

Through the estate grounds, green and strange as Eden, from Sunday School pacing, whisper-chanting by a tree, 'Yield not . . .'

'There's virtue for you,' he said in a mock Welsh voice.

'Please,' Chris said, and startled he looked fully at her and saw she was exhausted.

'Not far,' he said, driven, 'to the end of the island.'

Grey stone rubbed through the grass. Heather like skinned flesh led them on to a slope of loose rock. A piece dislodged under his foot and bounced and turned end over end until it splintered.

'Stay by my side.'

She hung back and he grabbed her arm and pulled her along.

'Don't be a fool. If I get ahead of you and set one of those rolling it could break a leg for you – or an arm. Or your stubborn head.'

'I'm not stubborn.'

Her voice flat and colourless might have been insolent; but she stumbled almost pulling him down and he saw she was crying. Terrible soundless tears brimmed from her eyes.

'Oh, Daddy! I'm sorry.' She slumped through his grasp and lay on her knees against him. 'If you let me rest only for a little. Please, don't be angry.'

In anguish, he touched her clumsily on the shoulder. 'Come on, Chris. There's no need for this. Don't let yourself down.'

She lay between his feet. Abandoned, her body had made its separate peace.

'You can't know how bad I've been. I couldn't bear to tell you. Filth. So much, much – dirty! You would hate me.' She rubbed at

109

her throat as if to clean something away. 'I'll tell you about Lolly. All of the filth, filth.'

There was no meaning he could attach to the repeated word. Unbidden, blue-movie stills ran in his head – he rejected each scene before the actors could move – in all of them his daughter had a part.

'Thank you for bringing me here. I can thank God now for bringing us here. I feel reborn – the wind blows me clean. The sea washes me clean'. She looked up at him, her face bloated with contrition.

Perhaps it was nothing more sinister than fastidiousness that left him no better response. 'And the lambs, plenty of them about here,' he said. 'Don't forget the lambs.'

Trying to understand, she stared up dazed, then taking him entirely by surprise she rebounded to her feet and before he could stop her was running. She, who had seemed entirely spent, went so furiously that at first he lost ground. She fell but was up at once. She ran on with the lagging rhythm of a music box almost unwound. The leaden effort of driving on angered him till with a lunge he caught her and lifted her kicking into the air.

'Enough,' he gasped. 'That's enough!'

'Let me go!' Her heel tore his shin. 'We've got to go to the end of the island. You know you said so.'

'And now I unsay it.'

By his weight, he forced her down.

'I only want to do what you said.'

'Then be still.'

'You wanted to go to the end of the island.'

He held her until she quietened.

'To hell with that.' As she rested, he thought, we've been to the end anyway. Over her head, he smiled at the thought. If not to the end, not quite, not yet, at least in sight of it.

As it happened, trying to return they were deceived into a slow climb that took them to a place from which they could look back. Like a tray of light glittering with a tremble of islets, the sea lay beyond the end of the island.

'So beautiful,' she whispered.

'I'm sorry. We've come too far. It will be a long walk back.'

By chance they came off the hill at an angle that avoided the

worst of the broken ground. It was as if they crossed the palm of
the giant's unclenched fist. When she had to rest, he was solicitous
and knelt by her. They moved painfully slowly and he was worrying
about a night in the open when they came over a low bank and saw
a beach with the sea at a great distance across it.

'Sheol,' he said aloud. 'They called it Sheol.'

Wearied to obsession, he had been puzzling to recall the name
the Hebrews had given to the place of their dead. They called it
Sheol.

'I want to go to the water,' Chris said.

From some appalling resource, she found the strength for a
quivering dipping flight that died in the floundering sand.

'Too far!' She stood submissive as he caught her by the arm. 'We
can't go all the way to the sea.' He squinted into the evening light.
'God, it looks miles.'

Her arm moved in his hand, a movement so faint and suppressed
so quickly that it suggested to him not protest but depths of
disappointment.

'Too far,' he tried to explain.

'I wanted to feel the sea on my face.'

They were walking towards the sea. Still he held her arm. He
was sure she had not pulled him into walking but had no sense of
voluntary effort in himself. As he thought about that, they came on
the sand firmed by the withdrawing tide.

'We can walk on this,' he decided, and turned her by the elbow,
keeping her by his side so that now they went parallel to the sea.
'It might take us all the way back. If we come to the bay where the
Lazy Charlotte is, we can strike up and find the house that way.'

Without protest, she moved with him; only, after a while, said
colourlessly, 'I wanted to feel the water on my face.'

'Among the rocks.' He pointed. 'There'll be water among the
rocks. Pools left behind. You can bathe your forehead and feel
better then.'

The rocks poked like a finger from the sea. They plodded towards
them with the slowness of nightmare. The tide had turned and ran
in deceptively fast. When they came to them, he saw the rocks
were shuffled like playing cards. It was like mounting a flight of
ruined stairs. On the first step, Chris knelt and with cupped hand
patted water over her eyes and cheeks.

Anxious, he scrambled on until he could look into the next bay. He walked along one edge of rock, stepped up, went back a little round a pool of water gone dark in the twilight, took the next step and saw, with a leap of relief, the *Charlotte* riding at anchor in the path of the setting sun. As he began to turn to call Chris, he brought into view marks of feet showing plainly, edged with deep shadows, in the sand.

A shudder of superstitious fear chilled his heart as he followed the line of steps to where about twenty yards off a figure shaped like a man knelt on the sand, its back to him, both hands raised to its head as if clasped in prayer.

TWELVE

The buzzing tried against his resistance to rouse him: a plane a dive-bomber belly opening on those quaint bombs that whistled as they fell twisting into a fat wasp that alarmed him awake.

The stranger blocked the light. He was tall, not quite six feet though, but extraordinarily broad across the shoulders. In front of the window, he stood with one elbow cocked in the air, pulling his neck first to one side then the other.

The door opened, brushing the foot of the sleeping bag. Chris came in, yawning and scratching the top of her thigh. She wore only a shirt in which she must have slept. Her feet were bare and dirty. He took in breath and she glanced down at him. He made himself into a single mime, 'Get out!'

The sound of the door closing made Ramsay – yes, Ramsay – turn.

'Good morning,' he said over the buzz, then with his thumb moved something and it was quiet. In the silence, sheep outside complained.

'Battery,' Ramsay said holding out the razor with a smile.

The sleeping bag entangled him. He wriggled and kicked until he was free. 'No, thank you.' Ramsay looked surprised – perhaps he had not been offering the razor. 'I'm letting mine grow. Seems the easiest way.'

Ramsay unscrewed the razor's head and blew. On that breath fine hairs flighted down a shaft of morning sunlight.

'Ah,' Ramsay said restoring the head with a deft turn, 'easiest?'

'Batteries won't last for ever,' Campbell said defensively.

'Why should they? I'll be here a long time short of for ever. Won't you, sir?' Added 'sir' like a polite young man – or in parody of an earlier generation of gentle young men.

Campbell sought an answer. Absurd, yet as a question not exactly simple to resolve coming upon him suddenly like that. He was

113

grateful for the diversion of Chris's return. She was wearing the same shirt top but had pulled on a pair of jeans, the shirt loose outside them.

'I was saying to your husband—' Ramsay broke off. 'Sorry.'

Campbell became conscious of his own bare legs, endlessly long and white, and hastened decently to cram them out of sight. Pulling up his zip with his back to them, he grunted, 'I'll take that as a compliment.'

'A compliment.' Ramsay weighed the word as if in a hand balance. Campbell wondered if he was slow-witted, and then it struck him that perhaps Ramsay had decided last night they were lovers and dismissed their claim to be father and daughter as some whimsical obscenity. His uncomfortable imagination provided a context – an office, a secretary perhaps, and the wife, there would be a wife, who wouldn't, naturally, understand, and then the voyage, some pretext invented, to a dirty old man's Shangri-la. Deeply offended, Campbell regarded his fiction.

'A compliment, Daddy,' Chris said, 'since you look so young.'

She knelt by the kitchen range. When she pulled open the door with the little hook from the hearth, Campbell saw a ripple of flame. She smiled over her shoulder, 'You've been busy,' looking up at this stranger.

Ramsay nodded at the table.

'And fetched water from the burn.'

'What I said. You've been busy.'

She poured water from the plastic bucket into a pan and set it on the ring, lifting off the cover plate.

'Will that heat it?' Campbell asked.

'Oh, certainly,' Ramsay said. 'There's sticks and peat in there. It'll give off plenty of heat.'

'We didn't think of trying a fire,' Campbell said. 'I thought the chimney would be blocked.'

The smell from the smouldering peat oiled his nostrils.

'Unless,' Chris said suddenly, 'what you were really compliment-ing was Daddy's good taste. In wives, I mean.'

For some reason, the idea of that pleased each of them. In the way of such things, whatever had begun badly righted itself and they sat down together and ate.

Later, Chris and Ramsay sat on the warm stones of the broken

114

wall drinking tea from the heavy plastic beakers. Campbell, prowling as he drank, said abruptly, 'Twa corbies.'

'What?' Chris and Ramsay asked on the same breath and then laughed.

'It's a poem,' Campbell explained. 'You reminded me of it. "In ahint yon auld fail dyke I wot there lies a new slain knight And naebody kens that he lies there But his hawk his hound and leddy fair . . ." I can't remember any more.'

'But what has it— '

Ramsay interrupted her. 'Don't you see? You and me. On the wall like this – twa corbies.'

'Crows,' Campbell said. 'Corbies are crows. It's a poem I learned at school.'

'How clever of you,' Chris said.

Into the pause, Ramsay tactfully interjected, 'You do a terribly good Scotch accent.'

'I went to school here.'

'On the island?'

'Oh, no. In Scotland, I meant.'

'It's quite a large place . . . Scotland.'

As he spoke, Ramsay looked thoughtfully around at the green slopes and the hills against open sky. Like a pulse, the sea made its faint persistent claim in each silence. Something in the tone reminded Campbell as he listened that the accent for which he had exchanged his childhood voice was still far from those lovingly distorted upper-class vowels of the younger man. 'I laugh every time I think of it,' he said abruptly.

'It?' Ramsay asked.

'Seeing you last night kneeling on the beach. I thought you were praying.'

'Your father thought I was praying,' Ramsay said to Chris. 'It must be all the texts hanging on the walls inside.'

'I put those up,' she said.

'My daughter the religious maniac.' He used his funny Jewish voice.

Chris jumped up and went inside, as if impatiently, but came out in a moment with the binoculars. In the spirit of the thing, Ramsay knelt holding them steady to his eyes. From the back, it was a pose that might have been mistaken for prayer.

115

'But what were you looking at last night?' Campbell asked, uneasy as the glittering discs centred on him.

'Tell me the names of sea birds you know,' the round stare commanded.

'Cormorant, gulls, of course, eh, blackheaded, isn't that one kind? And . . . sorry. What else? Fulmars? Puffins. Kittiwake – is that a sea bird?'

In Ramsay's hands, the binoculars looked small. With a conjuror's movement he spun them end for end.

'This way,' he said, 'you rush far off. You're only . . . so big.'

From behind the binoculars' blankness, he held out his left hand. The first finger and thumb indicated a minute separation.

'Buffoonery,' he said, standing up and putting the caps over the glasses. 'I have the holiday feeling – like the first day of the long vacation.'

Campbell saw that he was a young man. Last night's strangeness or simply the alarming physical bulk of Ramsay had hidden that plain fact. He might have been one of those students in distant London listening with veiled eyes to him unwind his spool of wisdom through the tedious hour of a summer afternoon.

'What's your subject?' he asked.

'Industrial design.' Ramsay held out his hands and turned them palm and back. 'It's practical. As well as being other things.'

'Aesthetically satisfying,' Campbell suggested, by temperament reluctant to leave a definition unexplored.

'Well paid,' Chris offered unexpectedly.

'Undemanding,' Ramsay added on his own account.

Campbell sprayed the dregs of tea from the beaker against the house wall. The image troubled him of these two at the back of a class passing alien inscrutable judgements.

'I had better think of letting Neil know where I am,' Ramsay said.

'Neil? Neil?' His voice flapped up like a bird springing from the cold shock in his chest.

If Ramsay was startled he controlled it.

'He's on the boat.'

'What boat?' Was the island to be full of people?

'I came on a boat,' Ramsay said reasonably.

'I thought you were alone,' Campbell said bewildered. He was

116

afraid to look at Chris. Yet he had no reason to be ashamed. 'I was sure you said that.'

'I will be once Neil goes. The boat will leave today. It's just that Neil didn't come ashore. He likes his comfort.'

Campbell tried hard to concentrate. They had been sleep-walkers stumbling up here last night. There was no way he could remember what had been said.

'Would you like to come with me? I'm going to the boat now to see Neil. I expect there'll be something to drink. That's Neil's style.'

'I don't think so.'

'I'd like to,' Chris said.

Before Ramsay could answer, Campbell said, 'Let me change my mind. Why not?'

They came off the hill and down between the crofts.

'We slept our first night there,' he told Ramsay pointing upwards to the house above the yellow field.

'What made you move?'

He looked back. Chris trailed behind.

'Rats,' he said softly, shaping the word with his lips a little in exaggeration.

Ramsay broke step laughing.

'Healthy enough creatures here,' he said. 'Different if you were in a slum in London.'

'Where?' The phrase in Ramsay's mouth was disturbing.

'It's their fleas,' Ramsay said. 'Rat fleas spread the black plague – only that was in the Middle Ages, of course.'

'Indeed,' Campbell allowed himself, 'that's one worry the less then.'

He looked quickly in search of a response. The fleshy, imminently heavy features of the younger man were immobile with solemnity. A light tremor crawled across his skin. 'Fleas or not, I'd hate to wake up to one running across my bed. Do you know in the morning after the one night we spent up there, I found a cheese box with the corner chewed off. It was made of plastic.'

They jumped a ditch and went up the ridge that backed on to the beach.

'They're rodents,' Ramsay explained. 'They have these rather special teeth, you see.'

Just then he seemed to Campbell rather a dull young man.

The two boats lay not more than thirty yards apart. Big waves were rolling beyond the point and away on the right tall white combers foamed on to the sand. Near the edge of the water another dinghy rested beside the one from the *Lazy Charlotte*.

'Your boat was hiding ours. Last night from where I was looking,' Campbell said. 'I was in just the wrong place.'

'Smell the sea. What a morning!' Ramsay said, and took an interminable breath. 'I say, look there!' The salt air exploded again in exclamation. With a single movement, he had the binoculars uncased and, palming the caps, raised up to his eyes. 'Here, have a look.'

Campbell took them automatically, then embarrassed lowered them to seek a direction from Ramsay's pointing finger.

'That's what I was watching when you saw me last night.'

Impatient with excitement, he took Campbell by the shoulder, who let himself be turned and set in position. 'Just by the edge – see! To the left – just off the line of the dinghy – your one. You'll be lucky to see a bird like that again!'

Into focus, he brought a dapper gull, but wavering surreptitiously right and left could find no other bird and so decided it must be something else, not a gull at all.

'There it goes!' Ramsay said and took back the glasses with a casualness that was offensive. At his head he moved them in a single arc that sped down. 'Like a stone! That fish is dead twice over – smashed and pulled out into the air.' Smiling, he had broad very clean teeth. 'This is going to be a lucky day.'

He ran in a sandslip down the side of the dune. Chris, caught up, followed in bounding leaps, risking and retaking balance like a clown on the slack wire. Campbell hesitated at their laughter. They seemed like youngsters anywhere on an outing by the sea. Carefully he stepped his way down after them.

Distracted by Ramsay holding out a hand as if to help him into the dinghy, he half slipped and soaked one leg to the knee. The younger man took the oars. At each beat, they surged forward spurning the surface; it was casual and impressive. Birds clustered on the rocks spun up squabbling. He was puzzled by a thin sound then realised Chris curled at the front of the dinghy was singing softly. The hand he had been trailing over the side was suddenly

braceleted with cold. 'Daddy, your fingers are like pork sausages' –
as he reached down to take her hand on a cold Sunday morning
walk. Daddy's clever girl. Next day at work he had told everyone.

Ramsay as they came near hailed the boat, but it was like a still
house. Some instinct in him sensed emptiness. They came along-
side and scrambled aboard in silence.

Yet Ramsay, popping his head up from the cabin, was entirely
astonished.

'He's not here!'

The three of them crowded in the swaying cockpit stared at one
another.

'Let me look,' Campbell said. The words were spoken before he
had time to examine them. Embarrassed by them, he tensed
waiting but Ramsay gave no sign of objection, scratching his head
as he settled on the bench seat.

Out of the light, his eyes traced golden scrolls on the dim
surfaces. There was a narrow door and he opened it, wrinkling his
nose at something stale and sour in the air. Under the forward
hatch liquid slopped gently in a plastic bucket.

'Well?' Ramsay called.

'Oh, nobody. Nobody here.'

There were two bunks, neatly made up so that there was no way
of telling if both of them had been used. Swiftly, furtively, he slid
doors open and shut. Behind one, he found a row of books.

'Well?' Ramsay called.

He read the titles: *The Instrument at the Door*, *The Self as
Agent*, Paton's *The Moral Law*—

Startled, he turned to see Ramsay watching him. 'Sorry.'

'I don't fancy,' Ramsay said, 'Neil wants to run a lending library.'

'The books are his?' Campbell asked.

'They're not mine.'

'They say you can tell about a man from the books he reads.'

'Do they?' Ramsay reflected. 'I don't know what you'd make of
Neil.'

He wondered suddenly if Neil existed at all.

'Was there another boat – a raft?'

Ramsay shook his head, watching him.

'He must have swum then.'

Chris, who was tugging on the line that held the dinghy, said without looking round, 'In which direction?'

For some reason, Ramsay found that extraordinarily funny. His laugh was high-pitched for so big a man and he laughed for what seemed to Campbell an unreasonable time. 'For America, eh?' he speculated and spluttered laughter.

Campbell took the line from Chris and pulled the dinghy close.

'Get in,' he told her.

She looked at him blankly.

'In, *in*,' he said harshly. 'Haven't we wasted enough time?'

She climbed down clumsily so that it bucked and almost tipped her into the sea.

'Careful, for God's sake!'

Ramsay came down after them with the compact neatness of an athlete. He took the oars again; in his hands they looked small. As he rowed his face swung close to Campbell's and receded.

'Waste of time?' he repeated. 'What is there here but all the time in the world? Isn't that why you came?'

'Why I came?' Campbell said. 'What do you mean, why I came?'

'For a holiday.' The heavy face, that looked now as if it had never smiled, swam close and receded. 'Your father needs this holiday, Chris. Too much business. Worrying about making money. Worrying about time.'

In the first class he had ever taught, there had been a boy with a withered arm whom he had disliked unreasonably and had been ashamed of disliking, for, though he had a shabby trick of goading his mates to violence and then begging off, he had the perspiration stench of authentic misery. It was stupid to be reminded of him by solid healthy Ramsay, rushing them over the blue water with his two powerful arms.

'I'm not a businessman,' he started to say but at the same instant they were at the beach and it was lost in the flurry of landing.

With Ramsay he pulled the dinghy above the tide line, then looked up to see Chris walking away. Something purposeful in her movement disturbed him.

'Where are you off to?' he called.

She stopped and, turning only her head, stared at him. During the moment in which he still expected her to speak it was all right, but then it was very bad. At last, she walked away.

120

'In the army,' Ramsay said cheerfully, 'they call that dumb insolence.'

Campbell found himself unable to answer.

'Sorry.' Ramsay had a quick way of apologising. 'She's . . . at the awkward age.'

By his tone sufficiently conscious of how much nearer he was to Chris's age than to Campbell's, his expression conniving at the mild absurdity, unexpectedly for the older man he exerted a power genuinely to charm. It was then in an altered tone, heard by himself as conciliatory, that Campbell asked, 'When do you start doing your – survey, is that what you'd call it?'

'No hurry.' In illustration, Ramsay settled himself comfortably on the sand. 'It's the ideal job. I did it last year too.'

'Here? On Breagda?'

It seemed merely a gesture to remain standing and so he sat down, making, however unintentionally, a gesture.

'God, no! I was sent to an uninhabited rock sixty miles south of here.'

'Breagda's uninhabited,' Campbell said drily. It was unreal to him that his father, his grandfather, all that unbroken line, had been born on Breagda. What right had he, made over into so much a Londoner, to resent for them this self-assured young man?

'My rock didn't have someone like you on it. Certainly, no one like your daughter.'

Her swift walk had lost its purpose; by the water's verge, she was drifting now towards the slabbed rocks that closed the beach. While Ramsay spoke, Campbell had been watching her. Now his attention, as if guiltily, seized on the younger man.

'Last year, when you were on your rock counting up birds for your notebook— '

'In the cause of science or something.'

'In the cause of ecology or student employment . . . I was at a conference in Exeter. We stayed in residences at the bottom of a hill like the side of a house. At the top of the hill was the lecture hall. Up and down we went – breakfast to lecture, lecture to lunch, lunch to seminar, seminar to dinner, after dinner usually back up for an evening lecture. The conference lasted a week. Exeter students must have legs like mountain goats.'

'I've never been in Exeter,' Ramsay said comfortably, as an

indication of his willingness to listen. Island time being as it was, he rested with his hands behind his head.

'It has a cathedral – full of statues and plaques commemorating local magnates – like a spiritual jumble-sale. And I remember a windy main street with two youngsters roaring up it on motor bikes that weren't muffled.'

'I expect there's more to it than that.'

'I suppose so.' A place visited once was always like that: a snapshot with the foreground blurred and unexpected things crystal clear in the distance. Exeter . . . 'There was a wine and cheese affair on the last night. We had been to the Gulbenkian Theatre the evening before. The star was a TV actress who took all her clothes off for one scene. The locals were quite eager to get tickets. Ours had come as part of the conference fee. I met a novelist at the wine and cheese who told me he'd sold his ticket to the manager of a butcher shop for double the price.'

'I hope the butcher got his money's worth.'

'I doubt it. The lights were dimmed and the pair of them crossed to one another and kissed – then the lights went out.'

'Very tasteful.'

'I was sitting near the back, of course – perhaps at the front . . .' He picked up a twist of dried seaweed. The brittle stuff shredded as he rubbed it between his fingers. 'I've always admired writers. I once overheard a colleague . . . a friend describing me: there's one of them in every audience, he said – George is the little man who rushes up after the talk and buttonholes the speaker. People who are witty don't always realise they're being hurtful. It's the temptation, I suppose. I'm trying to explain that I was ridiculously upset because this writer boasted he'd sold his ticket at a profit – and because he'd sold it to a butcher. Isn't that stupid? I didn't see at all that it was funny.

'So there I was – eating a cheese biscuit, and his wife, a hard-faced blonde who'd given up modelling to be an intellectual, kept asking me questions. Are you married? Yes. Any children? Yes. How many? I felt hounded, so for some reason I invented more on the spot. Four, I said. Any boys? she asked. Eh, one. Did he come last? she asked, like a cat pouncing on me.'

Ramsay opened an eye and laughed.

'No, but do you see? I've been too fair to her. You really have to understand the idiot cunning.' He sank into a malevolent whine. 'I'm a writer's wife. Plumbed the depths of life with Wally. Did *he* come *last?*"' In the heat of earnest excitement, he let slip the tag-line he had attached to the story in the privacy of his own head. 'Can you imagine the mind of a cunt like that?'

'Eh?' Ramsay's first surprise slipped into a sly exaggeration. 'A what?'

'It's a quote from Henry Miller,' Campbell said shamefacedly. 'I'm afraid I quote a good deal.'

Ramsay hitched up on one elbow to look at the beach and Chris meandering by the water's edge.

'What are you quoting from here?' he asked.

'Here?' Campbell repeated slowly, trying to get time to think. 'From a book I'll read too late – or one I've read and forgotten. Isn't that what we all—'

'Sweet God!' Ramsay said in pious disbelief and sat straight up.

A naked man had appeared from the sea, wading round the outcrop of rock. He was a red-headed man, barrel-chested and looking as broad as he was tall. Even at that distance, without being long-sighted, Campbell was in no doubt about his red-haired nakedness. At the same moment, Chris and the man apeared to sight one another, and the man came to a stop with the waves creaming round his knees. He had a bottle in each hand. Brought smartly to the position of modesty, the bottles glinted in the sunlight as he retreated step by backward step until trunk, shoulders and head were drawn behind the decent rocks.

'It's Neil,' Ramsay said and fell back laughing on the sand.

THIRTEEN

If he were to get angry or drunk, he looked big enough to pull the roof down on their heads. In jeans and a yellow sweatshirt, the red-headed Neil rested forearms like burned thighs on the table as harbour for a bottle of whisky and the set of plastic beakers. Yet since he had reappeared dressed from behind the rocks, apology had been his preoccupation.

'I'm as embarrassed as a terrier in a hen house. I swear to God I'd no idea there would be a mortal soul on Breagda, leaving aside your man here.'

Ramsay yawned by way of acknowledging the reference.

It was another difficulty for Campbell that only slowly had his ear settled to the tune of Neil's speech.

'I wonder,' he asked, 'are you from the islands? From Breagda perhaps?' But that was stupid – how could a young man be from this deserted place? He heard himself snuffle the deprecatory laugh he despised. 'You're a Highlander, I can hear that from your accent.'

'That's astonishing – and I was deluding myself I spoke the language like a native.'

'Well, that's about right,' Ramsay said.

Neil turned his head and looked at him, but then carried his attention back to Campbell.

'Ten years in Glasgow – some time at school in Inverness before that – but for what it's worth a man of the islands, you could say an islander.' He poured from the bottle, setting the beakers in a neat row. 'We're very fond of whisky. Did you know we poured it into our porridge?'

Campbell thought for a moment of claiming against this clumsy irony his own descent, but stopped since it seemed undignified – and anyway he was not clear in his mind where he belonged.

Chris spoke, startling him. She had sat so entirely effaced, curled down on the ledge by the empty hearth.

'Not for me,' she said as the bottle tipped over the fourth beaker. 'I couldn't take any.'

'A little one?' Neil coaxed, the bottle poised. 'I'd feel better about the bourach I made on the beach. Going about mother naked like a born idiot. I'd my clothes in a bundle to swim ashore, you see, and—'

'We've heard all that,' Ramsay said. He pushed one of the beakers over to Campbell who took it up after an imperceptible hesitation. He cupped it in his hands and the whisky tang tickled his nostrils with the faint sickliness of the plastic underneath.

'And it was such a fine night I chucked them on the sand and went walkabout in my pelt,' Neil finished. There was a chuckle beneath the surface good nature that bothered Campbell until, thinking about it, he decided it was only the storyteller under the politeness. No doubt the man would make a fine story of it, later, in other company; and then he saw the reiterated apologies as a kind of preliminary exercise in the polishing and elaboration that would go to make the completed anecdote. He had met men like that who spun companionable words out of the home movie they starred in every waking minute of their lives.

'Cheers!' Campbell said and sipped. The mild warmth ran across his palate.

'Slainthe!' Neil said and Ramsay grinned and repeated the word in what seemed like a close imitation. Both men emptied their drink in a single movement.

Campbell sipped again. 'I think I'll have water with it.' He started to get up but Ramsay gestured him back.

'I'll get some. Sit where you are.'

Campbell told himself it was a young man's courtesy, but then he was not old. It made him uncomfortable.

'More?' Neil said, and poured it in before he could answer. 'Don't be too slow over it – that's death. You can get drunk doing that. Slainthe!'

'Slainthe!' Campbell said carefully and took a full mouthful. Sour banjo notes plucked in each temple. However good the whisky, he was unused to drinking so fast. Neil nodded approval and he finished what was left.

Ramsay came back from outside carrying the little camping pan. He wiped the bottom of it across his sleeve and laid it on the table. It rocked gently, settling.

'Bourbon and burn water,' he said.

'The Americans sell the water too,' Neil nodded and poured a measure into the three beakers. He hesitated again over the fourth.

'You wouldn't mind her having just a small one?'

'A small one,' Campbell agreed.

'There now!' He seemed delighted. 'Your father doesn't mind – not a small one. If you were worrying about that . . .'

With a still look that resembled contempt, Chris got up without answering and went out. Campbell went to the window.

'Don't worry,' Neil said behind him. 'She can't get into much bother out there. Nothing but grass out there.'

By bending his head and twisting he could see her sitting on the broken lip of the dry wall. Before he could pull back, she had looked up and seen him watching. She stood up and moved out of sight but, as he returned to his seat at the table, the door opened and she went back in silence to her place by the hearth.

'Did I ever tell you,' Neil asked, 'about the time I was in Dublin? I'd been collecting – not birds though. I'd been on the west coast collecting songs. It was a summer job collecting for the Irish Folklore Commission – that was the first time I heard songs by Padhraic O Finneadha.'

Ramsay tapped the bottle and said, 'You must have got a start on us.'

'A drop. But a swim in the cold sea after it. Anyway, this fellow McArtney and I went up to visit friends of his. Introductions all round – Danny and Sean and another fellow and the girl. Oh, the girl – green eyes, long dark hair. I don't think the woman Naoise died for could have been more beautiful. And not a day over seventeen. After a while, Sean gets up and says, Bridget and I'll go next door for a grind. The girl gets up and away they go. Jesus! I think, but you don't want to appear unsophisticated, so I keep talking and watching the door which was lying just a tiny wee bit *open*. Then – this is true – the other fellow, the one whose name I've forgotten, gets up, stretches, Time for a grind – and he's away through. A bloody orgy! So I'm imagining what might happen next and hoping – I mean I was getting excited – but still keeping casual, you know. I mean you don't want to look unsophisticated.

'Next thing though McArtney's up on his feet and the fellow Danny's seeing us out and as we pass the open door do the three of them from inside not shout, Goodbye! Outside in the street, That's a hell of a carry on! I say. Eh? Back there – the girl – the grind. What? he says, blinks, thinks, roars with laughter. A big priest with a walking stick like a club stopped and gave us a hard look – till he was sure it was nothing personal. You daft bugger, McArtney says, they've an exam next week. Apparently, in their unsophisticated way, a grind's the name for a spell of studying. We always used grind for—'

'Don't spoil a story by explaining it,' Ramsay said.

Neil had been pouring helpings from the bottle and now Ramsay splashed out more for each of them. Campbell realised with surprise that he had emptied his beaker. He had been drinking too fast because he was angry, fearful, ashamed. People talking explicitly about sex in front of his wife or daughter, he disliked that; once or twice at parties – and Charlie, once he had spoken sharply to Charlie, that was a long time ago, Jan had laughed, Sylvia had been amused but pleased . . . it had been a long time ago.

It would sound silly to object. Would they think of Chris as innocent? He turned to look at her; his head dropped sharply almost to his chest and jerked up to find her. She seemed, sitting by the blackened hearth, like the child who was his daughter most truly.

'. . . about the poof.' Ramsay was speaking. He looked back and saw Ramsay pout his lips; they minced like tiny obscene buttocks. '. . . a second before time, I'll take the penalty, Wembley all silent, the score nothing each, I kick for the Cup, darling – and miss! What kind of ambition's that? his friend asks him. But imagine, sweetie, he says. – Standing there in those attractive little shorts while twenty thousand rough men scream, Fuck you!'

Chris should not have to listen to such sadness. He felt a terrible pity for all the sad people.

The little pan of water was empty but then someone must have gone out for later it was on the table again and he poured water into his whisky and hardly spilled a drop.

'I was a student,' he said but then he couldn't get the story he wanted to tell them arranged in his mind. Suddenly, he decided that what Ramsay had said was intolerable. He wanted to tell him so – but Ramsay had gone out.

'. . . with two girls,' Neil said, 'and there they are up against the wall. Two big policemen come into the lane and the sergeant shouts, "Out of there, you daft buggers! Don't you know this is a bakery? If the morning van backs in here in a minute, you'll be squashed flat." One morning roll and two sandwiches.'

'I was a student,' Campbell said, 'I mean *when* I was a student.' He had a picture of Chris seeing him like this; he saw himself as if in a mirror, slack, drunk, with stupid saliva oozing from the liver dark roots of his tongue. But when he looked, she wasn't sitting by the fire any more. '*After* that – I was a teacher. You never forget the boys in your first class. Fat Malcolm, one of the children from the fairground. He wasn't really fat – it was all muscle that looked like fat. And he wrote in an essay, "so I told her in the tent baby and me and Francie fucked her". Difficult problem of correction – I followed best traditions of the profession. Wrote "punctuation!" in red pencil in the margin.'

At the end of that term a malevolent one-armed boy had said, 'You did okay, sir. But you'd have been in bother wif the team we 'ad last year.'

'Little bastard,' he said aloud. 'Incredible! "The team we 'ad last year."'

'Come again?' Neil said, big, red and likeable, oh, enormously likeable. Likeable *and* enormous. He grinned at the neatness of his own joke. It was easy to like Neil as long as Ramsay wasn't there. Perhaps that was only because both of them together filled the room. They were too big. Where was Ramsay? Where was Chris?

His heart lurched with apprehension; but then Ramsay was there.

'Reinforcements,' he said and put a bottle of whisky that hadn't been opened and another one part full on to the table. 'Chris and I rowed out to the boat for them.' Behind him, Chris lurked a lean cat in the shadows.

'You went for a walk?' Campbell asked, but, instead of getting an answer from her, it was Neil who said, 'Nothing but sheep and gulls out there.'

Sheep, gulls, grass, scoured hills and salt winds: Breagda.

'. . . wipe their bums with sponges,' Neil said. 'That's why Indians never have piles.'

'Ladies present!' Ramsay said to Campbell's surprise. Then he wondered if it was mockery, but before he could think about who might be being mocked, Ramsay went on, 'Let me tactfully change the subject. Shall I, Neil? Would you like me to do that? Neil?'

'Could I stop you?' Neil said laughing.

'Could you?' Ramsay asked. He held out his hand and Neil took it and they wrestled with their elbows resting on the table. Campbell thought to himself that he recognised what they were doing – Indian wrestling it was called. He had not seen it since he was a child at school; he had never seen adults playing it. The object of the game was to force back your opponent's hand until it touched the table.

At first the two men seemed to be sitting quite still but then Campbell saw that they were locked in a single stress. Gradually the two hands began to tremble perceptibly and very slowly and at last with a rush Neil pressed down Ramsay's hand.

'Again,' Ramsay said.

'Let's leave it at that.'

'Again.'

This time, however, it was over almost at once. Ramsay was defeated for the second time.

'Again.'

'Oh, for Christ's sake!' Neil said, no longer smiling.

Ramsay leaned forward, elbow on the table, hand raised in readiness.

'It won't be any different,' Neil said.

'Let's see.'

'Do it a hundred times – it won't be any different.'

For a lengthening moment they held in the same violent stillness as the first time. Again, however, Ramsay's hand began to tremble and, very slowly, started to give way. He had taken a mouthful to drink just as they began and without warning sprayed it from his lips. A mixture of whisky and saliva ran down Neil's face. Ramsay took advantage of the moment of shock to swing his arm over and smash the back of his opponent's hand on the table.

'I think that was different,' he said.

Everything held perfectly still. Campbell waited attendance on the physical potential of great violence in the room, but at last Neil wiped his hand down his face and looked at what was smeared on it.

'Different?' he said in uncomplicated astonishment. 'I think you're a bloody lunatic, Lolly.'

'What?' Campbell said starting up from his seat. The sudden movement set the whisky singing in his head. 'What did you call him?'

'Eh?' Neil gathered his brows.

'Lachie,' Ramsay said. 'He called me Lachie. It's a name my friends use – from Lachlan – that's my middle name. Neil and I are old friends.'

Unintentionally, Campbell had provided the saving diversion.

'You're a weird bloody man,' Neil grumbled, but the realising focus that led to anger was overlaid by confusion. He scrubbed his sleeve over his face and yawned. The spontaneous moment was gone. He tipped back his chair and stretched one massive arm to pick a text from the wall. He laid it carefully on the table. At an angle, it showed Campbell a jumble of letters interlaced with flowers.

'"He that being often reproved hardeneth his neck shall suddenly be destroyed and that without warning",' Neil chanted.

'Proverbs Twenty-Nine and One,' Ramsay said turning the frame to read, and Neil gave a lash of laughter, and the flowers were tongues of fire.

'Did I ever tell you,' Neil said to Campbell, 'of the time your man here was in the asylum?'

'How could you have?' Campbell asked solemnly. They had only met that day. He tried to find words to explain this but Neil would not stop talking.

'. . . there was this older man who'd been a lecturer at the university. Was it classics? That's right. So your man here gets it into his head that he's as sane as . . . That he's sane, eh? Gives him little tests. Though how he could judge – well, I mean it was only a summer job, right? He hadn't taken a course or read a book on it. That's not fair, eh? He'd read a book on it – gave the little tests – decided the guy was sane. They'd sit and talk about philosophy and Roman history and the Church fathers. Very peaceful, was that how you described it?'

'Sitting in a patch of sunlight,' Ramsay said, 'it was peaceful.'

'So he's just getting ready to make an appeal to higher authority when he comes in one morning, a Monday after the weekend, and this guy's bed's empty. At first he thought, They've let him out. Seeing him talking with me, they've realised it was all a mistake.

'It wasn't though. Off to hospital that's where he'd gone. Operated on – blood transfusions, the lot. The cat had got him.'

'Cat?' Campbell had been trying hard to concentrate.

'He'd been feeding it scraps. Apparently it used to sit outside the window. When he'd got it tame enough, he grabbed it and took it to bed. It almost ripped his crotch off. Had to have transfusions and everything.'

'You really mustn't,' Campbell said. 'Not in front of Chris.'

'Chris,' Ramsay said.

For some reason, they all looked at her. She sat so still, white against the absurd wall splashed with paint and the carefully hung texts. It was as if she was obliterated.

'Ah, yes,' Ramsay said, 'ladies present.'

'Would you like something to drink?' Neil asked her.

She shook her head.

'Are you all right, Chris?' Campbell asked, but his tongue filled his mouth and the words came out badly. He fought himself because it was important and repeated very slowly and clearly, 'Are you all right, Chris?'

'That friend of mine,' Ramsay said. 'In the hospital. It wasn't funny. He knew what I was trying to do. I was there to sweep up and help with the strong-arm stuff. He was clever – he knew what my tests were about – but I was only there to sweep up. He taught me things I had never heard of. His bed was by the window, you know. You could hear them cutting the grass, while he talked. He was fascinated by suicide. Two for the price of one he called it – crime and punishment. There's a knack in cutting your throat.' He plucked up a fold of tight young skin under his ear as if to show them. 'It's quite tough. If you're only trying it on, you underestimate and that's it. With the others you get two or three little trial cuts and then they go into a frenzy. Quite often it's not a matter of "he cut his throat", all neat and tidy. They saw their heads half off.'

'Ladies present,' Neil mimicked and made a movement of disgust.

131

Campbell knew that something was terribly wrong; if only he could sit quietly for a moment and think.

'I had a friend—' he began, but Neil started up pushing back the table.

'I'm going to sleep on the boat,' he said and picked up one of the bottles. Campbell with a drunken shrewdness saw that though it was only half full, the others were empty.

Outside he was surprised by the dim light. The day had passed while they sat and drank. Ramsay by his side, they followed Neil who wandered thigh deep in the pale grass down the long field. In the croft street, Ramsay said, 'I have to go back – I'll only be five minutes.' Campbell found he was lying on the ground so perhaps Ramsay had been helping him to walk. He sat up. Cut-out houses against a draining sky; out of the twilight Ramsay's voice calling back, 'Two for the price of one. Maybe the character who kicked the ambulance man downstairs was fined for assault. After they'd sewn his head on again, of course.'

It was a St John's ambulance man . . . The man came out of his room with a great gash across his throat and kicked the St John's ambulance man down a flight of stairs. Who had told him that? Not Ramsay. Something was terribly wrong. Superstitious fears shook him like a fever. The night air chilled on his skin. If he could think for a moment, he would understand.

As he quietened into himself, a voice sang out of the stillness. The words of the song were not English. It drew him up to his feet. He recognised it as the tongue of the people of Breagda. The speech whispered from the peat workings, the fished seas, the nested cliffs, the fields. The dark brown houses singing had found a voice and the words made no sense to him and he believed if he could understand them Chris would be cured and he would find his way.

Yet, at the same time, he knew it was only Neil; and at the crest of the ridge, heard him below on the beach, the song changed to a refrain from a students' beer bar that broke off in curses. Following down, he lost his footing and rolled to the bottom until he came to rest with the world still spinning. Staggering along the furrows, he found Neil sitting, who handed up the bottle. He drank, gave it back with enormous carefulness and fell down on the sand.

'Where's himself? He didn't come?' Neil asked after a moment.

'He went back to fetch something.'

'Loot,' Neil said. 'I brought this beautiful thing with me.'

It was the clock Chris had found in a cupboard and sat upon a shelf. Seeing it, he felt the shadow of a householder's indignation, although, of course, it was no more his than Neil's. It was made of marble and was heavy, but Neil held it out towards him with one hand at arm's length. Above the square base in which the face was set, there rose in miniature the statue of a woman. The marble was folded in a garment from her waist and her tiny white breasts were bare.

'I wouldn't have thought they'd have approved of those.' He touched them with a fingertip in turn; they were perfectly shaped but cold.

'Who?'

'The islanders.'

'Maybe that's why they left the clock,' Neil said, 'when they went away.'

They drank in silence. A little of the whisky ran from the corner of Campbell's lips.

'That's an awful bloody man for loot. He has a dishonest bit in him,' Neil said yawning. 'We used to steal milk bottles off the doorsteps on our way home in the morning. They set a trap for us and this big policeman from Skye told his sergeant, "I heard one say to the other, 'Oh, see, they're early with the deliveries tonight.'" He had to translate it for the sergeant when they took us back to the station.'

'Translate?'

'Well, it was in Gaelic. The last words I heard before those two sets of big feet jumped out on us.'

'Ramsay spoke to you in Gaelic? Did he learn it?'

'Learn?'

Neil was lying back. The word came softly, a question on the edge of sleep. Campbell shook him. It seemed enormously important that he should find out. 'To speak Gaelic. Why, in God's name, should *he* learn to do that?'

Neil's head rolled and then spaced slowly the words came: 'He's my cousin. From the same village – only his father was a clever one.'

'But the way he speaks – not like you, not like you.'

133

'There's more than one Lachie and he has a voice for all of them.' Breath snored in his throat and he seemed to have drifted off, but opened his eyes again and said, 'It was as well his father sent him away to that good school. It would frighten you how much they hate one another.'

Suddenly, shocking Campbell, he sat up and gripped his shoulder in one enormous hand.

'You're hurting me!'

'I'll tell you a secret.' He put his face close until Campbell could see nothing else. 'Lachie will do well. He could be a great man.' He stopped and Campbell could hear the dry rasp of him swallowing. 'But I'll tell you a secret – no one who's ever known him has been any better for it.'

'Neil?'

But this time he was asleep beyond wakening. Only after a moment he said very clearly out of some dream, 'Oh, see, they're early tonight.'

Crouched, Campbell triumphed over the heavy drinkers. He had outlasted them. He reached to ease the bottle from Neil's outflung hand and lost his balance. With the grit of sand upon his lips, he saw close to his face the ugly white pucker of a scar. On hands and knees, he crawled in a crazy intent circle around the big man's body. Gently, he tugged the left arm out of shadow and found a second matching scar. At some time, not long ago, Neil had slashed open his wrists. Staring at the livid stripe, Campbell understood that with his talk of suicide Ramsay had spat for a second time into his cousin's face.

It came to him then that there had been something terribly wrong about Ramsay's telling of the story of the suicide but he was lying on his back beside Neil and the last of the whisky ran into his mouth and the world stopped.

134

FOURTEEN

Beat / through dazzling water / up scattering light / arms beat / too deeply dived / slowly beat / drowning / was drowning—

He threshed awake in a hollow of sand, blue sky overhead and a circle of wind-shaken grass for horizon. A soft hubbub under the wind's shushing said he had slept near the sea. When he turned his head, a beaked gull took fright on giant wings.

'Bloody vulture!'

He widened gummed eyes and tried to remember. When he thought of the previous day, something important was almost tangible and then escaped him in a slither of images – a bottle full of sunlight on a window ledge, two hands trembling palm against palm. From a place outside his body, he saw Chris and himself – her eyes watching a slack-lipped drunk. She was sitting by the fire, but the fire had gone out.

Where was Chris?

With a groan, he sat up. The hollow was hip high like a tin bath. The wind blew in his face.

On his way to the house, he fell heavily, knuckles of knotted grass and stony dust punching at his heart. He had no idea where Chris was. It would have been easy to lie motionless. He had no idea where Chris was.

As he climbed, he called her name. A stone turned under his heel and a spasm of pain seized his back. Limping, he hobbled towards the door.

'Chris!'

As if the walls were glass, he saw Chris sleeping quietly upstairs; on the kitchen floor, Neil and Ramsay stretching to wake. If they hear me, they'll think I've gone mad – and then instantly remembered: Neil was going back to the boat and then he fell asleep on the sand.

'Chris!'

The kitchen was empty.

With the painful steadiness of an old man, he crept up the narrow stairs. 'Are you there, Chris?' he asked more softly than in conversation.

He sat on the edge of the bed. She had hung texts here too and that disturbed him. The sun edged down the wall. There under the roof it became unbearably hot. He took off his jersey and dropped it on the floor. For a while after that he told himself he should pick it up. From childhood, he had never got over the habit of tidying things away, putting jackets on hangers, squeezing wads of paper into the toes of his shoes when he took them off – till Sylvia objected and bought little plastic shapes to use instead. On the few occasions in his life when he had gone to bed drunk, he had wakened in the morning to discover his trousers neatly folded on a chair. There were nails here to hang things on, but Chris had used them for the texts: hardeneth his neck . . . destroyed . . . utterly destroyed. His hands hung between his spread knees; as the heat solidified, he panted and sweat spread dark on his sides. Getting up, he tramped unnoticing over the jersey. Outside, as if he had carried it from the attic room, he moved in an envelope of that burning air. Without knowing how he had come there, he was on the street of crofts. The broken thunder of his heart made him afraid. No doctor, nurse, ambulance, no phone, no Samaritan crossing the crowd. Salt blind with his own sweat, he knuckled his eyes as he started up the opposite slope. The broken roof opened as he circled the house by the shore and a white distant cloud was framed in the gap. Like a film in his head, the dinghy crossed the blue water to Neil's boat and each time in silence, never a sound of birds or sea.

The *Lazy Charlotte* swung at anchor, the only boat in the bay. He had been deceived before. Crabwise he ran watching for Neil's boat to be unmasked from behind the *Charlotte*; ran past sense or hope until he fell and the warm sand cradled him.

What a fool he had been to believe their lies. To go back alone. Aloneliness: he made up the terrible word.

Human breath or speech muddled under the sea noises; sand tremors against his cheek; something fleeting and ungraspable warned him and he rejoiced and was humiliated. What dignity would this treacherous body allow him abandoned buttocks upward on the sand?

'Is he . . .' It was Chris's voice, breathless, a little way off.

A hand touched him and he jerked his shoulder away and then made the unconsidered movement into a stretching turn. Eyes clenched, he yawned away the time it took to shame them open.

'Are you all right?' Ramsay's face hung over him; his voice a male echo of Chris.

'Christ, I feel awful,' he said in self-defence.

'Did you sleep here all night?' She had stopped a few paces away. 'What's wrong with— ' He felt her eyes on his face.

He put up a hand: with fingertips realised grains of sand stuck to his cheek, moved fingers under his eyes –

'Have you been crying?' she asked. Was she triumphant? Reared up then out of the base sand, unfolded to his full height, in that flurry wiped at his cheeks.

'Where the hell have you been?'

He directed his anger at Chris but it was Ramsay who responded in a puzzled drawl, 'Been? Sorry, I don't follow.'

'You weren't at the house. I was looking for you. You weren't there.'

'That's true,' Ramsay agreed, attentive to some point waiting to be made.

'Where were you?' His voice broke annoyingly.

'I'm afraid we've been looking for you.'

'What the hell do you mean? What am I – something you've mislaid? If I'm lost, I've been lost and found again before you were born so don't – I mean don't you ever – come looking for me.'

Somewhere in the middle of that Ramsay gestured to Chris, a gesture delicately judged that did not exclude or even criticise him, a wry acknowledgement, even an apology; and at once moved away but again by some graceful instinct while the tirade ran without entirely presenting a dismissive back.

'Don't walk away when I'm talking to you!'

But the fishwife shriek chilled anger. Ramsay sketched under-standing, almost conspiracy – turned right about and set off briskly down the beach.

'I think you're mad,' Chris said and sounded timorously contemplative.

'Don't be stupid.'

He walked away, taking the opposite direction from Ramsay, but changed his mind after a few steps and came back.

'Stupid to talk like that. You forget why we're here. *I* don't want to be here. You thanked me yesterday.'

'Not yesterday,' she said.

'What?'

She shook her head and took her own occasion to walk away.

He was frightened by the strength of his desire to run after and strike her. Together with the impulse, he recalled Ramsay who was now on the island and might object; and had by some process swifter than thought an image of himself under restraint, confined in a dark place.

'Are you too ashamed to talk to me?' he shouted.

At that she half broke her stride and looking back mouthed something. He did not hear the word, Drunk, but read it in the ugly gape of her lips.

His body was heavy and reluctant. To his horror he found that the previous day was beyond his recovery. He remembered the bottle on the ledge and a glass: the sun made glittering circles of the rim and the narrow base and glistened on the ring inside where it had been left unwashed; a milky shadow spread from it full of slow movement. There was no value in this stamped memory. At some point in the afternoon he must have spent time staring at the ledge and the play of light, desperately concentrating to hold himself together and appear in control. He tried to remember when he had last eaten. Only the fresh wind from the sea held off spasms of nausea.

Just ahead of him, Ramsay was mounting the rocks, going with neat compact leaps across the gaps. His first impulse was to turn back, but then he knew they had to talk. He tried to hurry but gave up after a few yards and settled for perseverance. On the other side of the rocks, he came on Ramsay, his legs folded under him, quietly watching the sea.

'Would you mind,' he said without looking round, 'keeping still – only for a moment?'

Campbell felt himself sway as he stood.

'I'm sure it's there – at the triangle of rock.'

138

Ramsay moved up away from the water. As he followed, Campbell said, 'I want to talk to you about Chris.'

'Yes?' Ramsay bent and reached into a crevice. 'I heard it sing – churring, churring.'

Staring at his back, Campbell had the sudden fierce suspicion that this was idiot play-acting. Being asked for types of sea birds; to look through binoculars – the beach blank and empty, suddenly he was sure of that; what was it but mockery? If the rules lapsed, safety anywhere was an illusion.

But Ramsay came gently from the rock and a little bird lay in the palm of his hand. It was black with a white bar across the tail. Dazed by the light, it lay quiet, the head with its sliver of beak cocked as if listening. 'It's a storm petrel,' Ramsay said in a voice different from any he had heard him use. 'Nine months of the year it lives at sea and never comes to land. Look how small it is.' He laid his hand on the rock and the bird with an odd shuffling haste vanished into the dark cleft.

A storm petrel: for Campbell, names were realities. It wiped out all his doubts. Exhausted he let himself sit beside Ramsay.

'Chris,' he blurted out, 'is a very pretty girl.'

'Oh, more than that,' Ramsay said mildly, 'she's quite beautiful, you know.'

He rejected that, yet it was not because he failed to be conscious of her. The plaited generations in her face made words like beauty meaningless.

'She's a drug addict.'

Despite his resolution, tears filled his eyes. He despised them and looked away to hide them. In his teacherly time, he had preached the doctrine of the will. Now, distracted, it occurred to him – what he had always known – that the opportunist whirring upwards like a machine used no more of the will power upon which he congratulated himself than another man drew on to get up each morning and shave.

Ramsay watched him in silence.

'She was killing herself. I forced her to come here.'

'Forced?'

'Made her come. Yes, forced. I kidnapped her.'

The melodramatic word, that might once have shamed him, gave him a thrill of pride. He wet his fingers and touched salt water to his temples, reminding himself that he was the man who had taken that great decision.

'She looks healthy enough to me.'

'It's not a new thing with her. She's been ill and better and ill again, desperately ill. This last time a doctor told me there was no hope.'

'Oh, "hope".'

'She was – she wasn't alone. There was a man involved. But when I went to the flat he had left her all by herself. She didn't know me – in one of those worlds they make up where the colours are wrong and the people have both eyes on one side of their face—'

'Like a Picasso drawing.'

'I dressed her. She came away without any fuss. I don't know what was happening in her world. When I got to the boat, she was asleep. I put her on the bunk. If she'd resisted, I'd have made her come – I'd have knocked her out. But I didn't need to. I just laid her on the bunk. She tied up her hands – but that was herself. I'd do it again.' He pressed the salt-tipped fingers against his burning eyes. 'The doctor told me there was no hope. She'd relapsed too often. I had to be her hope. Do you see that?'

Ramsay gathered flakes of rock and vacated shells from the sand. When his palm was full, he began to flick them in the direction of the sea. Campbell watched him as if waiting for a verdict.

'I'm not sure I do,' Ramsay said apologetically. 'Doctors aren't a fetish of mine. Is that the right word?'

Campbell nodded his poor head judiciously.

'I mean you must have had great faith in this doctor.'

'I only met him that one time . . . My wife had been unwell. We were – away from home. He was an old man – he'd seen a great deal. He'd seen it all before. I'd known it but wouldn't admit it. Chris wouldn't get better. She would die, and I said no. No, I wouldn't let her die. Leukemia or tuberculosis, even peritonitis; but not die for nothing, for no reason except her own weakness. I wasn't going to allow that, and I brought her here where there are no drugs and she'll be cured.'

'How long do you intend to stay here?'

With casual accuracy, Ramsay flicked one of the shells into a pool.

'I'll stay for ever if we have to.'

He spoke without taking time to think, and, the words said, felt an enormous release.

'I had an acquaintance,' Ramsay said thoughtfully, 'one of the tribe of Neil, who refereed schoolboy football matches. One Saturday morning he collapsed and a white track suit bounded over to give him the kiss of life thinking he'd taken a coronary. Being a schoolboy game, there was bound to be a chap about who could be relied on to keep his head in an emergency. Which was, as it turned out, rather a pity. My acquaintance had a bad habit of chewing gum during the game and he'd swallowed the stuff at a moment of high drama in a tackle. The kiss of life blew it deeper into his windpipe.'

'What's that got to do with— '

'It's this doctor of yours that bothers me. If the track suit had left my second cousin twice removed severely alone, he would probably have coughed the gum up and still be with us. I'm not clear how much use father figures are – doctors, I mean. However much they claim to have seen.'

It had been important to explain things to this young man but it had all gone wrong. With an effort that was moral as much as physical, he lifted himself to his feet. The white beach and blue sky rocked like a deck. Captain, he struck away the black spot tipped him by this mutinous crew.

'Talk about something you understand. Jesus Christ, chewing gum! Why do you insult me with a story like that? Why won't you listen? I'm talking about my daughter who was dying.' He searched for the words that would make clear what was so obvious – but all he could think of was matted hair and the running lice filth Sylvia had uncovered. That would make the man understand but, for Chris's sake, he could not bear that Ramsay, a stranger, should think so badly of his daughter. 'I don't think you should stay with us. Not back at the house. The island's quite large.'

After a silence, Ramsay said, 'But that's all taken care of. I had to move anyway to be nearer the cliffs – for the birds. That's what I'm here for. Chris helped me shift my gear. We were on our way back when we met you – so it really is no problem.'

The wind ruffled his hair and he smiled his very white smile. After a long expectant moment as if foreseeing the necessary course of the older man's answer, he allowed his eager smile to fade, seemed puzzled, resigned, but only with a friendly anxiety and, turning, set off briskly, leaving Campbell to congratulate himself on an acquired immunity to student charm.

As he scrambled back over the barrier of rocks, it seemed strange to him that among the mix of his feelings he could not identify guilt. It was true that he had no reason to feel guilty; he believed that; but how often in how many situations of his life, the irrational taste of it had filled his mouth. He spat experimentally, then stopped to stare at the brown rust left him by the previous day's excitements thinning in strings on the surface of a rock pool.

On the shore of the bay, he paced along the line between water and land. It felt as if his strength had come back. The slight wind shading the curling tops of the near waves, the darkening of the sea as the sun went behind the one cloud in the sky: the salt air scoured his eyes clean. As he drew a deep breath, contentment took him by surprise. To himself it seemed that he had changed and become someone simpler.

This changed man had no reason to feel guilty, but in the old life knowing he was no weaker than others, nor worse, nor more unjust, had made no difference to the guilt – the contradiction senselessly reiterated had wearied him of his flesh. Now, the morning's fears were vanquished by facing them; Ramsay would pass his time on the island decently out of sight; Chris must be, Chris would be, cured.

The treadmill churned in his head but it was as if he stood aside watching it spin, his attention constantly drawn away by the sea lightening as the cloud drifted free of the sun, gull swoop and clamour, the bustling at the five gates of his senses, until on a final return he stared astonished at the treadmill come to a stop, its poor animal released.

FIFTEEN

'I was worried about you,' he said apologetically.

She was making herself something to eat. They had brought tins up from the first house in a cardboard box. He reached in to find something for himself and stopped in surprise.

'What's happened to the stuff?'

More than half of what should have been there had disappeared.

'Have you put it away somewhere?'

She bent her head over the tin; winding the lid open, the key was hard for her to turn. Her wrists looked thin and fragile. Angered, he put his hand over hers, holding them still. Instantly every part of her was held in the same stillness. He felt her blood tremble under his fingers.

'Did you give our food to him?'

How then would Ramsay have lived if they hadn't been there? The question occurred to him, but he did not put it to her.

'We need that food.'

She gave him a swift upward glance that made him pause. He did feel they needed it – all of it. The food here, the shelf in the other house, all that was stored on the boat.

He took his hand away and at once she began to turn the key again, frowning with the effort of getting it to go round. From the packet, he picked out two crispbreads and put a slice of cheese between them, then took the dry sandwich to the window. He chewed twenty-four hours' emptiness; the dry crumbs stuck to his mouth.

Behind him she said, 'It's not as if we're short of food.'

'No,' he chewed the dry word.

'I don't understand why we needed so much food.'

Her reasonableness bore no relation to his sense of the reality they occupied together. If she had walked across the ceiling, she would not have seemed more strange to him.

'On a cruise like this,' he said, still looking out, 'you bring lots of food. You want to pamper yourself. It's the holiday spirit.'

In the flawless weather everything was freshened as if with a rubber; the little sheep desultory in the heat cropped along the verge of the dyke. Crumbs, sprayed out as he coughed, stuck to the window. The sheep wound through the pattern they made.

'I told him the truth about you, Chris. I told him why we're here. All right, yesterday I was stupid, but that was yesterday. I told him. He might even be able to help. Chris, it's going to be all right. I'm not going to let it not be all right.'

But when he turned the door lay open and she was gone. He turned back to the window taking it for granted that he would see her outside; the landscape lay empty of life, not counting the little sheep, tumult of birds, worlds in the dry grass. He stirred crumbs with his finger and systematically began to brush them from the pane. Falling, some spotted the text Chris had laid on the window ledge. He dropped the unpalatable sandwich on top of it. As he closed the outer door behind him, it occurred to him that he had not taken in the words of the text.

She was nowhere to be seen. He set off in the direction of the shore and then changed his mind and turned inland. When he crossed the stream, he caught sight of her higher on the hill, walking steadily like someone with a direction to take. He had followed for some time before a movement of her head made him worry in case she glanced back and saw him; afterwards he let the patterns of sheep tracks angle him just below the ridge. Abruptly he climbed high enough to glimpse her on the farther side. The country ahead was open and, reassured there was no chance of losing her, he drifted back putting the hill between them and settled himself for a long walk. Soon he was suffering badly from thirst. The lie of the land must have drained the water to the opposite side for there were no streams. He began to ache from the effort of walking on the slope. The scanty turf was scattered with knuckles of grey rock. A tumbled cairn of them was like an upset midden of bones. He counted his steps as a way of keeping going; at first he started over at each hundredth step and then he made it fifty since that seemed easier, and that went on until he became confused. He thought of his wife's sister and was upset because for a moment he could not remember her name. Someone he knew so well; that he had known so long. Charlie drunk at a party,

144

singing, 'Why was she born so beautiful?' Sprawled out on the floor, his back against a chair: 'Why was she born at all?' She had jumped up in a fury: 'Is that me you're referring to, is it?' Looked up at her, pop-eyed with cunning: 'She's a fine bloody pair of knockers,' and, grinning, 'She's no bloody tits at all.' That had been silly; standing with the backs of her hands on her hips, that was obviously silly. 'You're obscene,' she had said. 'Sit up straight – you're obscene.' His shoe was sucked half off by black mud. White flags of bog weed fluttered all round. As he sank deeper, he panicked and rushed forward.

At once, he was on firm ground and looking up realised he had cleared the flank of the hill. He could see all the way back down the valley in which Chris had been walking. Ahead the land lay open without cover but there was no sign of her.

He began to run. Within minutes, he was exhausted and sank on his knees, crouching under the fierce pain in his side. Slowly it ebbed, he straightened painfully and, opening his eyes, saw a low grey building just ahead and to the left as if it had sprung from the ground.

As he sat there, Chris came through a door at the side and slowly towards him. He waited for her to speak. She came close and passed. Her look was private, solitary, contemplative, like the face of some-one he had never met. He turned crab fashion until he could watch her and she walked for a long time until the hill hid her.

The building was rectangular with a single door and windows on each gable wall. He peered in one and saw through the other a print of hills framed in jagged edges of glass. He walked round it again; a house of one room. The door opened easily and then jammed against the floor. There were seats thrown against the wall, broken. A tall desk stood in the corner, but it was only when he saw an edge of wood behind it and found a blackboard that he realised the place was a schoolroom. He went quickly outside, bruising himself against the door in his haste. The empty landscape confirmed his bewilderment. He put his hands on the building. Under one, stone warmed in the sun; under the other, he felt a long gash where wood of the door had been gouged.

Behind the door, inside, he found a sleeping bag folded beside a rucksack. Near it there was a camping lamp and a book. He flipped the rucksack cover open and was not surprised to see familiar cans

145

and packets. He folded it shut and threaded one of the ties through the buckle, but then he could not remember whether it had been fed in or lain loose. Pushing it in and easing it free again, he tried to decide.

The book was about nine inches by six with grey cardboard covers and a spine with a rough feel like cloth. The words 'Scribbling Diary' were printed on the front. The thought of being caught by Ramsay reading his diary made him sweat. Holding it, he went outside so that he would not be taken by surprise. At first, he sat against the wall of the house – but why should Ramsay approach from the front? The first knowledge of him might be as he rounded the corner only a few feet away. With the book under his arm, he paced out from the house. Always there would be one narrow path along which Ramsay might walk and not be seen, the house shielding him . . . He sat on a flat piece of rock that split made a back to lean against, and puzzled over the problem of watching for Ramsay. He worked at it very seriously, intently, but extraordinarily slowly like a runner far from the tape and beyond his strength. The book fell open and after a little slid from his lap on to the grass.

Though his eyes had shut, he saw the girl and wanted her but she walked away and stood by her own car, leaning her thighs against it. Then he looped ribbon – blue ribbon – over her shoulders and crossing it under her breasts (brushing them with the backs of his hands, he heard her sigh) drew it round the whole length of the car. Tied it in a bow. It was extraordinary how well he did that without leaving the driving seat of his car. She asked why he wanted her to come. It's only a run, he said, you need a change. But she knew what he meant and when she came back – after walking away, hesitating, oh, he saw her decide – so girlishly, he despised her corrupt innocence. Get in, he told her. I need a change, she said, a little trip. He resolved to make it quick and unlovely. The car wrenched into a main street of stone tenements. Out, he told them, out, you're home, and the two young girls on the back seat giggled. He touched one of them on the thigh as she climbed out; did it quite openly; was it already he had been with them? Omnipotent, he drove the car the shortest of distances, enough of a trip for her, images of humiliation. They stopped in a fearful place, a gaunt and empty corner, the stone itself in blocks missing, the wall gapped, black, a dereliction more terrible than anything he could ever have

146

imagined. He stood with the girl at an entry. Vaguely he had planned to find an empty flat in the deserted building – but then didn't he own a flat here? A place he could come in and out with perfect safety. A secret place. The place he used for girls like this. But the reality of the place was awful. The sides of the entry huddled close like a tunnel under the earth. Water ran on one wall. There was no light. A woman came out of the darkness. He said, I was looking for a friend. Standing there with his little daughter in his arms. The fat woman grinned out of an awful stupidity. Desperately he wanted to be safe in his car (lock the doors, lock the doors, drive at them). A little man tiny as a dwarf staggered past. How strange he must seem to these people – what could have brought him here, well-dressed, carrying his daughter in his arms? A shambling black man looked into his face; like pike in a pool decisions moving in the deeps of his eyes. He sobbed to see the open street loitered with men. And then a voice, awful, whining, Have you any money you could give? A staggering man with a livid eye who held out an empty sleeve that *touched* him. There were cars. Did he try his key in one? And beyond a waist-high black iron railing more cars. How could cars survive in a place like this? His car was gone. If he ran with her in his arms the pack would pull her down, turning slowly, the turning centre of a black pool, drawn under there would be no help for his white child daughter, his daughter, daughter he had brought her to this. Terror. Pity. They came from everywhere, running.

He clenched his eyes and opened them on the blue sky; slumped down, he sprawled into the shelter of the rock. Remaking his dream, he remembered two selves, one experiencing, the other sceptical and uncertain. Why were dreams so full of questions? In them the sceptic questioned the reality even of stones. Only the terror was never doubted.

The shadow covered him. For a moment, he felt it as a cloud, then confusedly as the shade of a tree and the tree was Ramsay who frowned down on him. Immediately he remembered the book he had stolen. Was he that kind of person? He did not want to be that kind of person. He bent to pick it up and at a glance read on the open page – 'George Campbell's Journey over the ocean and Exile at home on Breagda with the record of all his reasons.'

147

SIXTEEN

He closed the book tight in his hands and felt the question press down on him. What had he stolen? When he stood up, he was careful to do it slowly. Even so there was hardly space and that seemed to be deliberate. He put the book behind his body to shield it.

'You're my first visitor,' Ramsay said.

'What?' He blinked at the land of peat and rock.

'I didn't mean to startle you. That didn't look a comfortable place to sleep.'

'I wasn't drunk,' Campbell said and then because that sounded stupid added, 'I mean I'm not drunk now.'

It still sounded stupid, but Ramsay behaved as if he hadn't heard, walking them towards the schoolhouse, his hand on Campbell's elbow.

'How did you know where I was?' he asked.

'I'm not your first visitor,' Campbell said as if that was an answer.

'Is Chris inside?' Ramsay wondered.

They were at the door of the house. He was afraid to go back in. Ramsay's hand on his arm drew gently. He stared down at it.

'Sorry,' Ramsay said with his clean white smile, 'I was trying to help.'

Campbell disliked charm. It disconcerted him, but he felt its force – the boyish flop of very black hair, the smile that entirely changed the heavy mouth and jaw. He had been taken in a natural movement to the threshold before he was conscious that Ramsay stil gripped his arm. With a sharp movement, he pulled free. The younger man paid no attention. With a turn of his head as if listening, he called, 'Chris! . . . Hear that? – She's inside.'

She came back while I slept, Campbell thought, and stepped inside. After the bright sun, there was darkness sparkled with

148

golden rods that dulled and spread until the room was filled with an ordinary light.

'She's not here then,' Ramsay said and closed the door behind them. 'We made a mistake.'

'I don't want her here,' Campbell said. He felt trapped. 'I told you why.'

'Why she mustn't come here?'

'She can't be excited. I told you why.'

'Would here excite her so much?' Ramsay smiled. 'I can't imagine it. Or is that some kind of compliment? Anyway she isn't here, is she?'

'She was here. I followed her.'

'She'd been here, but you knew that. I told you she helped me with my stuff.'

He waved a hand and glanced casually towards his gear by the wall. Something seemed to catch his attention. Unhurriedly, he crossed and looked down at the lamp, the folded sleeping bag, the rucksack. He might have been counting them. Without turning, he said, 'If she comes here, I'll stretch her over my knee, smack her bottom and send her on her way. Would that do?' He hunkered down and with one finger pushed up the tie of the rucksack until it came free.

'This book,' Campbell said taking it from behind his back and holding it out, 'where did you get it?'

Ramsay looked up at it and then, with a surprise that was somehow exaggerated, back at the empty space beside the lamp.

'Is that— ? I think that was— ' Unexpectedly, he laughed, balanced solidly, ribbed rock of thigh muscles under the tight cloth. 'Sorry. I was about to be indignant. I'm always surprising myself. It seems I have a nice respectable middle-class sense of property. The fact is, of course, I have no more right to the book than you have.'

'It's my father's.'

With the word, the diary became precious to him and a thing which Ramsay must not insult.

'What's wrong? Are you ill?'

Ramsay's voice faded and roared. A wash of nausea made the sweat burst out on his skin. Was this the man she had been with in the flat – *my mother's home?* With a movement like tearing cobwebs he clutched away the image of Chris and Ramsay sprawled in his mother's bed.

'Do you take drugs?'

'What?'

Ramsay's feigned bewilderment maddened him. How stupid they must think he was.

'Don't be stupid – stupid.'

The word swelled and writhed in his mouth like a twist of cold fat. Half falling in his sickness, he grabbed at Ramsay intending to search in the sinewy hollow of his arm for the marks.

Breath gone, sky black, roof black, jagged lightning spoke, 'Old bastard!' hard bones of the floor grinding his face.

Ashamed, he made no sign. If all he believed was true, after such humiliation it would be right to kill. In his wet and fallen body a judgement was passed but whether on Ramsay or himself it was too early to be sure. He had a judge's temperament but law needed its dirty handed lesser officers to be complete.

'Old— '

An explosion of pain in his shoulder half lifted him. He spun grappling up and was held.

'You kicked me!'

'No,' Ramsay murmured, solicitous and shocked. 'You fainted. Not enough to eat – and after yesterday. Neil's a pig with drink. I stumbled over you.'

As if through Ramsay's eyes, he saw his own grimace, rubber-lipped, the chimpanzee smile of fear.

'Rest your back against the desk.' He was lifted and sat down like a puppet. 'I'll make something to drink.'

Slumped, he saw Ramsay's foot kick the book fallen open upon the floor; saw him bend – gravity-parodied, flesh pulled in heavy pouches over the eyes, made older; saw his hand lift it.

'I'll put this book where it came from – out of our way.'

He lurched upright to see Ramsay lift the desk lid and throw the book casually inside.

'I broke the lock. But the teacher won't ever be back. I wondered what would be inside.'

It was true. The burst wood was clean and white. He touched it with his finger and a splinter lifted away.

'I hate anything locked,' Ramsay said.

He lifted the lid Ramsay had closed. The book was there beside a bundle of blue exercise jotters. When he opened the top one, the pages were blank except where rust from the metal clips had left a double stain. There were flat tobacco tins, one with broken crayons, the other empty except for a sixpenny piece.

When he lifted the book, a leather belt half uncoiled from under it.

'For hitting children with,' Ramsay said, taking it out. 'Hand up!' He struck the edge of the desk heavily. 'God bless! Next, please!' On each exclamation, the thump of the leather made the broken lid bounce crazily. 'They called it education.'

He stood panting very slightly, the leather belt hanging from his fist as if forgotten.

'Put the book back, would you? After all I found it,' Ramsay said seriously. 'There's nothing else here to read.'

'It's my father's diary,' he explained for the second time. 'It's true. It truly is so.' His hands shook so badly he had difficulty in opening the book. He set it on the open lid.

'You can see it there. My father's name – George Campbell.'

'That's your name,' Ramsay said laughing.

'My father was called by my name.'

'There aren't many people can claim that,' Ramsay said, the smile gone from his face.

'My father . . .'

'There's no sense in it! I break open a desk on Breagda and find that. Your father's? A Londoner like you?'

'My – my father wasn't like me at all.'

There was a confused image of a man much simpler than himself – but the memory came to him of the story he had been told by the old man at his mother's funeral in Glasgow. His father had fled to Breagda alone across the lunatic ocean. He knew nothing about the man who had been his father; even that notion of a simpler man was based on nothing more than that his father had been a labourer while he had been to university – as if they ran degree courses in anguish of spirit.

'This would help me to know him.'

Ramsay flicked the book towards him. It hung on the edge ready to fall.

151

'Thank you.' Pain flared in his shoulder as he lifted the book. 'It's important to me. I'm going home now.'

'Home? Where is that?'

He put the diary under his good arm and walked towards the door. As it receded, he struggled to it through a terrible sickness. His left eye was too swollen and heavy to keep open; he had no memory of the blow. Behind him, he could not hear Ramsay, who moved so softly, but felt him close.

The door opened at the lightest of touches and he was outside, small in an empty land.

'This is an unbearable place. Only desolation.'

'In the winter perhaps. Now, it's full of life.'

For a hallucinated second he saw the place reflected in Ramsay's eyes, fish in the streams, birds exploding from nests underfoot, many-coloured moths and butterflies hinged on the altering air, six-legged nightmares in the grass, sheep and the worm that drove into their flesh.

'This is a good place for what I want,' Ramsay said.

'Why?' He was abandoned on the flat monosyllable, until he dredged from his heaviness: 'Birds?' He looked around helplessly. 'What's so good about this place?'

'Sea cliffs that way. Beach back there. Here is half way, with the rest of the island behind us.'

'And the children?'

Ramsay looked blankly.

'The children must have walked,' Campbell said. 'Why have them walk so far?'

'There's another village tucked back by the cliffs.' Ramsay shrugged. 'Islanders are strange. Perhaps they compromised and settled on half way. Wouldn't you have to be strange to live on a rock in the middle of the sea?' He pulled the door closed. 'I'll walk back with you. Keep you company.'

'No. I'm all right.'

'I think I will. To show you the way. It's easy for a townsman to get lost where there are no road signs.'

'My father was born here.'

'So he was,' Ramsay said soothingly. 'You told me.'

It was a hard journey for him. If he had been alone, it would not have been in his power, but Ramsay went unhesitatingly forward so none of his strength was wasted, and gradually he understood the delicacy with which the younger man took a line through the rough country to make it easier for him. Conscious of that, as he became more exhausted he grew obsessively appreciative of the rightness of each decision. There was a gradual peace at last in the entirety of such submission. When he fell, Ramsay waited without offering to help until he could get up unaided. For this, too, he was grateful.

With the book seized in a fierce unconscious grip, at the end of his efforts he followed Ramsay out of a stand of head-high bracken to the edge of a stony field. A summer-starved stream dwindled down it with the croft on the farther side.

SEVENTEEN

'My father,' Chris said and he thought she was angry – screwing up his eyes as she shimmered black and strange against the light – but she went on as if affectionately, 'my father the drunkard. If your students could see you now.'

'Or your mother,' he said, but she had turned away.

'I've made soup. Sit up.'

'We wouldn't have believed this,' he said meaning the change which saw him being cared for instead of her. He was disturbed to hear how clogged and hoarse his voice sounded. He made a play of effort in sitting up thinking to exaggerate his weakness, but his arm gave under him and he fell back. She laid the cup down and lifted and turned him until he was settled with the wall against his back for support. To his surprise, she held the cup to his lips and tilted it so that he could drink.

'This is ridiculous,' he said trying to push it away. 'Drinking soup for my supper.'

'Breakfast. You're having breakfast.'

She held it to his lips again and he drank. She had put less water in it than he would have liked but he decided not to complain.

'It's nearly ten o'clock. You slept the evening and the night and now half the morning away.'

'Half the morning!' It pleased him ridiculously to hear her say that; she had lain in her vomit days together. 'You've been up early.'

'What of it?'

He was afraid she had sensed some echo of his thought.

'I don't understand why I still feel like this. Sleeping for all that time – I should be strong.' He touched his forehead gently just on the heavy bone by his eye where it ached. 'I feel as if I've a hangover. But a very bad one. I don't think I ever had to face my students feeling like this.'

She bent close. 'I think you've given yourself sunstroke. Your eyes look funny – the pupils are too wide.'

'If that's all it is . . .'

'Rest today. Keep out of the sun.'

He said something in reply or dreamed he did. When he opened his eyes, the sun had crept across the floor to his shoulder. He turned his head and saw a flask with a cup beside it. There was no sign of Chris.

He shifted and something hard poked him. He fished down into the sleeping bag, but when he found the book at first he did not recognise it. It was very strange that he should have had his father's diary for more than a day and left it unread. The size of it was awkward for him to hold. It was heavy; its awkward weight turned his wrists until it flapped open on his belly. He edged up until he could read.

'. . . like that. The man with the glasses said war would come. How would it not come? How would that be possible? He did not say plague. I say plagues but not boils or egyptian evils. Of all that, I am necessarily free. There was waste ground opposite the tenement and that was the first time I saw boys playing football for it was not a game we had at home. My aunt told me to make friends, but when they heard how I spoke for I could hardly speak English they stood about me in a circle except for one boy who was kicking the ball into the air and calling on them to begin again. I tried to deceive myself they were friendly but they abused me and one boy I have not forgotten struck me on the face with his open hand. I burst through them and ran, no one ran after me, no one until that time in my life had ever struck me, if I had thought about it I would have been of the opinion that I would have injured anyone who did such a thing. I ran but away from our house all the way over the wasteground and stopped under a window and an old woman leaned out of it looking at me. Where her nose should have been there was a piece of sticking plaster. I made a little noise and she looked at me and lifted one corner of the plaster. There were two red pits. And yet I say there is no hell. I told my aunt of the old woman and showed her the window but she pulled me away by the hand and said God had* *punished that woman for her sin. There is a trick the black trout has of throwing his picture to the side so that when you go to catch him you pull out a cold handful of nothing. That is a trick to deceive children.'*

He tasted the salt of his tears. What he read made no sense. It made no sense. Surely trout were brown? It had been more than the desire to find out about his father which had made the diary so important to him. Because of the way it had come to him, by chance and coincidence beyond belief – to lie so many years in that locked desk . . . beyond belief, his mind drifted away from that thought – he had expected to find from his father's words a message meant for him. The thought shamed him. He had spied upon an unhappiness more confused than his own; out of the past not help but an echo of old disorder.

Brooding upon his loss, he slept. After a time the door opened. Pages of the diary ruffled and turned in the draught.

He wakened with an erection under the hot covering for he came out of sleep entangled in memory. He had committed adultery only twice during all his married life. Each of them, the first and the second, had been the affair of a single night. He did not count the times he had been with prostitutes: those dry encounters were beneath the dignity of adultery. For the first time, lying in the rumpled sleeping bag, doped with the sun, it occurred to him that perhaps he had never really achieved adultery. A hole to push himself into cost something; he had learned the price of that; but the higher pretences or even the techniques that substituted for them – came dearer than he had been prepared to afford. Once he had been going home carrying a box of eggs. He had worn a hat and there had been another parcel too – he couldn't remember what it had contained just that the brown paper was coming undone at one end and he kept reclosing it protectively. Some piece of clothing for Sylvia: he had taken it back to the shop at lunchtime and they had exchanged it. He had put the parcel on a chair and the eggs beside it on the floor. He sat his hat on top of the parcel. He had taken off his clothes. He had even taken off his shoes and socks since he had felt it would be foolish to wear them when he was naked. She had said she would take off her clothes too, but when he turned round she was lying on the bed with her breasts

156

still covered and a kind of corset round her middle. She explained why she needed to keep them on and the explanation disgusted him, but he lay on top of her and though he was softening had gone through the motions and come almost at once. There's a bucket, she said. He hadn't noticed it: a bucket between the bed and the wall with used sheaths writhing in it. The sheath he pulled from himself clumsily hung like hawked phlegm from the lip of the bucket. She had already taken his money. Just inside the door she had taken the clean notes from him one at a time. He put on his clothes again and his hat. He crouched down and picked up his box of eggs and the parcel with its brown paper springing loose. He didn't feel guilty, only cheated.

Passion must come dearer.

Then he slept again. He felt as if it lasted for a long time but he kept wakening very briefly and slipping away – wake sleep wake sleep – a stick across palings.

Later he was thirsty and wanted something to drink. He worked up to his feet against the wall. Swaying, he saw the flask on the floor and slid down again to his knees. It was surprisingly easier going down than getting up. He picked up the flask and the diary and made it to a chair by the table. There was a flat tin of sild on the table. He thought about the little fish head to tail in oil. His mind was clear that it would be wise to eat. He unpicked the bright wrapper and was left with the key and the plain tin. The key had a slot in the shaft. A protruding tongue of the lid went through the slot and was wrapped around the shaft until the tin opened. He sat for a while with the tin in one hand and the key in the other thinking about the process. It was less simple than it had appeared at first. Properly done, the shaft and the weakened section of the lid should be at right angles; the first few turns would decide the matter. He put the tin down and laid the key carefully inside the rim. With the book and the flask, he shuffled to the outer door. It was open and he could see the shadow of the house like a carpet thrown on the grass. He told himself it was important not to sit in the direct light of the sun.

The stone wall rubbed cold against the skin of his back. After a wearisome struggle, he had pulled off his shirt. One arm was still wrapped in a sleeve. He picked at the tangle. Everything took time: unscrewing the flask, pouring, replacing the cup. The liquid was warm and sweet. Normally he did not take sugar. He wondered if Chris had been careless or thoughtful. Sugar for energy: I lack the gift of gratitude, he decided. Sitting against the wall, the crumpled shirt between his knees, he thought about the things for which he should be grateful. Considering them, he fell asleep.

With Sylvia it was never passion.

He woke up not hearing the words but seeing them as if they were chalked on a blackboard held up before his eyes.

> '. . . *a child into the world is a thing of terror. A terror summoned. All around us in those slum rooms I could hear the children being born. The rooms stood in the air room piled on room and in every room children were born as purposelessly as the dirt they let fall in the lavatories on the stairhead. I could hear it all. I had developed my powers to the point where I could hear everything, everyone, but I had not foreseen there was no way to stop hearing. And then she told me we were going to have a child and I was guilty too. All life—*'

As his father's only child, he must have been the son unwillingly summoned.

'You're not safe to be on your own.'

It was Chris, and the sun had crept round the house and fallen on him.

She helped him inside and sat with her elbows on the table looking between her hands at him.

'There's no doctor here if you make yourself ill.'

He closed his eyes and thought. She seemed to have been gone for hours.

'I'm not quite sure yet,' he said, ungumming his eyes cautiously, 'but I really think that I feel better.'

'And what am I supposed to do? Offer you more soup?'

'If you do, would you add less water this time? It would improve the taste.'

'Perhaps you are feeling better,' she said gloomily,

She exaggerated, however, for as he looked up at her the room slid away like a saucer of mercury.

'Daddy?'

Her face shimmered close. The room settled. Bright dots swarmed away like constellations separating.

'You won't go away again?' he asked.

'Not before I make you soup. And this time with less water,' she said and tried to smile.

As she started to rise, he caught her by the hand.

'You've been kind to me.'

She pulled away.

'Kind?' Her voice rose sharply. 'I don't want to be *kind*. I want you to tell me what to do.'

'Are you going out again?'

He couldn't see her face for she had her back to him at the table. He heard the hiss of the camping stove. It was hard for him to keep awake. He pressed the back of his hand against his eyes and waited for her to answer. When she didn't say anything, he decided she hadn't heard him. He thought about repeating the question. Perhaps she had heard and was pretending. He saw her walking with someone on the edge of a cliff watching the gulls below white against the sea.

'Is he here?' he asked, but just then she turned and said something so perhaps again she had not heard.

She offered him the beaker and he had to hold it with both hands to drink. She did not offer to help.

'It tastes good. I mean made just right,' he said.

'Why wouldn't you go to Canada?'

'What?' In his surprise, the beaker slopped. He dabbed at soup dribbling on his chin. 'That was so long ago. You were only a baby.'

She shook her head.

'I know that Mummy— she argued and begged and pleaded with you. It was your chance of a new life. The university would have paid your fares and they had found you a house. It was so *easy* – but you were afraid. Everything would have been different.'

'Like a magic wand,' he said neutrally. He didn't believe that she remembered any of that. He had heard too many of these phrases out of Sylvia's mouth. It made him sick to think of how often behind his back they had been rehearsed to Chris. 'Your mother didn't understand.'

'She thought she did. She said that was when she knew you would never amount to anything.'

'Ah,' he said and sipped from the beaker.

'I hated her for saying that.'

'I'll sleep now.'

'She blamed you because I wasn't a boy. I should have been a boy, you know.'

He had been sitting on the sleeping bag against the wall and now, putting down the beaker, let himself lie back. His eyes closed. Long ago a child on a school trip, he had spent the night in a cave. Darkness had been absolute deprivation of light and he had lain unable to sleep thinking of the whole unimaginable weight of the mountain above him.

'Oh, Daddy,' Chris said, 'why did you have to get drunk yesterday?'

It was so dark it made no difference whether your eyes were open or closed. The cave was an accident, a temporary thing in the time of the mountain.

'Do you remember Bertie Deane?' he asked without opening his eyes. 'He used to be in and out of the house when you were young. He wanted you to call him Uncle Bertie, but then we lost touch with him. He came from a farm in Sussex. Big chap with red cheeks. He worried about being clumsy. Told me if he sat with strangers he always felt as if his feet were touching everybody else's under the table.'

There was a silence and he looked, suddenly afraid she had gone.

'We didn't come here because of me at all,' she said softly, as if understanding something she should have known before. 'You're the one who's in trouble.'

'That's not true!'

He struggled to sit up.

'You wanted to sleep,' she said. 'You may as well. You'll feel better if you sleep.'

'Chris! Chris!'

He shouted but she didn't come back. With an effort, he got up and went to the window. Perhaps, he thought, it would be like the previous day and she would be sitting by the wall. The sun was still shining but there were black clouds on the edge of the sky. He took a handful of biscuits from the packet and poured water from the pan into the beaker. Curds of the soup flecked the surface. Outside it was warm and he sat in his nesting place by the side of the house.

160

If Chris had stayed, he could have explained to her that he hadn't been afraid to go to Canada. Why hadn't he gone? Trying to think what he could have told her, he turned the pages of the diary.

'He kept arguing with me. I was grieved and angry but not to be persuaded. Do I command no respect at all? Isn't it a strange thing that I can't remember whether he asked me that or I asked him? I would go away when it became more than a man could bear and there were things to be done single-handed as I was on the boat alone but he was always there when I came below with the shadow of the lamp on his face. Why did I think they had all left? he asked me. Only a child how could I remember? Only a child how could I remember what they had left – the great storms of winter and the hungry springs, the winds that scoured the crops out of the earth and the babies that died, year after year in that time the men could not provide and the mother's labour was new born into the sure hand of death. God had judged that island and its people. Was there nowhere over the green round of the world to live but Breagda? He had sailed to the Americas and gone south about Africa and to the continents of the east. Everywhere men lived and what law could bind a man in justice only for being born on that bare rock? I hated that smooth wise old man who spoke like a law-giver, a captain, as if the mantle of acknowledgement hung from his shoulders. Old traitor why do you treat me like this? Do you think I am some stranger in a back-street bar of a port to be lied to and told what a great man you are? Don't you think I know what you are? What are you but a servant of masters? Have you ever in all your sailing chosen a course? How then in the round of the green world could any place matter to you? How do you imagine I wouldn't know the truth about you? Have you forgotten I'm your son? He darkened on me with a great grief and anger, shouting, Blasphemer! you know I have never been in a public house in my life or put my lips to alcohol or spirits.'

Maybe he should have said to Chris that when the offer to go to Canada came he had already travelled too far. If he had gone to Canada, he might never have been able to find his way back. He

dipped into the diary at random, jumping back and forward careful
to avoid the last pages. A glance had told him the writing stopped
just past the half way mark of the book and he kept to the first third
of its pages, reading a paragraph, a page or two, sometimes only a
sentence.

*'Not a day of my life has passed without my considering the
nature of God.'*

That angered him and in reaction he remembered the NATE
conference and the fat man who said, laughing, It's not a bit like
our usual – I haven't seen any jumping into bed yet. The stupid
words stuck in his head; they had chimed him awake in the morning
and buzzed to his razor and that night the music from the room at
the end of the corridor syncopated them. 'My lovely Scotsman!' she
said and hung like a lead pendulum swinging her drunken weight
in the crook of his arm. 'What?' he had bawled not able to believe
his ears, then opportunist had burred like a scratched 78 of Harry
Lauder and sounded to himself, caught between past and present,
like Alfred Tennyson, Poet Laureate and Lord, crying out of pre-
history through a horn gramophone, Break, break, break, On thy
cold gray stones, O Sea! Oh, yes, and half carrying her up to her
room, her bag opening and spilling keys and cash, groping round to
collect it all honestly, scrupulously, while hard-eyed a passing
colleague asked, You all right, Marge? wondering what kind of
bastard he, toothless dracula, might be. And, in fact, in her little
conventual cell – how did students stand them over the winter?
suicidal melancholy signalled from the walls in tiny cramped graffiti
– fell on the bed and passed out; and when he kissed her, tipping
over drunk himself, convulsed and said, I sleep alone, monsieur.
Yet the next night he left a drunken poetry fest at half one in the
morning and retraced his route across the silent campus, past a
desk where two student porters watched him, and her door opened
dream-like and she was spread out on the bed and looking at him
as if she had been expecting nothing else. There's a bottle of gin on
the table, she said, my head of department gave me it – pour me a
drink; and he did and later put it into her once, and remembered
legs in black stockings and half waking later at her urging and
getting it in again – or probably only miming with his little veined

162

peace-maker as limp as a fingerless glove. Next morning, going home, he had seen her on the station platform – not as tall as the night before, not exotic, not glamorous – and looked carefully in the other direction until a voice at his side said in a molten whisper, 'By the way, I forgot to tell you – I have cancer of the liver,' and as he spun round her back moved from him, lumped as a little old granny under a shawl. Home, he locked himself in the bathroom and scrubbed his privates until they squeaked pink like diners' lobster.

Was that passion? He blew his nose and the fat snot flew from his fingers among the grass. Even remembering her, almost sure she had lied, flesh crawled at the impression of his spoon stirring such corruption, a spirtle, the plain stick his mother had used, pulled from the pot crusted with strands of green and red vegetables.

Crying out, he clutched himself and wakened.

Fat drops of rain from an overcast sky splashed warm on his arms and shoulders. He lay submissive, not free of sleep, drifting, fantasising, warm separate drops heavy on his flesh . . . Like a baptism, he came awake.

Companionably, he would go in search of Chris and Ramsay. The word pleased him. He had been in a fever, full of fears and imaginings, and now it was purged. He began to walk and it was surprising how he felt, no doubt deceptively, that the warm bathing air and rain had been sent to restore him. Water ran down his bare sides; his trousers, the shirt he carried in his hand were quickly soaked but he felt no discomfort. Exhilarated, he rubbed his hand over his face, down across his streaming chest. The touch of flesh on flesh was a comforting excitement; he held out the belt from his waist and let the warm rain flow down his belly.

He had no sense of weariness. When he felt the land rising again, he knew vaguely that he had missed the schoolhouse but continued to climb without any thought of going back. He felt as if all his strength had returned. The ground when he fell did not hurt him. Driving rain forced down his head, closed his eyes, but the need to find Chris drew him forward. He followed the vernicle of her face on the storm, until the threshing ceased and he straightened slowly in an unexpected stillness.

It was like looking at the future of the shore village. Time and weather had plucked the houses apart and tumbled their stones.

Only outlines were left, a lithomancy of broken walls and isolated gables. As he rubbed his hands over his cheeks, the whine of the wind, mingled with a deep persistent tumult, emerged from beyond the immediate silence. Aimless, he wandered between the stones and came out at the foot of a steep slope cupped like a hand round the ruins. Now he was very tired and began to scramble upwards only from inertia of purpose.

Near the top the grass blew towards his reaching hands. In another moment the full force of the wind caught him and he staggered forward half a dozen steps blinded by the rain. His shirt had been dropped and lost; the hail of stinging drops beat on his chest and he faced about and walked backwards for a few steps to get relief. When he turned, he was on the edge of the cliff. The sea was a sky below him. Death's colour it threw up white hands to draw him down. His body froze rigid with shock. He felt himself sway forward and could do nothing. I'm going to die, he thought, and in the same instant heard the voice of the old doctor on the day of his mother's funeral. I took her to the door, he said, and pointed to the sky. I wouldn't want to go there on a night like this. There was no more talk of suicide.

The voice released him. Dear God, dear God! he sank to his knees and crawled backwards from the drop. At once he was safe but he could not bear to stand up. On hands and knees, staring at the grass, he edged backwards until stopped by an obstacle. He twisted his head round to see and gaped up at Ramsay, whose spread legs spurned and held him. In his confusion, the figure looked deformed; arms blown crooked by the wind. The mouth moved.

'What? What?' he cried in bewilderment.

He tried to stand and the figure yielded; then they were over the edge and tumbling down the sheltered face of the slope.

'What?'

His voice sounded extraordinarily loud. They had fallen into the same silence out of the wind. He untangled himself from the weight of Ramsay's thighs. They lay side by side.

'I was saying, we'll have to stop meeting like this. Not very funny.' Ramsay shook and choked on laughter. It went on for a long time; he would struggle to stop and then collapse again. His heavy lips writhed. It seemed as uncontrollable as a fit. 'I thought it was the moon backing towards me through the rain.'

'I didn't want to be blown over the cliff.'

'You're not worried by the cliff? What about your Breagda blood?'

'I'd rather not spill any of it.'

'No, but seriously.'

The endless laughter had cleared Campbell's mind with a fit of mortification. Now this 'no, but seriously' was a phrase he had come across out of the mouths of impatient dullards.

'Seriously, didn't you know the men of Breagda were famous climbers?' The trick of the hill gave Ramsay's voice a clear penetrating softness. 'They gathered eggs from the nests – and the young gannets, gugas they called them. Good eating those, like dishcloths boiled in seaweed.'

He laughed showing big morning-yellow teeth, not looking dull at all.

'No wonder the babies died,' Campbell said.

'The babies?'

'In my father's diary he writes about them. Two many of the babies died.'

Ramsay rolled over on his side and stared. His face blotted out the world.

'It was your father's diary then? But you don't find that almost unbelievable? Your father's diary lying in that desk so many years until you came along – fresh from Hounslow or wherever – to find it waiting for you.' Scowling, he looked older. But then he wiped the rain from his eyes and said, 'God, if I'd known I'd have read it. A chance missed,' and grinned, looking nineteen and only a little crazy. 'Read it to Chris.'

The name rang through him like a verdict.

'Where is she?'

But Ramsay jumped up as if he hadn't heard and went light and fast back up the slope.

When he reached the top, Ramsay was standing on the torn edge of the cliff. He groaned in anguish and forced himself to go forward. There was a terrible temptation to get down and crawl. He found barely enough pride not to do that. The wind seemed to alter direction. He felt it from the left and then on the right as if it tried to push him off balance. The space between the top of the slope and the cliff edge was about twice the length of a room. A grey tumult of water foaming into the grey turmoil of sky framed Ramsay and cringing he came close and yelled, 'Isn't she with you?'

Ramsay swung round. Was he saying anything? Could the wind be snatching the words away?

'Isn't she with you?'

Ramsay caught him by the arm, (if a wind blew him over, he'd carry me with him, the terror of falling,) his dark heavy face alive with curiosity and shouted, 'Are you a climber?'

Aphasiac, he understood the words but could not string them into sense: a, you, are, climber, climber . . .

Without waiting for an answer, Ramsay released him and went over the edge.

All his life he had hated heights, instability, uncertain footing, rocks slick with seaweed, iced pavements mirror treacherous. The wind shoved him back from the edge yet he inched towards it. At a sudden drop in the wind, the removal of its pressure seemed to suck him forward. Beyond shame, he crawled on his belly to the edge. The turf rubbed off into rock from which the rain bounced, gathered and slid out into space. His eyes clenched shut in a reflexive spasm.

And opened on Ramsay's face, each tooth as large as a grave marker for it seemed he was smiling.

'Look,' Ramsay said. 'No hands!'

Upraised fists flew up unclenching and almost touched his face. Horror and fright carried his senses out so that he felt, as if in his own body, the multitude of delicate unconsidered adjustments that kept Ramsay's balance above the emptiness of falling.

'Don't! Please, don't!'

'Your Breagda relatives shopped for their groceries on these cliffs.'

He did a little shuffle that dropped him a foot, a crazy dance step.

'Oh, Christ!' Glued to the sodden earth, clutching it. What was there to anchor to here? 'Hold on! You'll fall!'

'They say,' and he did it again, seeming to his inflamed gaze actually to fall before finding a new perch, 'the men of Breagda developed special feet for climbing. Their toes changed. Did you get that from your father?'

166

He didn't understand. Nothing made sense in this foreign place. Bawled not knowing if the water on his face was tears, 'Come up! You'll fall!' And with his own courage, 'Give me your hand!'; wanting to reach out though his belly shuddered – to hold this crazy boy though he be tugged over.

'Oh, please,' he moaned. 'Come up!' Heard himself, logical absurd old schoolmaster, adjudge, 'This is silly!'

'Silly?' Ramsay considered, looking up, his face smaller, beaten by rain after his last descent. He smiled. 'Of course, here,' and to his painful relief he saw him climb up one step and pull for the next, coming closer, 'here, give me your hand,' his hand, hand, the left clenched the muddy turf, tore up the earth seeking a grip, 'give me your hand. But be careful,' the right that should have gone out rested heavier than the past, a weight beyond his ability to raise, he saw them fall, heard their scream, his treacherous imagination stopped them above the sea then made a beach of rocks – on that the bodies fell, 'Careful. Don't want to pull you over,' looking up in simple puzzlement, toed in on blemishes, rock afterthoughts, his left hand with a grip at head height, his right thrown up eager to be caught.

He stared at the hand, not wanting to see Ramsay's face, and the expectation of being held left it, not suddenly but like the draining of grain from a sack, and as that happened the tension reshaped and folded it down until he stared at a fist, its four white knuckles shining on him like lamps. Ramsay's left hand must have lost its grip for with an awful cry both arms erect over his head he fell.

His own scream blotted out that cry with a mean individual anguish. What could he have done? If Ramsay was a madman lacking the ordinary saving cowardices; or if it had been less dangerous than it appeared, tricks, techniques, well-recognised devices of the craft? Ignorant, how could he have known his help was needed? Had been needed; a thin vomit ran over his teeth.

He rolled on to hands and knees and crawled again towards the edge. Ramsay's face not more than six inches below looked up at him.

Nothing could have been more terrible or unexpected. He could have touched it. As he stared, too paralysed by astonishment to react, Ramsay made little kissing movements of his lips, each mewing chirp clear, and smiled, wrinkling his nose like a flirtatious girl.

He threw himself back. On his feet, bent to the wind, yelled at the blank and hidden drop, 'Bastard!'

Two hands showed finding a grip and then, as if summoned, Ramsay drew himself over, twisted clear and came up on one knee.

'Did I ever tell you,' he asked, and grimaced like a man in pain, 'that never a day goes by without me considering the problem of God's nature? The nature of God?'

He ran. If the devil had been in pursuit, he could not have run faster. When he slipped, he heard Ramsay at his back, hawk-beaked to tear at him.

A voice called, 'And Chris? What about Chris?'

He had always been afraid of the irrational. The drugged, the drunk, the incalculable mad; above all of those who, surrounded by conspirators, prepared their mad defences in silence, ripping apart the afternoons of sunlight. He fled until he came among a place of stones; and couched there an endless time, hare-eyed and gone to ground.

Mist, cold smoke pouring off the sea, thickened about him into a room of grey walls. Head bent, he listened feverishly. The sea sounded very near and all around. He struggled through trenches of thick soaked grass. Obsessed with the danger of the cliff, he balked and veered. The grey room narrowed. Through its walls Holmes and Watson passed side by side in a London hansom cab. They went to and fro through the fog, side by side yet in his delirium implacably silent. They were looking for the lost girl, though they knew what they would find. Every journey ended in a death. The room was no larger than a coffin; on each grey wall he saw an image of Chris. Raped, thrown from the cliff, drowning, her legs broken lying alone. There was no shortage of subjects though the styles were simple, no high art here; comic-book gothic, a pornography of newsreels, a jumbled handful of illustrations from his aunt's copy of the Brothers Grimm. They buried the Naughty Little Girl but she pushed her arm up out of the earth and did it again and again no matter how often they thrust it down – until they sent for her mother who struck the arm a blow with the rod, when it was drawn under and that was an end of it. 'And Chris!'

168

His poor Chris! He had not forced Ramsay to tell where she was. Had run. Ran. Was running.

Something burst deep in his chest. When he tried to get up, his legs and arms shook in violent spasms. Dear God, he thought, I'm paralysed; and then as his brain churned an incoherency of prayers and promises the shuddering moderated until he lay trembling.

Now to keep going was a bestial anguish. Each painful step carried him towards what he had done. Too late he understood that bringing Chris to Breagda was the great gesture of his life. Nothing he had ever done compared in his own eyes to that act. How many obstacles he had swept out of the way. It had been heroic. It had been his. Only when it had been taken from him did he apprehend all that it might have meant. Ramsay had taken it in minutes on that hellish cliff. Lost, he came down off the turf among a stretch of low shrubs that stung his shins and ankles. A brown shape burst up from under his reaching foot. The uproar spread itself on the mist as a bird with outstretched wings. He crouched under the suddenness of it. Like the percussion of a skirmish, three more whirled up from the ground, each setting off the next in a perfected image of panic. But then, even as he recognised the event, the last bird was darkening in successive glimpses, the one beyond a ghost, a disturbance at the limit of sight, until both were sealed in mist and their clamour passed into the beating of his heart.

At first it was hard to hear the sea. It had fallen away far into the distance. He stood and listened for its be-silent and the grey room was a place of refuge.

Yet as soon as he began to move he was more tormented than ever. But now instead of fear, rage stretched him on the rack. He cursed Chris for her spoiled life and despised himself for that and so cursed himself, Sylvia, Trish until all the muddied tributaries poured into a single anger whose object was Ramsay. Repeatedly he fell and leapt up until one fall filled his mouth with blood. It would be a release to sleep. He coughed and blood sprayed out in thick drops. Briefly it stained the grass by his face and he watched it soak away and touched the place where it had been. He would have to go back. By stages, he came to his feet. He would go back, find Chris, settle with Ramsay. The grey walls were at arms' length: as he turned trying to find the way back, a drifting corridor opened ahead of him and he stumbled into it.

After a dozen steps, the mist closed tight again. There was no doubt he was going more slowly but he did not fall so often. Walking with head bent, he watched for changes that might pull him down. He recognised his wisdom in going like this, not allowing fear or hate to drive him. The wise thing as he had done was to harness them. How else would he have been able to go on? The universe narrowed to the moving circle of gorse and stones about his feet; he followed what seemed to be paths, trails of sheep or winter streams that split and were lost. It seemed to him that he was smiling at the memory of a ploughing match he had seen in Cumberland. In holiday spirits, he had pointed out one of the young ploughmen and said to Sylvia, 'Lil' Abner, do you see?' – broad shoulders, head bobbing behind the plough, sleeves wadded above bunched biceps. His head bobbed reflectively; fallen into just that slow rocking pace, he ploughed the salt grass. Then he was lying on his side so he must have fallen. Later he lived in the round universe where all that mattered was the endless movement of one foot past the other. When they had first met, Sylvia and he had been young. He remembered that because there was a photograph of its truth. There was a seaside kiosk and a fragment of beach behind it and she was wearing a blazer and he looked excited and confident, their two hands clasped swung out towards the camera. And passion? It seemed to him that passion was not what Sylvia and he had felt even in their earlier good times. He wondered if it was less common than all the talk, the jokes, the fictions pretended. Then like light rushing from an open door, he saw Sylvia's face with the scar new drawn; she was just out of hospital; he kissed her and she turned her face away and in a fury of pity he seized her by the chin and hauled her to face him; she cursed words he would not have believed she knew, spitting obscenities and he held her tight her jaw squirming and jumping in his fist and he put one finger on the wrinkled crimson flesh and stroked the length of the scar saying over and over poor Sylvia poor Sylvia and they did things that night naked that surely must be all there was of passion. But she never let him touch the scar again – even after the plastic surgery when it was only a white thread and often not really easy to see at all.

His feet were on sand white under the bright sun. He watched them as closely as before but mirages of space pressed on him until he ploughed down on to his knees and the trance was broken. Just before him the sea came in tranquil wavelets to the shore. How could the sea be at peace? He ran and fell among the waves that hissed small in a shimmer of white bubbles. The sun was hot on his back and the shallow water warmed by the sand. Kneeling up, he saw the crooked arm of land that sheltered the bay and the *Lazy Charlotte* rocking on calm waters like a promise of home.

He took water in his hand and let it dribble into the corner of his neck. With the turning of his head, he shivered to see how close the fog was. As the last of the water dripped from his hand, a woman laughed.

He had been more alone in his anguish than at any time in his life. Round the whole horizon now, he was conscious of nothing human. Every animal fibre twisted, aching for flight, he crouched searching the empty beach and the sea. Everywhere in the sunlight there was no place of concealment.

The laughter came again, and surely it was nearer. Separate notes of laughter like moaning. It had a familiarity more terrible than strangeness. Very slowly, he turned towards the drifting edge of fog. The laughter sobbed and there might have been words, and then he heard under them another noise, the movement of someone wading through shallow water.

As he stared, every sound died except the splash and little surge of someone walking. The voice, the laughter, were silent. He thought he saw a shape and then it stretched and angled away. Like a kneeling statue, without breath, his whole life in his eyes, he watched.

First as a shadow among shadows, a whiter darkness, then as a shape that became the ideogram of a naked woman, wiping back her hair with one wrist from her eyes, Chris waded out of the mist at the land's edge. She must have fallen for her body was beaded with water drops that the sun, its boiling verge near the distant rim of the sea, turned into a shimmering outline of each small long-nippled breast and the stringy curve of her belly. In the sparse bush between her legs lanterns glowed and darkened. She waded slowly on before him. He heard her murmur, 'If you want me to', and laugh as if she was afraid.

'Chris,' he cried softly, rousing a sleep-walker.

She took another step and he called out sharply, 'Chris!'

She looked blindly towards him. He pretended for a moment to think she was drunk. The brilliant bruised eyes. The strangely altered mouth, thick-lipped like the rough painting of some over-worked whore. He had seen them before. They were horribly familiar to him. He groaned.

'Poor Lolly!' she said.

As he knelt, fixed in awful fascination, she moved gently to him through the parting waters.

'Poor Lolly!'

Before he could imagine what might happen, she took his head between her hands and drew his face into the nest of her groin. He tasted salt. He opened his mouth and tasted her; felt the rough hair at his lips. His tongue ran out between his parted teeth—

He struck up with both hands and the heels of his palms smashed into her thighs as he yelled incoherent rage. She staggered back and he tried to hit her, falling short so that he splashed up gouts of water like a childhood game. Too confused and furious to think of getting up, he sprawled after her flailing the water. And then a final blow that would have smashed her down carried him off balance. The sea ran into his lungs, salt light bruised blue in his eyes. Choking, he fought up out of the drowning wave and was close to her, crouched, the water lapping her breasts. He had never seen any human face so distorted by fear; and that look of hellish fright was concentrated on him.

'Oh, Chris,' he said. The bitter sea burned at the top of his lungs.

'Daddy,' she screamed, hands held up against some springing beast. 'Don't hurt me!'

The hair bristled on his neck.

'God forgive me,' he whispered. 'I'm sorry.'

But as he got to his feet, she screamed again, a keening that sent the gulls brokenly answering up from the waves. 'Daddy, I want you! Help me!'

As he held out his arms, she whirled and ran from him. He froze in astonishment then went after her, calling, 'It's all right. Daddy's here!'

Terror drove her at such a speed there was no chance of him catching her. When she splashed out of the sea, he followed along the hardening edge till another swerve took her up on the soft beach. At each step sand clung like a marsh. In his exhaustion it was something he had experienced before without placing where –

172

this great effort and the agonising slowness which repaid it. He grew afraid that his heart would burst. He had no breath now to call her name and could do nothing as she left him hopelessly further behind. One step, another, after an endless moment, a third. He stood beaten watching her go and she fell, leapt up screaming, and came back. Moving as if on grass, her face contorted with terror, blind, she ran straight at him and he grabbed her pinning both arms and fell on her with all his weight.

Retching for air, he lay on her. His heart shook against her.

'Chris?'

With the most delicate of movements, she raised her groin against him. He felt it press against his thigh and a shock like electricity ran through his whole body. He was afraid to let go in case she escaped; he could never catch her; but when he shifted his weight, trying to ease away, she wriggled with him. Against his swollen sex, she rose and fell with a slow increasing insistence.

He was angry with her. He said confused things. What he was trying to tell her was that she degraded him; she drew him into the filth of her drugged fantasy; he longed to punish her. He reared up his upper body, bending down his head to see her face; it was turned away, her chin resting on her shoulder, long hair like a veil strung across her eyes. He was afraid to let go her wrists. He held them stretched out on either side. To punish her, he pressed down – or to force her to be still. But then against her sharp young hips and the cleft apple that nibbled him, he relaxed, and pressed again and passed into a full movement that ended only when a sweet shuddering agony flushed over his belly.

With a groan of terror, he rolled away from her to the full extent of his outflung arm yet held her fist-chained by one frail wrist.

Afraid, he watched a cloud drifting to the east. She tugged and he tightened his grip, so hard the bones turned in his fist, but she did not groan or complain. The sky darkened. He felt against the roots of his middle fingers the hop and hurry of her pulse. It tapped and scurried, and then he lost it altogether. Suddenly he was conscious of the coldness of the hour and that she was naked and full of drugs and she might fall sick and die. Yet he could not bring himself to look at her. Like a trap forced open, he unclenched the hand that held her wrist. He waited but her thin bones rested in the palm of his open hand. Stealthily, he slid his hand free. Now

173

no part of him touched her. He waited, thinking she would move or say something to him. He half expected her to get up and run – and wondered vaguely if he would go after her. If she got up and ran, he felt, without being clear why that should be, somehow everything would be simpler.

The gulls reproached him. He couldn't hear Chris. There was no stir or sigh. He could not hear her breathing.

Panic-stricken, he rolled up with a convulsion that carried him half across her, kneeling with his hands on the sand by her shoulder. Her face was calm but too still. As he looked down on her in awe and terror, she touched her cheeks with the tips of her fingers and with the same caressive fondling touch drew them down her throat and came to rest on the nipple of each breast. As if to ease herself, she lifted her hips and spread her legs apart. When her eyes opened, she seemed normal and undisturbed. Her eyes were a shade of particular deep blue which was the colour of his own, their size and shape too resembled his; people remarked on that, although in other ways they did not look much alike. It was as if he stared down into his own eyes. Holding his gaze, she smiled and a turmoil of questioning rose in him but before he could find words she silenced him with the smallest movement of her head.

From the private smile, obscenely isolated above that naked self-absorbed body, there dribbled a parody of laughter colder and more wretched than mist and sea distance.

EIGHTEEN

He wakened and kept still, listening, before he opened his eyes. The sun through the narrow window glanced rainbows of light from the line of framed texts. Becalmed, the Gospel Ship lay full-rigged in the storm. The word WARNING was picked out in red along the prow. In her sleeping bag, Chris huddled under it.

Ramsay had not come to find them yet.

What a fool he had been to bring her back here! Pain pressed on his skull and drew the roots of his nose with a dry throbbing. The pressure of a full bladder knuckled each side of his pelvis. Last Christmas he had celebrated the season by going to a cinema alone; twice Sylvia had got ready and changed her mind despite his pleading; the film had been set in New York, blown refuse, beatings, neon lights, the camera in a night club lingering over faces no make-up girl could have made so ugly or so lost; coming out, he had thought, Dear old London! and down the side street where his car was parked come on a teenager drunk in the gutter; as the two girls with her staggered about trying to lift her, a thick gush of yellow liquid spurted from under her raised skirt. What a fool he had been. On the day of the funeral when he had gone to his mother's flat and found it locked against him, Ramsay had been there wrapped in some filthy act with Chris. The corrupter. He understood suddenly that the diary, his father's diary, must have been in the flat among his mother's possessions. His mother had preserved it all these years, even after his father's death, and Ramsay had touched it and read it and brought it with him to the island. The corrupter. He sickened at the thought.

Where was the diary? He had been sitting outside yesterday and then he had gone to look for Chris. As he tried to think, something struck the window. He was on his feet in the middle of the floor without any sense of having moved, but when he went close there was nothing to see. It could have been a bird or some fragment

175

blown against the glass. The window was as he had checked it the night before: sagged tight, sealed by neglect, its cobwebs strung with insect husks.

The window was a fact, shut and tight. Looking at it, he recognised other things as fact also. Unless Ramsay had supernatural powers he could not have known to follow them to Breagda and so Ramsay was not the man in the flat; he was not the mysterious Lolly. Only a student, Ramsay had come to earn vacation money by surveying birds on an island in summer. His friend Neil who had brought him here would come back again in his boat to fetch him.

Those things seemed to him certainly to be true. Even though he shuddered at the memory of the previous day, he was a reasonable man and valued that in himself. Ramsay's behaviour yesterday could be explained. He was an unpleasant young man who – what was it his friend Neil had said? – 'hated his father'. Today perhaps he would be ashamed of how he had behaved. Probably now he would stay away from Chris and himself.

Last night he had tried to lock the outside door by jamming the plastic bucket by its handle across the two knobs. It had sprung loose and lay on the floor. A stupid idea, but then he had been very tired as well as frightened. He went outside and relieved himself against the wall. Turning away, he saw the diary where he had dropped it on the grass. It had been rained on. The cardboard cover had been blown back and the pages were curled up, sodden and stuck together. When he unpicked them, they were spoiled. Only a paragraph in one place, a few pages elsewhere, could still be read; the last part, the end of what his father had written, was in the worst condition – no one could ever read it now. The feeling of loss was unbearable. As he closed the book, a yellow butterfly wavered across the grass and then coming to the house rose over it effortlessly. He had forgotten they were strong enough to do that. The air was already warm and smelled of the sea. The weather would be good today.

He tapped on the window to waken Chris. When she didn't move, he knocked again more loudly. He put his head against the pane blocking the light so that her shape dimmed. She lay in exactly the same position so she must be asleep after all and not pretending. His breath fogged the glass.

When he went back inside, the sun had moved off the text. Word starved, he read it automatically.

WARNING: He that being often reproved hardeneth his neck shall suddenly be destroyed and that without remedy.

Proverbs Twenty-Nine *and* One: he made the old rhythm of that and smiled to himself. While he made a hot drink, he clashed the beakers and clattered the pan down noisily on the camping stove. He sipped his drink looking down at her. She seemed to be lying face down. She had slid into the bag so that only a corner of the shirt he had put on her was showing. Abruptly, he crouched beside her.

'Chris? Chris? Are you all right?'

Her shoulder turned under his hand and his stomach retched for there was no resistance of bone: her body felt as if it had been pulped. Two responses happened then which were almost instantaneous: he was filled with the knowledge that, although he had no memory of it (remembered bringing her here, persuading her to sleep), in some moment of despair and madness he had beaten her to death; and at once knew the impossibility of that and believed that Ramsay had done this terrible thing. He heard a pitiful sound and did not recognise it as his own voice; and then he clenched his fist on what he held and pulled out a tangle of clothing, jeans, a jersey, the old shirt trailing a sleeve. He grabbed up the bag and shook until a half-crushed carton and then a sandal fell from it. They lay beside the clothes, a discarded bundle of oddments that had made the illusion of Chris.

He searched the house, looking behind doors, coming back over and over again to the same places. As long as he did this, he could keep the horror at bay. Yet he knew that he would not find her. Chris might have risen in the night and wandered away; it was even conceivable she might have hidden herself somewhere in the house; but she would not have prepared the sleeping bag to deceive him with the illusion of her presence. Ramsay had been here. Ramsay had stepped over him in the dark. He had come and taken Chris away again – yet had delayed to construct that childish hoax of clothes and cardboard . . . It was more than malice. Ramsay was trying to drive him mad, utterly to destroy him. Yet he had done nothing to deserve any of this; except try to save Chris. Was that a reason for so much hatred?

He broke a twig under his heel and realised he was outside. The long grass of the field parted like water as he waded down through the yellow morning light and the same light lay across the spread sheet of the bay. The *Lazy Charlotte* was gone.

He was alone on Breagda.

That was too much to bear, and so he told himself at once that it was important not to be deceived. It might be that Ramsay wanted him to think they were gone and that he was left alone. Luckily his mind was very clear. He went slowly back up the hill to the house and checked again all the places in which he had already looked. When he decided to go and search in the old schoolhouse where he had found Ramsay once before, he turned back after a few steps and went to where his father's diary was lying on the grass. It would not do to leave it behind. He had done that once before and ruined everything. It was fortunate that his mind was so clear.

The bracken came up past his waist. The house was an empty box far below. He began to run, hitting at the fronds with the book in his clenched fist until one clumsy sweep brought him down. When he touched his cheek, the hand came away red against the buzzing green he lay in. Like a thing emptied, one spray swung loose on a broken stalk. He punished it, made it pay for his hurt, bent and ripped it down. The blood of the plant oozed between his fingers.

A shadow covered his outstretched arm. As he blinked up painfully, an extraordinary thing happened. From a torn curtain of cloud shining columns stretched down to earth. The edge of the tear was bruised grey and then white and through it he could see the sky. The endlessness of space reared up on slender pillars of marble and permanence was unveiled. The curtain twitched and it was made nothing.

Single drops of rain fell. He retraced in some fashion the path of the previous day, mechanically attentive to the alterations of the ground under his feet. Wandering, he settled for each step as a separate act.

A triangle of trees stood in one place in an entire isolation. He had lost his way for he had not seen them before. Someone had told him there were no trees on Breagda. Stunted and combed down by the winter gales, still they had survived, and he was comforted and knelt among them. The big muscles in each thigh fluttered like sick hearts. Yes, I will, he repeated senselessly, yes, I will. When his Aunt Jess died, his mother's relatives had come to London from Glasgow for the funeral. The crematorium had been set beside a field and yellow leaves from a great chestnut tree had flown between black-clad strangers who surrounded his living mother as if to guard her. They had come far south for their ritual of parting. Kneeling, while he waited for the little increment of resolution that would get him to his feet again, he noticed a broken branch near his hand, but when he picked it up for a support it crumbled into powdery fragments.

When he came down at last on to the flat land, it seemed to him that he had made innumerable decisions to go on, a new one for every step, and that all of them had changed him. It was possible to be the same man and yet to change.

Quite soon, he saw the schoolhouse. After the first shock, he realised that it was still a long way off. By good fortune, he came on a stick from which the bark had peeled so that it shone as if it had been polished in the sea. There were no trees anywhere near it. In the middle of the moor, the stick floated on buoyant bushes of heather.

He took it in his hand and went forward cautiously. The schoolhouse slept beside its shadow. He made a half-circle so that he would not pass in front of the window, imagining that they might be watching for him. With his hand on the door, he listened. The house was a husk; like dead wood it would crumble into corruption at a touch. He had been in the grip of a madness. It had been the madness of hope to believe that anyone could be here. Then as he pushed the door open he heard the sigh of someone taking breath and he knew that Ramsay was inside ready to attack him. He raised the stick and ran into the room, the flesh of his back cringing until he could turn.

He stared at the blank wall where the door juddered to rest. The broken flap of the desk gaped, dust danced in the shaft of light which had followed him; sleeping bag, rucksack, any sign of Ramsay was gone. The stick unnoticed slipped through his fingers and rattled on the floor.

'The glass is broken out of the windows. It has rained terribly all last night and the day before. The rain wet all the

floor excepting one corner and I lay there. At first I was cold but as I gathered my great power of listening I grew warm and then I burned and threw off my coat for I could hear everything. I heard all the cities of the world. A wide room full of people. Every city was a man and there was no man who did not weep. I had not known there were so many cities. I heard my son weep in his mother's womb. My child pitied me and yet I could not stop listening and at last I heard the steps of One who sought me. He goes about the island seeking. I am no longer alone. It is light enough to write this down. I am staying in this corner because it is hidden for soon God's face will come to my window. He will think I am caught not knowing this is the trap I have prepared. I am the hunter now and will wrestle like Jacob with the angel until—'

On the first line over the page there was a word that might have been 'question'. The rest was lost.

Poor madman. He sat with the book on his knees spreading the pages flat with an absent brushing of his hand. In the same cleft rock that had sheltered him once before, he watched the moor darkening and thought that if he were not there the house would go down into a darkness of the earth. Only his attention settled it like an image in shaken water. He could sleep outside and did not want to go back inside the schoolhouse. The approaching night would be warm and still – but he was alone on the island. To be outside and alone would be unbearable. Space without limit crushed him. He was stalked by the endless land. He had no one to care for and the sky hung over his head like the thumb of God.

He lay down in a corner of the room too exhausted to sleep. Like the highest pure note of a singer, he heard the moonlight spread its radiant stain upon the planked floor. Its touch cooled his burning eyes, and as it washed over him he drowned gliding through deeps and deeps. On the bed of an ocean, his body stirred to the nuzzling of blind fish.

One fist clenched and slackened, clenched.

He heard a voice and memory and love surprised the roots of his life. 'Grandpa?' he cried and sat up, wondering in a child's confusion how the voice had come to him under the sea. 'Grandpa?' Now his questions would be answered and he would understand all the

180

things that God let happen. But it was like before, when his mother had been weeping for his father's death, the voice spoke in a language whose words he did not know. There was no sense in the words and he made them curses. The door shook as if the man outside were fumbling to find the handle.

In a moment of great terror, the moonlight glimmered on a peeled snake and he recognised the stick he had picked up for his protection. It writhed on the floor towards his hand. Without knowing how he got there, from a single spasm made up of separate acts all trembling with a fury of haste and silence, he stood behind the opening door with the stick raised. The door struck his foot. The shape of a man came into the room as if going towards the desk then turned. A silver round of moonlight shone into the hollow flesh at its temple. All his misery, his fear, his great hatred of Ramsay gathered in him, the mad drugged eyes of Chris shone out of the dark, blood flowed over his tongue, and the swung stick beat its very tip into the silver coin and Ramsay was falling and the treacherous stick broke in two with a crack that was followed by another as the open lid of the desk caught the head of the falling man and threw the body to one side.

From his animal shape, he unbent slowly. First, for a way out, he looked over his shoulder to where the opened door framed a silver bush with stars in its branches. His shadow crept ahead of him until it covered the feet of the fallen man. The stick in his hand was a fragment; he was left with nothing to defend himself. He pressed it into the figure's side. His hand slid along the stick until he laid the tips of his fingers on the ribs at the side of the chest and they were still. In the moonlight the man's hair had been black. Ramsay's hair was black. Now the head was so close that he could reach out and touch it. He crept round the body until he could see the face. It had been beaten out of shape. The corner of the mouth was ripped. Everything above it was so pulped and swollen that it was impossible to tell where the eye was or if it was there at all. Only the red hair told him that the man on the floor was Neil.

He edged away from it stealthily. Not until he was outside did he get to his feet. His shadow stretched black from him through the open door to where fingers of an outflung hand quivered. He understood it was a trick of the moonlight and backed away until claws tore at his shoulders and slashed him across the eyes. Blind, he struggled in the silver bush, groaning softly for fear of being overheard.

The ruined village on top of the cliff was a poor comfort but he could not be in the schoolhouse or bear to be alone under the open sky. When he came upon it, he huddled against the remnant of a wall and waited for the morning to come. Night clouds unravelled off the edge of a broken chimney. He could hear the hunters in the grass and the sigh of outspread wings. From the cliff face there drifted up an occasional squabbling of birds. He did not exist. Gradually the chill that gripped his legs and the lower part of his body crept upwards. Twice scurrying things ran over him indifferently since he was so still.

With the last of the darkness greying, his body began to shudder. Bent arms fist-clenched, jaw, head, shook uncontrollably. With every spasm he gasped until he was drunk on air. By the neck, he was shaken to life. Holding to the wall, he dragged himself up. At first he could not walk; his joints burned and swelled under his skin. An old man limped out of the ruins, but instead of taking the easier slope he began to edge upwards with the small steps of a child.

The day was very new. A fresh pale radiance covered the world. In its vast saucer, the sea wrinkled out of sunlight into shadow. He stood so close that half of one foot rested over the drop. He had crawled here and lain on his belly, reaching down to Ramsay and pleading with him. Where he had crawled, now he stood. To swim down morning air in the sea to be quietened—

Carefully, he took a step from the edge and then a second. If Neil had only pretended to leave the island, then his boat must be anchored somewhere out of sight and hidden. But if that was so, then it was possible that the *Lazy Charlotte* might be in that secret anchorage too and with Ramsay and Chris still on board. What had happened to Neil? Who had beaten him so badly? Ramsay was his friend. Perhaps they had quarrelled over Chris. At the thought a thickness like vomit rose in his throat.

Why had Ramsay been here that day at the top of the cliff? Could he have climbed up from below? He thought of that awful gulf of air and shuddered. At the memory of his fear, he had to force himself to inch forward to where the land ended.

There was a path. It started under the lip of rock to his right, a flaw wide enough for a man to walk on safely, perhaps half the width of a staircase. Ramsay when he had let go had fallen only a foot or perhaps two on to that ledge. It was nothing. Anyone could do it, who had no vision of landing badly, staggering back into air and falling . . .

If Chris was alive she was at the bottom of that path. Ramsay would be there also. He would walk along the cliff, not climb down, only walk along the top and try from above to trace where the path went. His legs were cold, stiff, heavy; it was hard to move. As the sky lightened, a breeze nudged him backwards.

The beginning of the path jutted within a dozen steps only three feet below him. He blinked water from his eyes looking down to where raucous birds circled and returned. In the corner of the ledge, grass and tiny plants had rooted in a smear of soil. With no drop underneath, he could have set one hand on the turf and vaulted down. He lay on his belly and reached blindly with his feet, scrabbling, until they rested on the rock of the ledge. Then hand after hand he moved his clutches of earth until he leaned on the very edge of the cliff as if yearning inward to the island. He began to move very slowly, keeping his eyes fixed on the rock in front of his face until he stumbled; after that he inclined his head and watched his feet shuffle along against the inner place where rock met rock. When he stole a quick glance up, the cliff edge already appeared to be far above him, two or three times the height of a man; a flowering bush nodded out into the air. He moved slowly but never came to a stop. The round hill of the sea at his eye corner rose to the top of the world. His eyes fixed on the moving edge where rocks met, he had no sense of it happening gradually – suddenly the path was halved in width. Like an automaton, his body shuffled forward. The path became just wide enough and then not wide enough at all and then a pace ahead it ended, a card tamped back into the deck.

He had done more than his nature was shaped to bear. Yet he looked down.

Bright sparkles struck off the links of a metal chain pinned into the rock at his feet and running to a second ledge perhaps ten feet below. He crouched infinitely slowly and took the chain with his right hand. As his left searched for a grip, he overbalanced and fell. The wrench almost tore his hand from the chain and then his kicking feet found a hold and he went down step by step. Looking up, feet on the lower ledge, both hands holding the chain, he saw where rests had been cut into the rock to make it easy. He heard the sobbing of his breath and felt the shaking of his heart. He knew that he had to release his hold on the chain. Time passed and he did so. This ledge was narrower. He went with his hands at chest level against the rock. The tension of his muscles told him he was being taken upwards, the ledge was on a rising incline, but that was too cruel to believe. He looked up, moving his eyes more than his head, and the rock had gathered to an overhang, shutting out the sky like a crypt of shadows. On some strange impulse, he touched the rock with his tongue. It was smooth and very cold. He had never felt anything so cold. He took a step with his right foot and brought the left up to it, and did that again, and again – and there was nothing on either side but open sky. He had stepped into a maelstrom of birds. To the right, from where he hung on the outermost turn of the cliff's shoulder, in every crack and cranny they ruffled and squabbled. The air was giddy with them. They called *fall, fall, fall*. A jet like bile covered his right fist and by chance he saw the bird that swelling its throat spat its vomit at him. Released, he edged back. When he came to the chain, he went past it and on upon the lower ledge because it was too late, and perhaps not possible, to return. The ledge went steadily on a downward slope. It widened until he could walk upon it normally. He came on to turf and followed a long descent that led across a headland busy with cropping sheep and ended in a rough scramble down to a beach of stones.

He chose a direction and walked out of the shadow into a stripe of sun. Beyond exhaustion, he had passed into a state of very pure attentiveness, which, however, was not always directed to the present. From the sun's position, he realised with surprise that it was still early morning. The shore was laden with seaweed, twined green and black, uncertain footing. When he fell, the familiar taste of blood comforted him. 'Grandpa?' He had heard a voice and looked around startled, but it was only the crying of the gulls.

The cove was a very secret place. Even knowing it must be there, the sight of it carried a shock to the heart. The shore had ended in a rock platform that swung out in a spur lashed by waves so that he had to wait and run limping between them for fear of being washed off – and found himself at the mouth of the cove, so small it seemed he could reach across it. That was a deception caused by its great height, the sides meeting overhead like steepled fingers. The boat, Neil's boat, was lying inside in the glassy stillness of some accident of rock and tide. There was space beyond it and a dark glitter of water going back under the cliff. As he went in upon a ledge of rock, he found himself just above the level of the deck where Ramsay was standing with his legs apart.

'Why don't you go and sleep? You're being a bore.'

The sea and gulls' clamour was hushed and, though he spoke quietly, the man's voice carried clearly with a faint echo. As if suddenly conscious of being watched, he looked up. He showed no surprise but smiled, the unexpected grin that transformed the heaviness of his mouth and jaw.

'She's being a bore,' he said pleasantly.

Chris was kneeling in front of Ramsay. When he understood why, he cried out and she fell back and turned her head. So close it seemed he might reach out to her, his daughter looked ill and half insane.

'Daddy?' Chris asked in a puzzled voice, and swaying got to her feet.

She was wearing only a shirt; he remembered the one he had pulled on her and how it had been used to deceive him. The shirt hung open and the triangle of hair was black against the whiteness of her belly.

'She's like a child,' Ramsay said. 'Wait a bit and she'll put her thumb in her mouth,' and he laughed, standing with one hand rooting into her from behind.

'Chris,' he shouted. 'Yes! It's Daddy! I'm coming!'

'Ah . . .' Ramsay said. 'How marvellous.'

He walked Chris forward and putting one hand on the nape of her neck bent her head forward so that she was looking down into the water.

'Daddy's coming. But how? How are you going to come?'

The ledge was high above deep still water. Farther on, it finished in a rubble of stones; a grey beach, chill and drained of light. He looked at the bleak water and wondered if he had strength left to swim.

'We're waiting. Your baby's waiting.'

185

It would be a cold place to die. He could not get on board without help. At the thought of Ramsay's hand touching him, he shuddered.

'Chris?'

'She's in splendid form. Daddy's little girl, aren't you?' He nodded her head up and down. 'See? She's saying yes.'

She did not seem to know what was happening; who they were perhaps or where she was.

'You.' The word was heavy in his mouth. 'You.' And then the admission came in a hoarse cry that tore adhesions of remorse deep inside him. 'You should be dead. I thought I'd killed you.'

'What?' He let Chris fall discarded to the deck. 'I think after all I'll come to you.'

As Ramsay paddled closer, Campbell looked about on the ledge and found a piece of broken stone that made him grunt to lift it. He clasped it to his chest and waited. His muscles anticipated the strain and relief. He heard bone burst apart and saw the living brain splash out – and then Ramsay pulled away to the side and had landed on the beach. The stones grated turning under his feet.

Campbell let the stone fall and with a cry followed it into the water. By instinct, he swam. He used the breast stroke, pushing out his arms, kicking back. Nothing seemed to happen; the terror of death by drowning possessed him. Till suddenly another pull took him into a length of sunlight. The warmth bathed his head. It would not be possible to drown in that light. He looked back and saw Ramsay sitting on the shore, making no attempt to follow, content it seemed for the moment to watch. His legs went numb. 'Chris!' he called and tried to cry again on each forced out breath.

Her white clown's face, child breasts and scribbled bush reversed above him.

'You have – to help me. Give me – your hand.'

He was too weak to get on board without her help. As he tried to reach up, she turned away and disappeared.

'Chris!'

The slanting plane of the boat's hull; above, in place of blue sky, black rock like an ogre's frown. Slowly, he trod water.

'Chris!'

Thank God! she came. He imagined himself raised, the boat on the open sea, her rescued, his life vindicated.

Over the rail, the marble clock, the naked Venus Neil had stolen, drunkard's loot, was held out between her living hands. Did she say 'Daddy'? Better to think of her as maddened. He was monster, nightmare, a shape out of a dream. Never Daddy. Oh, God! The child hands parted and the shrouded goddess of love trod him down.

Sank in unshed tears and was willing to be at peace. Held breath was agony but someone else's. He was willing . . . In a column, light from the surface fell past him and illuminated under his kicking feet the shifting outline of a boat. Something in him rebelled against death's voyage and he rose thrashing until he gasped air. As he tried to swim, anguish stamped like hooves. He sank and struggled to rise. His right shoulder had taken the blow. The arm was derelict and useless. He cradled it with his left hand and lay on his back. He would not die. He floated, slanted his head to breathe, frog-kicked and surged out of the round eye of sunlit water.

On the beach, pebbles stretched like a perspective of hills. They ground into his cheek and hurt down the length of his body. He retched sea water. On giant boots the mountain smashed towards him.

'You spoiled everything,' Ramsay said.

Enormous and unknowable he stared down.

'I never meant Neil to be hurt,' Ramsay said. 'You made me hurt him.' He sounded as if he would weep. 'You spoiled everything. Neil felt sorry for you – you had no right to make him feel sorry for you.'

Campbell's left hand closed on a stone. As Ramsay waited, he came infinitely slowly to his knees and then on to his feet. He shielded his left hand holding the stone.

'I thought it was you,' Campbell said. 'I killed him with a stick.'

'I'm not dead. It's not so easy.'

Campbell swayed as if he would fall. It brought him a half-step nearer. He stared at the hollow in Ramsay's temple where he would strike. It was no larger than a coin.

'I won't let you take Chris,' he said.

'What does it matter what you want?' Ramsay asked. 'Who cares about her or you? You were told there was no hope for her. But you had to know better. You wouldn't listen.'

At the look on Ramsay's face, he realised that Ramsay hated him not for his weakness but for this hope in him which would not die.

'There's always hope,' he said.

'Nobody cares,' Ramsay said. 'Not even your wife. I went to your house looking for Chris. It was your wife who told me you'd taken her to Breagda.'

His left fist loosened. The stone fell at his side.

'You bloody old lunatic!' he heard Ramsay say as if from far away and then as he was falling another word was cried out in a language he knew but did not understand. As he fell, the giant foot flew towards him. His shoulder exploded in darkness.

He came round hearing waves as waves; under their patient murmur, heard another sound sighing and recognised it for what it was. The boat was drifting towards the mouth of the cove. Ramsay stood alone at the wheel. Beyond the boat, he saw white spray. With his left hand, he scrabbled up pebbles and threw them out. They cast up an artillery of little splashes. He had to save Chris.

'For God's sake,' he whispered, 'you'll be smashed to pieces.'

Along the path of sunlight, the boat drifted to destruction. Pebbles clacked and spattered under his running feet. He leant on his hands to scramble up to the ledge and pain took him to the edge of the dark place. He fought it and crawled belly flat on to the rock.

The boat moved so immeasurably slowly that he came abreast of it.

'Leave Chris!'

Ramsay's face blurred and swayed. He concentrated on it desperately. In pantomime, Ramsay cupped his hand behind his ear like an old deaf man.

'Please!' And he kept on saying it in a whisper that did no good; please please.

Ramsay turned abruptly and disappeared below. He thought that was the end – but then he came back pushing Chris into sight. She was naked and at the touch of sunlight shrank back and was thrown forward. As she fell, he saw Ramsay with his foot still raised.

'Chris! Jump! Swim to me!'

I can't, he thought in terrible shame, swim to you. If only she would, this time he could save her. This time Ramsay would die. This time he would kill him for ever.

Chris swayed on hands and knees. Her long hair swung like a curtain.

'Don't do this,' he cried. It was the wrong time of the tide. They would be smashed. 'For God's sake!'

He could come no nearer; the ledge curved away from the boat. Its bow turned slowly towards the place of destruction.

'Take me! Don't leave me!' he cried.

The boat hesitated on the edge of chaos. For a moment, it recoiled from the sea. Ramsay reached forward and drew up Chris's head. 'Say goodbye!' he shouted but at which of them it was impossible to tell. The boat swayed and he let go to save himself. Chris slumped down.

'Look out!'

Please. He thought they were both about to die in front of him.

Ramsay pulled Chris up by the hair and punched her in the face. 'Say goodbye,' he shouted and pulled back his fist. 'Tell her goodbye!'

Afraid to see her hurt again, terrified that she would drown if Ramsay did not save her, he heard himself bawl, 'Goodbye! Goodbye!' like an idiot parent on some fond pier. Goodbye, Chris.

Ramsay put her hands on the rail. She knelt there staring ahead. Goodbye, Chris.

He watched Ramsay move swiftly. She clung, a white butterfly spread and pinned with thick-fingered delicacy. Goodbye, Chris.

Cupped hands of rock re-echoed the roar of the engine. Pistons smashed him. He held her face between his hands, corpse flesh, looked into her eyes. She had been the meaning of his life and he had lost her. She had been the hope of his life who now despaired. She had been the salvation of his life and he had not saved her. On the sea the boat half spun, straightened, was gone.

Goodbye, Chris.

Now the sun flooded the cove with light. It spread across the floor of water and lapped his fingers where they clutched the rock's edge. Yellow light on the rock. Ten sticks salt cleaned. Fish shadow snaking. The sand of the bed lit in the visible sea. Snake shadow . . . Into a bush, a tree, a mast.

The *Lazy Charlotte* shimmered under the clear water, and there seemed no way in which he could leave that place or any reason ever to try.

NINETEEN

'I don't see why a ship should ever come,' he said aloud, forgetting that where soldiers had been once with their guns it was likely they would come again.

Cloud or clearing, the sky hung in the balance. For the last week it had rained for part of each day. Somewhere below, the sea was swirling past the still cove where Ramsay had sunk the *Lazy Charlotte* to maroon him on Breagda. As he watched, the sun came out and away to the horizon every crest struck a glittering signal of light. This was the first time he had been back to the cliff and he had brought his father's diary here to read whatever was left. The ledge ran below where he stood and, leaning out to trace its course, he could not remember what there had been in dying to make him so afraid.

They had crispbreads from the last packet. He had spread them with margarine and they ate them with leathery slices of processed cheese. It was a habit he had fallen into to have one meal in the day with a companion. It worked best with friends he hadn't seen since university or with one of the self-absorbed colleagues with whom he had spent too many years of his life. Anyone closer asked about Chris, and would argue with him until he was afraid he would go mad. Today it was Gerry's turn and they talked about timetables and reminisced about the blonde student who had later been cited in a second divorce case. 'Is that wot's teaching the kids naow?' he asked, doing his Cockney mum, and generous Gerry laughed. But when the meal was finished, it would have been too dangerous to have Gerry stay, and instead he laid his father's diary on the grass and turned the pages. There was nothing to read. At first glance, everything it seemed was spoiled.

After such pain, how to begin again? It would have been better if he had gripped that outstretched hand and drawn Ramsay with him to swim down air into the silence where all harm ended. It would

190

have been better if he had let the salt sea fill their mouths until they choked.

He wanted to sleep. All that he wanted now was quiet sleep. Without allowing the image of what he was going to do to form in his mind, he retraced his steps to the edge of the cliff. He came to the last cleared place extraordinarily quickly and with no fatigue or any sense of effort. As high as this it was never still and he leaned back against the wind and gazed down on the sea far below. Under him the guillemots circled out crying from the cliff's shoulder white splashed with their dung. It was not true that you worried about what lay on the other side of death. He was so tired that he would welcome a sleep without waking. If you were tired enough, all you wanted was to sleep. He swayed forward.

The diary was awkward to hold with one hand. His right arm was folded and strapped against his chest with Neil's belt. He had gone back to the schoolhouse, perhaps because of a last glimpse of a hand in the moonlight quivering. By then he had been in so much pain that when he could find nothing else he had unbuckled the belt and pulled it free. It had been at that moment Neil opened his eyes.

He came down the brief slope from the rostrum of the cliff and through the village of tumbled stones and fallen roofs. It had been abandoned a long time ago; before the people had been forced to leave the island, they had given up this village to the elements. He recognised the wall against which he had huddled waiting for morning on the day when he found and lost Chris for the last time on Breagda. 'I don't see any reason why a ship would ever come,' he said aloud. His father's diary had fallen in front of him and pinning it with his knee he began to tear out its pages. They came easily until tough stitching and too large a handful brought him to a pause. He looked with horror on what he had done. When he tried to gather up the loose sheets, crouching on his knees and reaching out, the wind flicked and harried them away. It was the last betrayal.

His outstretched hand rubbed the rough stone of the wall by which he knelt. His fist held crumpled leaves of his father's diary and now he saw writing there, faint and splashed with dew but still legible.

'The Catechist set me Job's words, Chapter 23, Verse 2 – My stroke is heavier than my groaning.'

191

'What could be the meaning of such a cry?

'Last night I dreamed I was a child who could not answer the Catechist come to put me to the question and when I looked up my mother was weeping. I wakened in great agony of spirit.

'I am writing this out of the wind under a ruined wall, all that is left of the house where May Gillies the widow lived with her daughters Belle and Davina. Even though she died before I was born, I know her story. My grandfather had all the histories of the people in his head and on the evening of a gathering after the singing they would turn to him and listen. One night when I was only a young boy, all the people who were left came to my father's house and prayed and sang together. And afterwards when it was late – so late I was expecting every minute to be packed to my bed but no one minded me that night – my grandfather told some stories and one of them was the story of May Gillies the widow. The next day the boat came and all of us were taken from the island not ever to return.

'When the well failed, my grandfather said, everyone came down to the shore village for there was no living without it. But the widow would not leave and, at the first of it, her two daughters would not leave either but stayed with her. The missionary spoke to her and the teacher and her own brother pleaded with her but it made no difference. She was a stubborn woman. It just was not possible to live there lacking the well. And at last her daughter Belle knew it was hopeless and came down and asked to live with her uncle. He would not take the girl in though until he had asked her mother's permission. And my grandfather called the widow truly a mother in Israel for despite her hurt she would not have her brother turn the girl away but told him to take her in. Davina then was angry not with her sister but with her sister's lack of faith. She grieved for her sister as one lost to the Lord. The next Thursday after that – and it was a Fast Day – she prayed and set the pail down into the dry well. It came up overflowing with water, abundant as the spring of Moses in the land of exile, sweet as the promise of Canaan. From that hour, Davina was marked as a saintly woman and one exercised in the Lord.

'That was the story my grandfather told, and we listened

192

though all of us knew the well in this place was choked with dry stones.

'When we came to Glasgow, there was more whisky than stories and soon Mungo dead of the tumour that ate his mind and Hamish spitting red blood into the handkerchiefs my mother always kept so white for him. As a man, I put those old tales away as childish things. And yet since I have been alone here so many days they come into my head, more and more of them. Every rock and bush has a story that comes back to me. For the last week, I have risen every day determined to set sail from Breagda. Yet I could not bring myself to leave. I long towards my unborn son and yet I could not bring myself to leave.

'But here on the cliff above Ach-nan-uaigh the story of May Gillies the widow came back to me and I have thought about it an hour together. I am set free. In the morning I draw the anchor and leave Breagda behind.

'The day passes and I wander from place to place hearing the voices that will never be—'

He had fed upon his hatred to survive. For hours in the sun and under the rain, he had daydreamed of the ways in which he would kill Ramsay. Under a wall in the broken village, he learned that even hate was not enough to make him want to live.

The crumpled sheets and what was left – covers, blank leaves at the end, pages unreadable because of the rain – he folded together carefully. For the ruined village, out of his brief stay on the island he could furnish memories. When he came to the plain of crouching bushes and worn rock, to the stream with flags of white flowers, to where in the water's crook the ground went to marsh – for none of them had he anything; no memory of legend, no anecdote, nothing of childhood. No community; no belief; no identity. With no company but his man time, he limped on bribing himself with promises of rest, breaking each promise until by a rock backed like a seal his legs gave under him.

Late in the afternoon when the sun broke through the clouds, he sat outside the schoolhouse. Neil was asleep, and he sat with one of the blue exercise jotters on his knee. He had taken it from the bundle under the flogging strap coiled in the desk. 'God bless!

Next!' The burst wood of the lid bouncing crazily under the thump of the leather. What had Ramsay said? 'They called it education.'

In the middle of the jotter, the two metal clips had rusted and left a symmetrical shape like the seed case of an apple. He turned back to the blank page at the beginning and wrote: *The day my grandfather came, they were holding a party for Tam Maclean who was going off to the war.* It took an endless time to write that, left-handed, in a scrawl that shook and trembled. Staring ahead, he tried to remember what Mrs Maclean looked like. But that was hard too. He doubted if he would ever manage it. His past was a bare landscape. How could he hope to recover in the wavering hand of a child so much he had spent a lifetime determined to forget? Yet sharp and unbidden there came into his mind the image of a little rod of iron with a hole in one end for tightening the frame of an old-fashioned bed. It looked nothing like a key.

Things it seemed were harder to forget than people.

On the first morning, he had left Chris lying on the bunk and swum from the *Charlotte* across the bay to the shore – tiny waves like a plain of hills full of movement and light as he turned his head one way and the other to draw a breath, rocking, stretching – travellers on moon worlds could not have moved more freely. There was one meal left. Yesterday he had made his last trip to the shore village and, though able to carry so little, had brought back all of the food that was left from his store of supplies. The rest had been taken by Ramsay or spoiled by him. The sun's warmth could not reach the place at the top of his right lung where there was a dull and constant ache.

If you were tired enough, no one could blame you for wanting to sleep.

There was a crash from the house. Not giving himself time to decide, he rushed inside. Neil had fallen near the desk. For a terrible second he thought the big man had struck his head but then there was a groan and he stirred as if trying to rise. His courage almost failed him as it had done each time he came near the injured man, not fearing the wrecked face but made timid by his own guilt and the fear of being reproached. Mostly what could be understood as words seemed to be in Gaelic, however, and even the snatches of English suggested a life far in the past. Nothing recent had appeared in what passed with him for speech. He took

194

Neil by the shoulders and turned him. At that moment each time before, the ruined mask had dissolved in animal fear. In its eyes, he would see himself again, a one-armed man dark against the light. It was this which had become more than he could bear.

He got him to his feet. There was no paralysis, but the sense of balance was gone so that without help after a few steps he would fall. He held him by the elbow and they paced steadily out to the open air. It was only when he sat him down against the wall that he realised what had gone wrong. The smell of urine drew his eyes to the stain. 'It's all right,' he said automatically, unbuttoning the trousers and easing them off as he had done before. When he rolled down the underpants, they were heavy with excrement. Looking up, he was surprised to see tears running down the cheeks of the mask. 'It's all right,' he said in a different tone. He wiped between the massive thighs and had gathered the bundle of clothes when a noise made him turn back.

'It's juniper,' Neil said. From around his neck, fumbling he tugged and brought free a cross of wood threaded on a length of cord. He held it out on the palm of his hand. 'A sure protection against—'

Those words came startlingly clear and then the last one was lost and the mask grimaced and was silent.

'Against what?' he wondered sourly. 'All of this?'

The mask was silent.

'Why juniper? Can't it make up its mind, Christian or pagan?'

Did it matter? It was being given.

'You want me to have it?' he asked. 'Are you sure?' he wondered, as if there could be any doubt, and only then and at last took it as if reluctant. 'Thank you,' he said, reaching out, accepting.

He laid the soiled bundle away from them on the grass. Later, when he had more strength, he would wash the clothes and spread them to dry in the afternoon warmth. It seemed to him that Neil had improved; that his fall had come about because he was trying to care for himself. Perhaps his balance gradually would steady. Such things were possible. Speech and memory had been known to repair.

Coming back from the cliffs, he had fallen in weariness by a rock backed like a seal. 'I don't see why a ship should ever come,' he had cried out. Thinking about that now, he knew it as foolish since

195

the island in its abandonment had not been without visitors: fisherfolk and naturalists and once a commune of young people who had turned their backs on the city and all its works. It occurred to him that, out of then and now, for the grey seal rock he had made a memory.

On this day Neil had given him a gift. He turned the little cross with a finger on his palm. A sure protection. Against drowning perhaps. This was the day of the gift. As for the rest, there were birds on the island and the small sweet-fleshed sheep. Somehow they would live. Ignorant, he would learn and keep them alive till help came. A one-armed man would save them.

A calm sureness like peace touched him. One day they would get free of the island. He would find Chris again; and seek out Ramsay, not for revenge but justice. He believed in justice.

George Campbell rested in the sun at the door of the schoolhouse on Breagda.